Tom Sawyer ABROAD

Here is one of Samuel Clemens' most beloved characters—and indeed one of the most delightful boys in all of literature—in another exciting and hilarious adventure.

When Tom and his friends Huck and Jim find themselves in accidental, but sole possession of a balloon, they are overcome by wanderlust and start on a series of journeys over the Atlantic Ocean in a machine which none of them has ever flown before! Flying over the Sahara Desert, the three travelers manage to anchor on a pyramid where they settle their problem in an unexpected though typically riotous manner.

Boys and girls who have laughed over the adventures of Tom Sawyer will enjoy catching up with their hero's incredible but always entertaining pranks.

The professor never stirred till the sun was overhead

SAMUEL CLEMENS

Tom Sawyer
ABROAD

ILLUSTRATIONS BY
GERALD McCANN

COMPANION LIBRARY

Grosset & Dunlap

PUBLISHERS
NEW YORK

Contents

Illustrations

Tom Sawyer ABROAD

1: *Tom Seeks New Adventures*

Do you reckon Tom Sawyer was satisfied after all them adventures? I mean the adventures we had down the river, and the time we set the darky Jim free and Tom got shot in the leg. No, he wasn't. It only just p'isoned him for more. That was all the effect it had. You see, when we three came back up the river in glory, as you may say, from that long travel, and the village received us with a torchlight procession and speeches, and everybody hurrah'd and shouted, it made us heroes, and that was what Tom Sawyer had always been hankering to be.

For a while he *was* satisfied. Everybody made

much of him, and he tilted up his nose and stepped around the town as though he owned it. Some called him Tom Sawyer the Traveler, and that just swelled him up fit to bust. You see he laid over me and Jim considerable, because we only went down the river on a raft and came back by the steamboat, but Tom went by the steamboat both ways. The boys envied me and Jim a good deal, but land! they just knuckled to the dirt before TOM.

Well, I don't know; maybe he might have been satisfied if it hadn't been for old Nat Parsons, which was postmaster, and powerful long and slim, and kind o' good-hearted and silly, and bald-headed, on account of his age, and about the talkiest old cretur I ever see. For as much as thirty years he'd been the only man in the village that had a reputation—I mean a reputation for being a traveler, and of course he was mortal proud of it, and it was reckoned that in the course of that thirty years he had told about that journey over a million times and enjoyed it every time. And now comes along a boy not quite fifteen, and sets everybody admiring and gawking over *his* travels, and it just give the poor old man the high strikes. It made him

sick to listen to Tom, and to hear the people say
"My land!" "Did you ever!" "My goodness
sakes alive!" and all such things; but he
couldn't pull away from it, any more than a fly
that's got its hind leg fast in the molasses. And
always when Tom come to a rest, the poor old
cretur would chip in on *his* same old travels and
work them for all they were worth; but they
were pretty faded, and didn't go for much, and
it was pitiful to see. And then Tom would take
another innings, and then the old man again—
and so on, and so on, for an hour and more, each
trying to beat out the other.

You see, Parsons' travels happened like this:
When he first got to be postmaster and was
green in the business, there come a letter for
somebody he didn't know, and there wasn't any
such person in the village. Well, he didn't know
what to do, nor how to act, and there the letter
stayed and stayed, week in and week out, till the
bare sight of it gave him a conniption. The
postage wasn't paid on it, and that was another
thing to worry about. There wasn't any way to
collect that ten cents, and he reckoned the
gov'ment would hold him responsible for it
and maybe turn him out besides, when they

*He had told about that journey over
a million times*

found he hadn't collected it.   Well, at last he
couldn't stand it any longer.   He couldn't sleep
nights, he couldn't eat, he was thinned down to
a shadder, yet he dasn't ask anybody's advice, for
the very person he asked for advice might go
back on him and let the gov'ment know about
the letter. He had the letter buried under the
floor, but that did no good; if he happened to
see a person standing over the place it'd give
him the cold shivers, and loaded him up with
suspicions, and he would sit up that night till
the town was still and dark, and then he would
sneak there and get it out and bury it in another
place.   Of course, people got to avoiding him
and shaking their heads and whispering, because, the way he was looking and acting, they
judged he had killed somebody or done something terrible, they didn't know what, and if
he had been a stranger they would've lynched
him.

Well, as I was saying, it got so he couldn't
stand it any longer; so he made up his mind to
pull out for Washington, and just go to the
President of the United States and make a clean
breast of the whole thing, not keeping back an
atom, and then fetch the letter out and lay it

before the whole gov'ment, and say, "Now,
there she is—do with me what you're a mind to;
though as heaven is my judge I am an innocent
man and not deserving of the full penalties of
the law and leaving behind me a family that
must starve and yet hadn't a thing to do with it,
which is the whole truth and I can swear to
it."

So he did it. He had a little wee bit of steam-
boating, and some stage-coaching, but all the
rest of the way was horseback, and it took him
three weeks to get to Washington. He saw lots
of land and lots of villages and four cities. He
was gone 'most eight weeks, and there never was
such a proud man in the village as he when he
got back. His travels made him the greatest man
in all that region, and the most talked about;
and people come from as much as thirty miles
back in the country, and from over in the Illinois bottoms, too, just to look at him—and
there they'd stand and gawk, and he'd gabble.
You never see anything like it.

Well, there wasn't any way now to settle
which was the greatest traveler; some said it was
Nat, some said it was Tom. Everybody allowed
that Nat had seen the most longitude, but they

had to give in that whatever Tom was short in longitude he had made up in latitude and climate. It was about a stand-off; so both of them had to whoop up their dangerous adventures, and try to get ahead *that* way. That bullet-wound in Tom's leg was a tough thing for Nat Parsons to buck against, but he bucked the best he could; and at a disadvantage, too, for Tom didn't set still as he'd orter done, to be fair, but always got up and sauntered around and worked his limp while Nat was painting up the adventure that *he* had in Washington; for Tom never let go that limp when his leg got well, but practiced it nights at home, and kept it good as new right along.

Nat's adventure was like this; I don't know how true it is: maybe he got it out of a paper, or somewhere, but I will say this for him, that he *did* know how to tell it. He could make anybody's flesh crawl, and he'd turn pale and hold his breath when he told it, and sometimes women and girls got so faint they couldn't stick it out. Well, it was this way, as near as I can remember:

He come a-loping into Washington, and put up his horse and shoved out to the President's house with his letter, and they told him the President was up to the Capitol, and just going to start for Philadelphia—not a minute to lose if he wanted to catch him. Nat 'most dropped, it made him so sick. His horse was put up, and he didn't know what *to* do. But just then along comes a darky driving an old ramshackly hack, and he see his chance. He rushes out and shouts: "A half a dollar if you git me to the Capitol in half an hour, and a quarter extra if you do it in twenty minutes!"

"Done!" says the darky.

Nat he jumped in and slammed the door, and away they went a-ripping and a-tearing over the roughest road a body ever see, and the racket of it was something awful. Nat passed his arms through the loops and hung on for life and death, but pretty soon the hack hit a rock and flew up in the air, and the bottom fell out, and when it come down Nat's feet was on the ground, and he see he was in the most desperate danger if he couldn't keep up with the hack. He was horrible scared, but he laid into his work for all he was worth, and hung tight to the arm-loops and made his legs fairly fly. He yelled and shouted to the driver to stop, and so did the crowds along the street, for they could see his legs spinning along under the coach, and his head and shoulders bobbing inside through the windows, and he was in awful danger; but the more they all shouted the more the darky whopped and yelled and lashed the horses and shouted, "Don't you frct, I's gwine to git you dah in time, boss; I's gwine to do it, sho'!" for you see he thought they were all hurrying him up, and, of course, he couldn't hear anything for the racket he was making. And so they went ripping along, and everybody just petrified to see it; and when they got to the Capitol at last it was the quickest trip that ever was made, and everybody said so.

The horses laid down, and Nat dropped, all tuckered out, and he was all dust and rags and barefooted; but he was in time and just in time, and caught the President and give him the letter, and everything was all right, and the President give him a free pardon on the spot, and Nat give the darky two extra quarters instead of one, because he could see that if he hadn't had the hack he wouldn't 'a' got there in time, nor anywhere near it.

It *was* a powerful good adventure, and Tom

Sawyer had to work his bullet-wound mighty lively to hold his own against it.

Well, by and by Tom's glory got to paling down gradu'ly on account of other things turning up for the people to talk about—first a horse-race, and on top of that a house afire, and on top of that the circus, and on top of that the eclipse; and that started a revival, same as it always does, and by that time there wasn't any more talk about Tom, so to speak, and you never see a person so sick and disgusted.

Pretty soon he got to worrying and fretting right along day in and day out, and when I asked him what *was* he in such a state about, he said it 'most broke his heart to think how time was slipping away, and him getting older and older, and no wars breaking out and no way of making a name for himself that he could see. Now that is the way boys is always thinking, but he was the first one I ever heard come out and say it.

So then he set to work to get up a plan to make him celebrated; and pretty soon he struck it, and offered to take me and Jim in. Tom Sawyer was always free and generous that way. There's a-plenty of boys that's mighty good and friendly when *you've* got a good thing, but when a good thing happens to come their way they don't say a word to you, and try to hog it all. That warn't ever Tom Sawyer's way, I can say that for him. There's plenty of boys that will come hankering and groveling around you when you've got an apple and beg the core off of you; but when they've got one, and you beg for the core and remind them how you give them a core one time, they say thank you 'most to death, but there ain't a-going to be no core. But I notice they always git come up with; all you got to do is to wait.

Well, we went out in the woods on the hill, and Tom told us what it was. It was a crusade.

"What's a crusade?" I says.

He looked scornful, the way he's always done when he was ashamed of a person, and says:

"Huck Finn, do you mean to tell me you don't know what a crusade is?"

"No," says I, "I don't. And I don't care to, nuther. I've lived till now and done without it, and had my health, too. But as soon as you tell me, I'll know, and that's soon enough. I don't see any use in finding out things and clogging up my head with them when I mayn't ever have any occasion to use 'em. There was Lance Williams, he learned how to talk Choctaw here till one come and dug his grave for him. Now, then, what's a crusade? But I can tell you one thing before you begin; if it's a patent-right, there's no money in it. Bill Thompson he—"

"Patent-right!" says he. "I never see such an idiot. Why, a crusade is a kind of war."

I thought he must be losing his mind. But no, he was in real earnest, and went right on, perfectly ca'm.

"A crusade is a war to recover the Holy Land from the paynim."

"Which Holy Land?"

"Why *the* Holy Land—there ain't but one."

"What do *we* want of it?"

"Why, can't you understand? It's in the hands of the paynim, and it's our duty to take it away from them."

"How did we come to let them git hold of it?"

"We didn't come to let them git hold of it. They always had it."

"Why, Tom, then it must belong to them, don't it?"

"Why, of course it does. Who said it didn't?"

I studied over it, but couldn't seem to git at the right of it, no way. I says:

"It's too many for me, Tom Sawyer. If I had a farm and it was mine, and another person wanted it, would it be right for him to—"

"Oh, shucks! you don't know enough to come in when it rains, Huck Finn. It ain't a farm, it's entirely different. You see, it's like this. They own the land, just the mere land, and that's all they *do* own; but it was our folks, our Jews and Christians, that made it holy, and so they haven't any business to be there defiling it. It's a shame, and we ought not to stand it a minute. We ought to march against them and take it away from them."

"Why, it does seem to me it's the most mixed-up thing I ever see! Now, if I had a farm and another person—"

"Don't I tell you it hasn't got anything to do with farming? Farming is business, just common low-down business: that's all it is, it's all you can say for it; but this is higher, this is religious, and totally different."

"Religious to go and take the land away from people that owns it?"

"Certainly; it's always been considered so."

Jim he shook his head, and says:

"Mars Tom, I reckon dey's a mistake about it somers—dey mos' sholy is. I's religious myself, en I knows plenty religious people, but I hain't run across none dat acts like dat."

It made Tom hot, and he says:

"Well, it's enough to make a body sick, such mullet-headed ignorance! If either of you'd read anything about history, you'd know that Richard Cur de Loon, and the Pope, and Godfrey de Bulleyn, and lots more of the most noble-hearted and pious people in the world, hacked and hammered at the paynims for more than two hundred years trying to take their land away from them, and swum neck-deep in blood the whole time—and yet here's a couple of sap-headed country yahoos out in the backwoods of Missouri setting themselves up to know more about the rights and wrongs of it than they did! Talk about cheek!"

Well, of course, that put a more different light on it, and me and Jim felt pretty cheap and ignorant, and wished we hadn't been quite so chipper. I couldn't say nothing, and Jim he couldn't for a while; then he says:

"Well, den, I reckon it's all right; beca'se ef

dey didn't know, dey ain't no use for po' ignorant folks like us to be trying to know; en so, ef
it's our duty, we got to go en tackle it en do de
bes' we can. Same time, I feel as sorry for dem
paynims as Mars Tom. De hard part gwine to
be to kill folks dat a body hain't been 'quainted
wid and dat hain't done him no harm. Dat's it,
you see. Ef we wuz to go 'mongst 'em, jist we
three, en say we's hungry, en ast 'em for a bite to
eat, why, maybe dey's jist like yuther people.
Don't you reckon dey is? Why, *dey'd* give it, I
know dey would, en den—'"

"Then what?"

"Well, Mars Tom, my idea is like dis. It ain't
no use, we *can't* kill dem po' strangers dat ain't
doin' us no harm, till we've had practice—I
knows it perfectly well, Mars Tom—'deed I
knows it perfectly well. But ef we takes a' ax or
two, jist you en me en Huck, en slips acrost de
river tonight arter de moon's gone down, en
kills dat sick fam'ly dat's over on the Sny, en
burns dey house down, en—"

"Oh, you make me tired!" says Tom. "I
don't want to argue any more with people like
you and Huck Finn, that's always wandering
from the subject, and ain't got any more sense

than to try to reason out a thing that's pure theology by the laws that protect real estate!"

Now that's just where Tom Sawyer warn't fair. Jim didn't mean no harm, and I didn't mean no harm. We knowed well enough that he was right and we was wrong, and all we was after was to get at the *how* of it, and that was all; and the only reason he couldn't explain it so we could understand it was because we was ignorant—yes, and pretty dull, too, I ain't denying that; but, land! that ain't no crime, I should think.

But he wouldn't hear no more about it—just said if we had tackled the thing in the proper spirit, he would 'a' raised a couple of thousand knights and put them in steel armor from head to heel, and made me a lieutenant and Jim a sutler, and took the command himself and brushed the whole paynim outfit into the sea like flies and come back across the world in a glory like sunset. But he said we didn't know enough to take the chance when we had it, and he wouldn't ever offer it again. And he didn't. When he once got set, you couldn't budge him.

But I didn't care much. I am peaceable, and don't get up rows with people that ain't doing nothing to me. I allowed if the paynim was satisfied I was, and we would let it stand at that.

Now Tom he got all that notion out of Walter Scott's book, which he was always reading. And it *was* a wild notion, because in my opinion he never could've raised the men, and if he did, as like as not he would've got licked. I took the book and read all about it, and as near as I could make it out, most of the folks that shook farming to go crusading had a mighty rocky time of it.

2: *The Balloon Ascension*

WELL, Tom got up one thing after another, but they all had tender spots about 'em somewheres, and he had to shove 'em aside.   So at last he was about in despair.   Then the St. Louis papers begun to talk a good deal about the balloon that was going to sail to Europe, and Tom sort of thought he wanted to go down and see what it looked like, but couldn't make up his mind. But the papers went on talking, and so he allowed that maybe if he didn't go he mightn't ever have another chance to see a balloon; and next, he found out that Nat Parsons was going down to see it, and that decided him, of course.

He wasn't going to have Nat Parsons coming back bragging about seeing the balloon, and him having to listen to it and keep quiet. So he wanted me and Jim to go too, and we went.

It was a noble big balloon, and had wings and fans and all sorts of things, and wasn't like any balloon you see in pictures. It was away out toward the edge of town, in a vacant lot, corner of Twelfth Street; and there was a big crowd around it, making fun of it, and making fun of the man—a lean pale feller with that soft kind of moonlight in his eyes, you know—and they kept saying it wouldn't go. It made him hot to hear them, and he would turn on them and shake his fist and say they was animals and blind, but some day they would find they had stood face to face with one of the men that lifts up nations and makes civilizations, and was too dull to know it; and right here on this spot their own children and grandchildren would build a monument to him that would outlast a thousand years, but his name would outlast the monument. And then the crowd would burst out in a laugh again, and yell at him, and ask him what was his name before he was married, and what he would take to not do it, and what

It was a noble big balloon

was his sister's cat's grandmother's name, and all
the things that a crowd says when they've got
hold of a feller that they see they can plague.
Well, some things they said *was* funny—yes, and
mighty witty too, I ain't denying that—but all
the same it warn't fair nor brave, all them people pitching on one, and they so glib and sharp,
and him without any gift of talk to answer back
with.   But, good land! what did he want to sass
back for?   You see, it couldn't do him no good,
and it was just nuts for them.   They *had* him,
you know.   But that was his way.   I reckon he
couldn't help it; he was made so, I judge.   He
was a good enough sort of cretur, and hadn't no
harm in him, and was just a genius, as the papers said, which wasn't his fault.   We can't all be
sound: we've got to be the way we're made.   As
near as I can make out, geniuses think they
know it all, and so they won't take people's
advice, but always go their own way, which
makes everybody forsake them and despise
them, and that is perfectly natural.   If they was
humbler, and listened and tried to learn, it
would be better for them.

The part the professor was in was like a boat,
and was big and roomy, and had watertight

lockers around the inside to keep all sorts of
things in, and a body could sit on them, and
make beds on them, too. We went aboard, and
there was twenty people there, snooping around
and examining, and old Nat Parsons was there,
too. The professor kept fussing around getting
ready, and the people went ashore, drifting out
one at a time, and old Nat he was the last. Of
course it wouldn't do to let him go out behind
us. We mustn't budge till he was gone, so we
could be last ourselves.

But he was gone now, so it was time for us to
follow. I heard a big shout, and turned
around—the city was dropping from under us
like a shot! It made me sick all through, I was
so scared. Jim turned gray and couldn't say a
word, and Tom didn't say nothing, but looked
excited. The city went on dropping down, and
down, and down; but we didn't seem to be
doing nothing but just hang in the air and stand
still. The houses got smaller and smaller, and
the city pulled itself together, closer and closer,
and the men and wagons got to looking like ants
and bugs crawling around, and the streets like
threads and cracks; and then it all kind of
melted together, and there wasn't any city any

*We didn't seem to be doing nothing but just
hang in the air and stand still*

more: it was only a big scar on the earth, and it seemed to me a body could see up the river and down the river about a thousand miles, though of course it wasn't so much. By and by the earth was a ball—just a round ball, of a dull color, with shiny stripes wriggling and winding around over it, which was rivers. The Widder Douglas always told me the earth was round like a ball, but I never took any stock in a lot of them superstitions o' hers, and of course I paid no attention to that one, because I could see myself that the world was the shape of a plate, and flat. I used to go up on the hill, and take a look around and prove it for myself, because I reckon the best way to get a sure thing on a fact is to go and examine for yourself, and not take any-body's say-so. But I had to give in now that the widder was right. That is, she was right as to the rest of the world, but she warn't right about the part our village is in; that part is the shape of a plate, and flat, I take my oath!

The professor had been quiet all this time, as if he was asleep; but he broke loose now, and he was mighty bitter. He says something like this:

"Idiots! They said it wouldn't go; and they

wanted to examine it, and spy around and get the secret of it out of me. But I beat them. Nobody knows the secret but me. Nobody knows what makes it move but me; and it's a new power—a new power, and a thousand times the strongest in the earth! Steam's foolishness to it! They said I couldn't go to Europe. To Europe! Why, there's power aboard to last five years, and feed for three months. They are fools! What do they know about it? Yes, and they said my airship was flimsy. Why, she's good for fifty years! I can sail the skies all my life if I want to, and steer where I please, though they laughed at that, and said I couldn't. Couldn't steer! Come here, boy; we'll see. You press these buttons as I tell you."

He made Tom steer the ship all about and every which way, and learnt him the whole thing in nearly no time; and Tom said it was perfectly easy. He made him fetch the ship down 'most to the earth, and had him spin her along so close to the Illinois prairies that a body could talk to the farmers, and hear everything they said perfectly plain; and he flung out printed bills to them that told about the balloon, and said it was going to Europe. Tom got so he could steer straight for a tree till he got nearly to it, and then dart up and skin right along over the top of it. Yes, and he showed Tom how to land her; and he done it first-rate, too, and set her down in the prairies as soft as wool. But the minute we started to skip out the professor says, "No, you don't!" and shot her up in the air again. It was awful. I begun to beg, and so did Jim; but it only give his temper a rise, and he begun to rage around and look wild out of his eyes, and I was scared of him.

Well, then he got on to his troubles again, and mourned and grumbled about the way he was treated, and couldn't seem to git over it, and especially people's saying his ship was flimsy. He scoffed at that, and at their saying she warn't simple and would be always getting out of order. Get out of order! That graveled him; he said that she couldn't any more get out of order than the solar sister.

He got worse and worse, and I never see a person take on so. It give me the cold shivers to see him, and so it did Jim. By and by he got to yelling and screaming, and then he swore the world shouldn't ever have his secret at all now, it had treated him so mean. He said he would sail his balloon around the globe just to show what he could do, and then he would sink it in the sea, and sink us all along with it, too. Well, it was the awfulest fix to be in, and here was night coming on!

He give us something to eat, and made us go to the other end of the boat, and he laid down on a locker, where he could boss all the works, and put his old pepper-box revolver under his head, and said if anybody come fooling around there trying to land her, he would kill him.

We set scrunched up together, and thought considerable, but didn't say much—only just a word once in a while when a body had to say something or bust, we was *so* scared and worried. The night dragged along slow and lonesome. We was pretty low down, and the moonshine made everything soft and pretty, and the farmhouses looked snug and homeful, and we could hear the farm sounds, and wished we could be down there; but, laws! we just slipped along over them like a ghost, and never left a track.

Away in the night, when all the sounds was late sounds, and the air had a late feel, and a late smell, too—about a two-o'clock feel, as near as I could make out—Tom said the professor was so quiet this time he must be asleep, and we'd better—

"Better what?" I says in a whisper, and feeling sick all over, because I knowed what he was thinking about.

"Better slip back there and tie him, and land the ship," he says.

I says: "No, sir! Don't you budge, Tom Sawyer."

And Jim—well, Jim was kind o' gasping, he was so scared. He says:

"Oh, Mars Tom, *don't!* Ef you teches him, we's gone—we's gone sho'! I ain't gwine anear him, not for nothin' in dis worl'. Mars Tom, he's plumb crazy."

Tom whispers and says: "That's *why* we've got to do something. If he wasn't crazy I wouldn't give shucks to be anywhere but here; you couldn't hire me to get out—now that I've got used to this balloon and over the scare of being cut loose from the solid ground—if he was in his right mind. But it's no good politics, sailing around like this with a person that's out of his head, and says he's going round the world and then drown us all. We've *got* to do something, I tell you, and do it before he wakes up, too, or we mayn't ever get another chance. Come!"

But it made us turn cold and creepy just to think of it, and we said we wouldn't budge. So Tom was for slipping back there by himself to see if he couldn't get at the steering-gear and land the ship. We begged and begged him not to, but it warn't no use; so he got down on his hands and knees, and begun to crawl an inch at a time, we a-holding our breath and watching. After he got to the middle of the boat he crept slower than ever, and it did seem like years to me. But at last we see him get to the professor's head, and sort of raise up soft and look a good spell in his face and listen. Then we see him begin to inch along again toward the professor's feet where the steering-buttons was. Well, he got there all safe, and was reaching slow and steady toward the buttons, but he knocked down something that made a noise, and we see him slump down flat an' soft in the bottom, and lay still. The professor stirred, and says, "What's that?" But everybody kept dead still and quiet, and he begun to mutter and mumble and nestle, like a person that's going to wake up, and I thought I was going to die, I was so worried and scared.

Then a cloud slid over the moon, and I 'most cried, I was so glad. She buried herself deeper and deeper into the cloud, and it got so dark we couldn't see Tom. Then it began to sprinkle rain, and we could hear the professor fussing at his ropes and things and abusing the weather. We was afraid every minute he would touch Tom, and then we would be goners, and no help; but Tom was already on his way back, and when we felt his hands on our knees my breath stopped sudden, and my heart fell down 'mongst my other works, because I couldn't tell in the dark but it might be the professor, which I thought it *was*.

Dear! I was so glad to have him back that I was just as near happy as a person could be that was up in the air that way with a deranged man. You can't land a balloon in the dark, and so I hoped it would keep on raining, for I didn't want Tom to go meddling any more and make us so awful uncomfortable. Well, I got my wish. It drizzled and drizzled along the rest of the night, which wasn't long, though it did seem so; and at daybreak it cleared, and the world looked mighty soft and gray and pretty, and the forests and fields so good to see again, and the horses and cattle standing sober and thinking. Next, the sun come a-blazing up gay and splendid, and then we began to feel rusty and stretchy, and first we knowed we was all asleep.

3: *Tom Explains*

WE went to sleep about four o'clock, and woke up about eight. The professor was setting back there at his end, looking glum. He pitched us some breakfast, but he told us not to come abaft the midship compass. That was about the middle of the boat. Well, when you are sharp-set, and you eat and satisfy yourself, everything looks pretty different from what it done before. It makes a body feel pretty near comfortable, even when he is up in a balloon with a genius. We got to talking together.

There was one thing that kept bothering me, and by and by I says:

"Tom, didn't we start east?"

"Yes."

"How fast have we been going?"

"Well, you heard what the professor said when he was raging round. Sometimes, he said, we was making fifty miles an hour, sometimes ninety, sometimes a hundred; said that with a gale to help he could make three hundred any time, and said if he wanted the gale, and wanted it blowing the right direction, he only had to go up higher or down lower to find it."

"Well, then, it's just as I reckoned. The professor lied."

"Why?"

"Because if we was going so fast we ought to be past Illinois, oughtn't we?"

"Certainly."

"Well, we ain't."

"What's the reason we ain't?"

"I know by the color. We're right over Illinois yet. And you can see for yourself that Indiana ain't in sight."

"I wonder what's the matter with you, Huck. You know by the *color?*"

"Yes, of course I do."

"What's the color got to do with it?"

"It's got everything to do with it.   Illinois is green, Indiana is pink.   You show me any pink down here, if you can.   No, sir; it's green."

"Indiana *pink?*   Why, what a lie!"

"It ain't no lie; I've seen it on the map, and it's pink."

You never see a person so aggravated and disgusted.   He says:

"Well, if I was such a numskull as you, Huck Finn, I would jump over.   Seen it on the map! Huck Finn, did you reckon the states was the same color out-of-doors as they are on the map?"

"Tom Sawyer, what's a map for?   Ain't it to learn you facts?"

"Of course."

"Well, then, how's it going to do that if it tells lies?   That's what I want to know."

"Shucks, you muggins!   It don't tell lies."

"It don't, don't it?"

"No, it don't."

"All right, then; if it don't, there ain't no two states the same color.   You git around *that,* if you can, Tom Sawyer."

He see I had him, and Jim see it too; and I tell

you, I felt pretty good, for Tom Sawyer was
always a hard person to git ahead of. Jim
slapped his leg and says:

"I tell *you!* dat's smart, dat's right down
smart. Ain't no use, Mars Tom; he got you *dis*
time, sho'!" He slapped his leg again, and says,
"My *lan'*, but it was smart one!"

I never felt so good in my life; and yet *I* didn't
know I was saying anything much till it was out.
I was just mooning along, perfectly careless, and
not expecting anything was going to happen,
and never *thinking* of such a thing at all, when,
all of a sudden, out it came. Why, it was just as
much a surprise to me as it was to any of them.
It was just the same way it is when a person is
munching along on a hunk of corn-pone, and
not thinking about anything, and all of a sudden bites into a di'mond. Now all that *he*
knows first off is that it's some kind of gravel he's
bit into; but he don't find out it's a di'mond till
he gits it out and brushes off the sand and
crumbs and one thing or another, and has a look
at it, and then he's surprised and glad—yes, and
proud too; though when you come to look the
thing straight in the eye, he ain't entitled to as

much credit as he would 'a' been if he'd been *hunting* di'monds. You can see the difference easy if you think it over. You see, an accident, that way, ain't fairly as big a thing as a thing that's done a-purpose. Anybody could find that di'mond in that corn-pone; but mind you, it's got to be somebody that's got *that kind of a corn-pone*. That's where that feller's credit comes in, you see; and that's where mine comes in. I don't claim no great things—I don't reckon I could 'a' done it again—but I done it that time; that's all I claim. And I hadn't no more idea I could do such a thing, and warn't any more thinking about it or trying to, than you be this minute. Why, I was just as ca'm, a body couldn't be any ca'mer, and yet, all of a sudden, out it come. I've often thought of that time, and I can remember just the way everything looked, same as if it was only last week. I can see it all: beautiful rolling country with woods and fields and lakes for hundreds and hundreds of miles all around, and towns and villages scattered everywheres under us, here and there and yonder; and the professor mooning over a chart on his little table, and Tom's cap flopping in the rigging where it was hung up to dry. And one thing in particular was a bird right alongside, not ten foot off, going our way and trying to keep up, but losing ground all the time; and a railroad train doing the same thing down there, sliding among the trees and farms, and pouring out a long cloud of black smoke and now and then a little puff of white; and when the white was gone so long you had almost forgot it, you would hear a little faint toot, and that was the whistle. And we left the bird and the train both behind, *'way* behind, and done it easy, too.

But Tom he was huffy, and said me and Jim was a couple of ignorant blatherskites, and then he says:

"Suppose there's a brown calf and a big brown dog, and an artist is making a picture of them. What is the *main* thing that that artist has got to do? He has got to paint them so you can tell them apart the minute you look at them, hain't he? Of course. Well, then, do you want him to go and paint *both* of them brown? Certainly you don't. He paints one of them blue, and then you can't make no mistake.

It's just the same with the maps. That's why they make every state a different color; it ain't to deceive you, it's to keep you from deceiving yourself."

But I couldn't see no argument about that, and neither could Jim. Jim shook his head, and says:

"Why, Mars Tom, if you knowed what chuckleheads dem painters is, you'd wait a long time before you'd fetch one er *dem* in to back up a fac'. I's gwine to tell you, den you kin see for you'self. I see one of 'em a-paintin' away, one day, down in ole Hank Wilson's back lot, en I went down to see, en he was paintin' dat old brindle cow wid de near horn gone—you knows de one I means. En I ast him what he's paintin' her for, en he say when he git her painted, de picture's wuth a hundred dollars. Mars Tom, he could 'a' got de cow fer fifteen, en I *tole* him so. Well, sah, if you'll b'lieve me, he jes' shuck his head, dat painter did, en went on a-dobbin'. Bless you, Mars Tom, *dey* don't know nothin'."

Tom lost his temper. I notice a person 'most always does that's got laid out in an argument. He told us to shut up, and maybe we'd feel

better. Then he see a town clock away off down
yonder, and he took up the glass and looked at
it, and then looked at his silver turnip, and then
at the clock, and then at the turnip again, and
says:

"That's funny! That clock's near about an
hour fast."

So he put up his turnip. Then he see another clock, and took a look, and it was an hour
fast too. That puzzled him.

"That's a mighty curious thing," he says. "I
don't understand it."

Then he took the glass and hunted up another clock, and sure enough it was an hour fast
too. Then his eyes began to spread and his
breath to come out kinder gaspy like, and he
says: "Ger-reat Scott, it's the *longitude!*"

I says, considerably scared:

"Well, what's been and gone and happened
now?"

"Why, the thing that's happened is that this
old bladder has slid over Illinois and Indiana
and Ohio like nothing, and this is the east end
of Pennsylvania or New York, or somewheres
around there."

"Tom Sawyer, you don't mean it!"

"Yes, I do, and it's dead sure. We've covered about fifteen degrees of longitude since we left St. Louis yesterday afternoon, and them clocks are *right*. We've come close on to eight hundred miles."

I didn't believe it, but it made the cold streaks trickle down my back just the same. In my experience I knowed it wouldn't take much short of two weeks to do it down the Mississippi on a raft.

Jim was working his mind and studying. Pretty soon he says:

"Mars Tom, did you say dem clocks uz right?"

"Yes, they're right."

"Ain't yo' watch right, too?"

"She's right for St. Louis, but she's an hour wrong for here."

"Mars Tom, is you tryin' to let on dat de time ain't de *same* everywheres?"

"No, it ain't the same everywheres, by a long shot."

Jim looked distressed, and says:

"It grieves me to hear you talk like dat, Mars

Tom; I's right down ashamed to hear you talk like dat, arter de way you's been raised. Yassir, it'd break yo' aunt Polly's heart to hear you talk like dat."

Tom was astonished. He looked Jim over wondering, and didn't say nothing, and Jim went on:

"Mars Tom, who put de people out yonder in St. Louis? De Lord done it. Who put de people here whar we is? De Lord done it. Ain' dey bofe his children? 'Cose dey is. *Well*, den! is he gwine to *scriminate* 'twixt 'em?"

"Scriminate! I never heard such ignorance. There ain't no discriminating about it. The Lord made the day, and he made the night; but he didn't invent the hours, and he didn't distribute them around. Man did that."

"Mars Tom, is dat so? Man done it?"

"Certainly."

"Who tole him he could?"

"Nobody. He never asked."

Jim studied a minute, and says:

"Well, dat do beat me. I wouldn't 'a' tuck no sich resk. But some people ain't scared o' nothin'. Dey bangs right ahead; *dey* don't care what happens.   So den dey's allays an hour's diff'unce everywhah, Mars Tom?"

"An hour?   No! It's four minutes difference for every degree of longitude, you know. Fifteen of 'em's an hour, thirty of 'em's two hours, and so on.   When it's one o'clock Tuesday morning in England, it's eight o'clock the night before in New York."

Jim moved a little way along the locker, and you could see he was insulted. He kept shaking his head and muttering, and so I slid along to him and patted him on the leg, and petted him up, and got him over the worst of his feelings, and then he says:

"Mars Tom talkin' sich talk as dat! Choosday in one place en Monday in t'other, bofe in the same day! Huck, dis ain't no place to joke —up here whah we is. Two days in one day! How you gwine to get two days inter one day? Can't git two hours inter one hour, kin you? Can't git two gallons of whisky inter a one-gallon jug, kin you? No, sir, 'twould strain de jug. Yes, en even den you couldn't, *I* don't believe. Why, looky here, Huck, s'posen de Choosday was New Year's—now den! is you gwine to tell me it's dis year in one place en las'

year in t'other, bofe in de identical same minute? It's de beatenest rubbage! I can't stan'
it—I can't stan' to hear tell 'bout it." Then he
begun to shiver and turn gray, and Tom says:

"*Now* what's the matter? What's the trouble?"

Jim could hardly speak, but he says:

"Mars Tom, you ain't jokin', en it's *so?*"

"No, I'm not, and it *is* so."

Jim shivered again and says:

"Den dat Monday could be de las' day, en dey
wouldn't be no las' day in England, en de dead
wouldn't be called. We mustn't go over dah,
Mars Tom. Please git him to turn back; I
wants to be whah—"

All of a sudden we see something, and all
jumped up, and forgot everything and begun to
gaze. Tom says:

"Ain't that the—" He catched his breath,
then says: "It *is,* sure as you live! It's the
ocean!"

That made me and Jim catch our breath, too.
Then we all stood petrified but happy, for none
of us had ever seen an ocean, or ever expected
to. Tom kept muttering:

"Atlantic Ocean—Atlantic. Land, don't it

sound great! And that's *it*—and *we* are looking
at it—we! Why, it's just too splendid to believe!"

Then we see a big bank of black smoke; and
when we got nearer, it was a city—and a monster she was, too, with a thick fringe of ships
around one edge; and we wondered if it was
New York, and begun to jaw and dispute about
it, and, first we knowed, it slid from under us
and went flying behind, and here we was, out
over the very ocean itself, and going like a cyclone.   Then we woke up, I tell you!

We made a break aft and raised a wail, and
begun to beg the professor to turn back and
land us, but he jerked out his pistol and motioned us back, and we went, but nobody will
ever know how bad we felt.

The land was gone, all but a little streak, like
a snake, away off on the edge of the water, and
down under us was just ocean, ocean, ocean—
millions of miles of it, heaving and pitching and
squirming, and white sprays blowing from the
wave-tops, and only a few ships in sight, wallow-
ing around and laying over, first on one side and
then on t'other, and sticking their bows under

and then their sterns; and before long there warn't no ships at all, and we had the sky and the whole ocean to ourselves, and the roomiest place I ever see and the lonesomest.

4: *Storm*

AND it got lonesomer and lonesomer. There was the big sky up there, empty and awful deep; and the ocean down there without a thing on it but just the waves. All around us was a ring, where the sky and the water come together; yes, a monstrous big ring it was, and we right in the dead center of it—plumb in the center. We was racing along like a prairie-fire, but it never made any difference, we couldn't seem to git past that center no way. I couldn't see that we ever gained an inch on that ring. It made a body feel creepy, it was so curious and unaccountable.

Well, everything was so awful still that we got to talking in a very low voice, and kept on getting creepier and lonesomer and less and less talky, till at last the talk ran dry altogether, and we just set there and "thunk," as Jim calls it, and never said a word the longest time.

The professor never stirred till the sun was overhead; then he stood up and put a kind of triangle to his eye, and Tom said it was a sextant and he was taking the sun to see whereabouts the balloon was. Then he ciphered a little and looked in a book, and then he begun to carry on again. He said lots of wild things, and, among others, he said he would keep up this hundred-mile gait till the middle of tomorrow afternoon, and then he'd land in London.

We said we would be humbly thankful.

He was turning away, but he whirled around when we said that, and give us a long look of his blackest kind—one of the maliciousest and suspiciousest looks I ever see. Then he says:

"You want to leave me. Don't try to deny it."

We didn't know what to say, so we held in and didn't say nothing at all.

He went aft and set down, but he couldn't

seem to git that thing out of his mind. Every now and then he would rip out something about it, and try to make us answer him, but we dasn't.

It got lonesomer and lonesomer right along, and it did seem to me I couldn't stand it. It was still worse when night begun to come on. By and by Tom pinched me and whispers:

"Look!"

I took a glance aft, and see the professor taking a whet out of a bottle. I didn't like the looks of that. By and by he took another drink, and pretty soon he begun to sing. It was dark now, and getting black and stormy. He went on singing, wilder and wilder, and the thunder begun to mutter, and the wind to wheeze and moan among the ropes, and altogether it was awful. It got so black we couldn't see him any more, and wished we couldn't hear him, but we could. Then he got still; but he warn't still ten minutes till we got suspicious, and wished he would start up his noise again, so we could tell where he was. By and by there was a flash of lightning, and we see him start to get up, but he staggered and fell down. We heard him scream out in the dark:

"They don't want to go to England. All right, I'll change the course. They want to leave me. I know they do. Well, they shall— and *now!*"

I 'most died when he said that. Then he was still again—still so long I couldn't bear it, and it did seem to me the lightning wouldn't *ever* come again. But at last there was a blessed flash, and there he was, on his hands and knees crawling, and not four feet from us. My, but his eyes was terrible! He made a lunge for Tom, and says, "Overboard *you* go!" but it was already pitch-dark again, and I couldn't see whether he got him or not, and Tom didn't make a sound.

There was another long, horrible wait; then there was a flash, and I see Tom's head sink down outside the boat and disappear. He was on the rope-ladder that dangled down in the air from the gunnel. The professor let off a shout and jumped for him, and straight off it was pitch-dark again, and Jim groaned out, "Po' Mars Tom, he's a goner!" and made a jump for the professor, but the professor warn't there.

Then we heard a couple of terrible screams, and then another not so loud, and then another

He made a lunge for Tom, and says, "Over-
board you go!"

that was 'way below, and you could only *just* hear it; and I heard Jim say, "Po' Mars Tom!"

Then it was awful still, and I reckon a person could 'a' counted four thousand before the next flash come. When it come I see Jim on his knees, with his arms on the locker and his face buried in them, and he was crying. Before I could look over the edge it was all dark again, and I was glad, because I didn't want to see. But when the next flash come, I was watching, and down there I see somebody a-swinging in the wind on the ladder, and it was Tom!

"Come up!" I shouts; "come up, Tom!"

His voice was so weak, and the wind roared so, I couldn't make out what he said, but I thought he asked was the professor up there. I shouts:

"No, he's down in the ocean! Come up! Can we help you?"

Of course, all this in the dark.

"Huck, who is you hollerin' at?"

"I'm hollerin' at Tom."

"Oh, Huck, how kin you act so, when you know po' Mars Tom—" Then he let off an awful scream, and flung his head and his arms back and let off another one, because there was a white glare just then, and he had raised up his face just in time to see Tom's, as white as snow, rise above the gunnel and look him right in the eye. He thought it was Tom's ghost, you see.

Tom clumb aboard, and when Jim found it *was* him, and not his ghost, he hugged him, and called him all sorts of loving names, and carried on like he was gone crazy, he was so glad. Says I:

"What did you wait for, Tom? Why didn't you come up at first?"

"I dasn't, Huck. I knowed somebody plunged down past me, but I didn't know who it was in the dark. It could 'a' been you, it could 'a' been Jim."

That was the way with Tom Sawyer—always sound. He warn't coming up till he knowed where the professor was.

The storm let go about this time with all its might; and it was dreadful the way the thunder boomed and tore, and the lightning glared out, and the wind sung and screamed in the rigging, and the rain come down. One second you couldn't see your hand before you, and the next you could count the threads in your coat-sleeve, and see a whole wide desert of waves pitching and tossing through a kind of veil of rain. A storm like that is the lovelist thing there is, but it ain't at its best when you are up in the sky and lost, and it's wet and lonesome, and there's just been a death in the family.

We set there huddled up in the bow, and talked low about the poor professor; and everybody was sorry for him, and sorry the world had made fun of him and treated him so harsh, when he was doing the best he could, and hadn't a friend nor nobody to encourage him and keep him from brooding his mind away and going deranged. There was plenty of clothes and blankets and everything at the other end, but we thought we'd ruther take the rain than go meddling back there.

5: *Land*

WE tried to make some plans, but we couldn't come to no agreement. Me and Jim was for turning around and going back home, but Tom allowed that by the time daylight come, so we could see our way, we would be so far toward England that we might as well go there, and come back in a ship, and have the glory of saying we done it.

About midnight the storm quit and the moon come out and lit up the ocean, and we begun to feel comfortable and drowsy; so we stretched out on the lockers and went to sleep, and never woke up again till sunup. The sea was sparkling like di'monds, and it was nice weather, and pretty soon our things was all dry again.

We went aft to find some breakfast, and the first thing we noticed was that there was a dim light burning in a compass back there under a hood. Then Tom was disturbed. He says:

"You know what that means, easy enough. It means that somebody has got to stay on watch and steer this thing the same as he would a ship, or she'll wander around and go wherever the wind wants her to."

"Well," I says, "what's she been doing since—er—since we had the accident?"

"Wandering," he says, kinder troubled— "wandering, without any doubt. She's in a wind now that's blowing her south of east. We don't know how long that's been going on, either."

So then he p'inted her east, and said he would hold her there till we rousted out the breakfast. The professor had laid in everything a body could want; he couldn't 'a' been better fixed. There wasn't no milk for the coffee, but there was water, and everything else you could want, and a charcoal stove and the fixings for it, and pipes and cigars and matches; and wine and liquor, which warn't in our line; and books, and maps, and charts, and an accordion; and furs, and blankets, and no end of rubbish, like brass beads and brass jewelry, which Tom said was a sure sign that he had an idea of visiting among savages. There was money, too. Yes, the professor was well enough fixed.

After breakfast Tom learned me and Jim how to steer, and divided us all up into four-hour watches, turn and turn about; and when his watch was out I took his place, and he got out the professor's papers and pens and wrote a letter home to his aunt Polly, telling her everything that had happened to us, and dated it *"In the Welkin, approaching England,"* and folded it together and stuck it fast with a red wafer, and directed it, and wrote above the direction, in big writing, *"From Tom Sawyer, the Erronort,"* and said it would stump old Nat Parsons, the postmaster, when it come along in the mail. I says:

"Tom Sawyer, this ain't no welkin; it's a balloon."

"Well, now, who *said* it was a welkin, smarty?"

"You've wrote it on the letter, anyway."

"What of it? That don't mean that the balloon's the welkin."

"Oh, I thought it did. Well, then, what is a welkin?"

I see in a minute he was stuck. He raked and scraped around in his mind, but he couldn't find nothing, so he had to say:

"*I* don't know, and nobody don't know. It's just a word, and it's a mighty good word, too. There ain't many that lays over it. I don't believe there's *any* that does."

"Shucks!" I says. "But what does it *mean?* —that's the p'int."

"*I* don't know what it means, I tell you. It's a word that people uses for—for—well, its ornamental. They don't put ruffles on a shirt to keep a person warm, do they?"

"Course they don't."

"But they put them *on*, don't they?"

"Yes."

"All right, then; that letter I wrote is a shirt, and the welkin's the ruffle on it."

I judged that that would gravel Jim, and it did.

"Now, Mars Tom, it ain't no use to talk like dat; en, moreover, it's sinful. You knows a letter ain't no shirt, en dey ain't no ruffles on it, nuther. Dey ain't no place to put 'em on; you can't put 'em on, and dey wouldn't stay ef you did."

"Oh, *do* shut up, and wait till something's started that you know something about."

"Why, Mars Tom, sholy you can't mean to say I don't know about shirts, when, goodness knows, I's toted home de washin' ever sence—"

"I tell you, this hasn't got anything to *do* with shirts. I only—"

"Why, Mars Tom, you said yo'self dat a letter—"

"Do you want to drive me crazy? Keep still. I only used it as a metaphor."

That word kinder bricked us up for a minute. Then Jim says—rather timid, because he see Tom was getting pretty tetchy:

"Mars Tom, what is a metaphor?"

"A metaphor's a—well, it's a—a—a metaphor's an illustration." He see *that* didn't git home, so he tried again. "When I say birds of a feather flocks together, it's a metaphorical way of saying—"

"But dey *don't*, Mars Tom. No, sir, 'deed dey don't. Dey ain't no feathers dat's more alike den a bluebird en a jaybird, but ef you waits till you catches *dem* birds together, you'll—"

"Oh, give us a rest! you can't get the simplest little thing through your thick skull. Now don't bother me any more."

Jim was satisfied to stop. He was dreadful pleased with himself for catching Tom out. The minute Tom begun to talk about birds I judged he was a goner, because Jim knowed more about birds than both of us put together. You see, he had killed hundreds and hundreds of them, and that's the way to find out about birds. That's the way people does that writes books about birds, and loves them so that they'll go hungry and tired and take any amount of trouble to find a new bird and kill it. Their name is ornithologers, and I could have been an ornithologer myself, because I always loved birds and creatures; and I started out to learn how to be one, and I see a bird setting on a limb of a high tree, singing with its head tilted back and its mouth open, and before I thought I fired, and his song stopped and he fell straight down from the limb, all limp like a rag, and I run and picked him up and he was dead, and his body was warm in my hand, and his head rolled about this way and that, like his neck was broke, and there was a little white skin over his eyes, and one little drop of blood on the side of his head; and, laws! I couldn't see nothing more for the tears; and I hain't never murdered no creature since that warn't doing me no harm, and I ain't going to.

But I was aggravated about that welkin. I wanted to know. I got the subject up again, and then Tom explained, the best he could. He said when a person made a big speech the newspapers said the shouts of the people made the welkin ring. He said they always said that, but none of them ever told what it was, so he allowed it just meant outdoors and up high. Well, that seemed sensible enough, so I was satisfied, and said so. That pleased Tom and put him in a good humor again, and he says:

"Well, it's all right, then; and we'll let by-gones be bygones. I don't know for certain what a welkin is, but when we land in London we'll make it ring, anyway, and don't you forget it."

He said an erronort was a person who sailed

around in balloons; and said it was a mighty sight finer to be Tom Sawyer the Erronort than to be Tom Sawyer the Traveler, and we would be heard of all round the world, if we pulled through all right, and so he wouldn't give shucks to be a traveler now.

Toward the middle of the afternoon we got everything ready to land, and we felt pretty good, too, and proud; and we kept watching with the glasses, like Columbus discovering America. But we couldn't see nothing but ocean. The afternoon wasted out and the sun shut down, and still there warn't no land anywheres. We wondered what was the matter, but reckoned it would come out all right, so we went on steering east, but went up on a higher level so we wouldn't hit any steeples or mountains in the dark.

It was my watch till midnight, and then it was Jim's; but Tom stayed up, because he said ship-captains done that when they was making the land, and didn't stand no regular watch.

Well, when daylight come, Jim give a shout, and we jumped up and looked over, and there was the land sure enough—land all around, as far as you could see, and perfectly level and yaller. We didn't know how long we'd been over it. There warn't no trees, nor hills, nor rocks, nor towns, and Tom and Jim had took it for the sea. They took it for the sea in a dead ca'm; but we was so high up, anyway, that if it had been the sea and rough, it would 'a' looked smooth, all the same, in the night, that way.

We was all in a powerful excitement now, and grabbed the glasses and hunted everywheres for London, but couldn't find hair nor hide of it, nor any other settlement—nor any sign of a lake or a river, either. Tom was clean beat. He said it warn't his notion of England; he thought England looked like America, and always had that idea. So he said we better have breakfast, and then drop down and inquire the quickest way to London. We cut the breakfast pretty short, we was so impatient. As we slanted along down, the weather began to moderate, and pretty soon we shed our furs. But it kept *on* moderating, and in a precious little while it was 'most too moderate. We was close down now, and just blistering!

We settled down to within thirty foot of the land—that is, it was land if sand is land; for this wasn't anything but pure sand. Tom and me

clumb down the ladder and took a run to stretch
our legs, and it felt amazing good—that is, the
stretching did, but the sand scorched our feet
like hot embers. Next, we see somebody coming, and started to meet him; but we heard Jim
shout, and looked around and he was fairly
dancing, and making signs, and yelling. We
couldn't make out what he said, but we was
scared anyway, and begun to heel it back to the
balloon. When we got close enough, we understood the words, and they made me sick:

"Run! Run fo' yo' life! Hit's a lion; I kin
see him thoo de glass! Run, boys; do please heel
it de bes' you kin. He's bu'sted outen de menagerie, en dey ain't nobody to stop him!"

It made Tom fly, but it took the stiffening all
out of my legs. I could only just gasp along the
way you do in a dream when there's a ghost
gaining on you.

Tom got to the ladder and shinned up it a
piece and waited for me; and as soon as I got a
foothold on it he shouted to Jim to soar away.
But Jim had clean lost his head, and said he had
forgot how. So Tom shinned along up and told
me to follow; but the lion was arriving, fetching
a most ghastly roar with every lope, and my legs

shook so I dasn't try to take one of them out of the rounds for fear the other one would give way under me.

But Tom was aboard by this time, and he started the balloon up a little, and stopped it again as soon as the end of the ladder was ten or twelve feet above ground. And there was the lion, a-ripping around under me, and roaring and springing up in the air at the ladder, and only missing it about a quarter of an inch, it seemed to me. It was delicious to be out of his reach, perfectly delicious, and made me feel good and thankful all up one side; but I was hanging there helpless and couldn't climb, and that made me feel perfectly wretched and miserable all down the other. It is most seldom that a person feels so mixed like that; and it is not to be recommended, either.

Tom asked me what he'd better do, but I didn't know. He asked me if I could hold on whilst he sailed away to a safe place and left the lion behind. I said I could if he didn't go no higher than he was now; but if he went higher I would lose my head and fall, sure. So he said, "Take a good grip," and he started.

"Don't go so fast," I shouted. "It makes my head swim."

The lion was arriving, fetching a most ghastly roar with every lope

He had started like a lightning express. He slowed down, and we glided over the sand slower, but still in a kind of sickening way; for it *is* uncomfortable to see things sliding and gliding under you like that, and not a sound.

But pretty soon there was plenty of sound, for the lion was catching up. His noise fetched others. You could see them coming on the lope from every direction, and pretty soon there was a couple of dozen of them under me, jumping up at the ladder and snarling and snapping at each other; and so we went skimming along over the sand, and these fellers doing what they could to help us to not forgit the occasion; and then some other beasts come, without an invite, and they started a regular riot down there.

We see this plan was a mistake. We couldn't ever git away from them at this gait, and I couldn't hold on forever. So Tom took a think, and struck another idea. That was, to kill a lion with the pepper-box revolver, and then sail away while the others stopped to fight over the carcass. So he stopped the balloon still, and done it, and then we sailed off while the fuss was going on, and come down a quarter of a mile off, and they helped me aboard; but by the time we was out of reach again, that gang was on hand once more. And when they see we was really gone and they couldn't get us, they sat down on their hams and looked up at us so kind of disappointed that it was as much as a person could do not to see *their* side of the matter.

6: *It's a Caravan*

I WAS so weak that the only thing I wanted was a chance to lay down, so I made straight for my lockerbunk, and stretched myself out there. But a body couldn't get back his strength in no such oven as that, so Tom give the command to soar, and Jim started her aloft.

We had to go up a mile before we struck comfortable weather where it was breezy and pleasant and just right, and pretty soon I was all straight again. Tom had been setting quiet and thinking; but now he jumps up and says:

"I bet you a thousand to one *I* know where we are. We're in the Great Sahara, as sure as guns!"

He was so excited he couldn't hold still; but I wasn't. I says:

"Well, then, where's the Great Sahara? In England or in Scotland?"

" 'Tain't in either; it's in Africa."

Jim's eyes bugged out, and he begun to stare down with no end of interest, because that was where his originals come from; but I didn't more than half believe it. I couldn't, you know; it seemed too awful far away for us to have traveled.

But Tom was full of his discovery, as he called it, and said the lions and the sand meant the Great Desert, sure. He said he could 'a' found out, before we sighted land, that we was crowding the land somewheres, if he had thought of one thing; and when we asked him what, he said:

"These clocks. They're chronometers. You always read about them in sea-voyages. One of them is keeping Grinnage time, and the other is keeping St. Louis time, like my watch. When we left St. Louis it was four in the afternoon by my watch and this clock, and it was ten at night by this Grinnage clock. Well, at this time of the year the sun sets at about seven o'clock.

Now I noticed the time yesterday evening when the sun went down, and it was half-past five o'clock by the Grinnage clock, and half-past eleven A.M. by my watch and the other clock. You see, the sun rose and set by my watch in St. Louis, and the Grinnage clock was six hours fast; but we've come so far east that it comes within less than half an hour of setting by the Grinnage clock now, and I'm away out—more than four hours and a half out. You see, that meant that we was closing up on the longitude of Ireland, and would strike it before long if we was p'inted right—which we wasn't. No, sir, we've been a-wandering—wandering 'way down south of east, and it's my opinion we are in Africa. Look at this map. You see how the shoulder of Africa sticks out to the west. Think how fast we've traveled; if we had gone straight east we would be long past England by this time. You watch for noon, all of you, and we'll stand up, and when we can't cast a shadow we'll find that this Grinnage clock is coming mighty close to marking twelve. Yes, sir, I think we're in Africa; and it's just bully."

Jim was gazing down with the glass. He shook his head and says:

"Mars Tom, I reckon dey's a mistake somers. I hain't seen no darkies yit."

"That's nothing; they don't live in the desert. What is that, 'way off yonder? Gimme a glass."

He took a long look, and said it was like a black string stretched across the sand, but he couldn't guess what it was.

"Well," I says, "I reckon maybe you've got a chance now to find out whereabouts this balloon is, because as like as not that is one of these lines here, that's on the map, that you call meridians of longitude, and we can drop down and look at its number, and—"

"Oh, shucks, Huck Finn, I never see such a lunkhead as you. Did you s'pose there's meridians of longitude on the *earth?*"

"Tom Sawyer, they're set down on the map, and you know it perfectly well, and here they are, and you can see for yourself."

"Of course they're on the map, but that's nothing; there ain't any on the *ground.*"

"Tom, do you know that to be so?"

"Certainly I do."

"Well, then, that map's a liar again. I never see such a liar as that map."

He fired up at that, and I was ready for him,

and Jim was warming his opinion, too, and next minute we'd 'a' broke loose on another argument, if Tom hadn't dropped the glass and begun to clap his hands like a maniac and sing out:

"Camels!—Camels!"

So I grabbed a glass and Jim, too, and took a look, but I was disappointed, and says:

"Camels your granny; they're spiders."

"Spiders in a desert, you shad? Spiders walking in a procession? You don't ever reflect, Huck Finn, and I reckon you really haven't got anything to reflect *with*. Don't you know we're as much as a mile up in the air, and that that string of crawlers is two or three miles away? Spiders, good land! Spiders as big as a cow? Perhaps you'd like to go down and milk one of 'em. But they're camels, just the same. It's a caravan, that's what it is, and it's a mile long."

"Well, then, let's go down and look at it. I don't believe in it, and ain't going to till I see it and know it."

"All right," he says, and give the command: "Lower away."

As we come slanting down into the hot weather, we could see that it was camels, sure

enough, plodding along, an everlasting string of
them, with bales strapped to them, and several
hundred men in long white robes, and a thing
like a shawl bound over their heads and hanging
down with tassels and fringes; and some of the
men had long guns and some hadn't, and some
was riding and some was walking. And the
weather—well, it was just roasting. And how
slow they did creep along! We swooped down
now, all of a sudden, and stopped about a hundred yards over their heads.

The men all set up a yell, and some of them
fell flat on their stomachs, some begun to fire
their guns at us, and the rest broke and scam-
pered every which way, and so did the camels.

We see that we was making trouble, so we
went up again about a mile, to the cool weather,
and watched them from there. It took them an
hour to get together and form the procession
again; then they started along, but we could see
by the glasses that they wasn't paying much attention to anything but us. We poked along,
looking down at them with the glasses, and by
and by we see a big sand mound, and something
like people the other side of it, and there was
something like a man laying on top of the

mound that raised his head up every now and then, and seemed to be watching the caravan or us, we didn't know which. As the caravan got nearer, he sneaked down on the other side and rushed to the other men and horses—for that is what they was—and we see them mount in a hurry; and next, here they come, like a house afire, some with lances and some with long guns, and all of them yelling the best they could.

They come a-tearing down onto the caravan, and the next minute both sides crashed together and was all mixed up, and there was such another popping of guns as you never heard, and the air got so full of smoke you could only catch glimpses of them struggling together. There must 'a' been six hundred men in that battle, and it was terrible to see. Then they broke up into gangs and groups, fighting tooth and nail, and scurrying and scampering around, and laying into each other like everything; and whenever the smoke cleared a little you could see dead and wounded people and camels scattered far and wide and all about, and camels racing off in every direction.

At last the robbers see they couldn't win, so their chief sounded a signal, and all that was left of them broke away and went scampering across the plain. The last man to go snatched up a child and carried it off in front of him on his horse, and a woman run screaming and begging after him, and followed him away off across the plain till she was separated a long ways from her people; but it warn't no use, and she had to give it up, and we see her sink down on the sand and cover her face with her hands. Then Tom took the hellum, and started for that yahoo, and we come a-whizzing down and made a swoop, and knocked him out of the saddle, child and all; and he was jarred considerable, but the child wasn't hurt, but laid there working its hands and legs in the air like a tumblebug that's on its back and can't turn over. The man went staggering off to overtake his horse, and didn't know what had hit him, for we was three or four hundred yards up in the air by this time.

We judged the woman would go and get the child now; but she didn't. We could see her, through the glass, still setting there, with her head bowed down on her knees; so of course she hadn't seen the performance, and thought her child was clean gone with the man. She was nearly a half a mile from her people, so we

thought we might go down to the child, which
was about a quarter of a mile beyond her, and
snake it to her before the caravan people could
git to us to do us any harm; and besides, we
reckoned they had enough business on their
hands for one while, anyway, with the wounded.
We thought we'd chance it, and we did. We
swooped down and stopped, and Jim shinned
down the ladder and fetched up the kid, which
was a nice fat little thing, and in a noble good
humor, too, considering it was just out of a battle and been tumbled off of a horse; and then we
started for the mother, and stopped back of her
and tolerable near by, and Jim slipped down
and crept up easy, and when he was close back of
her the child goo-goo'd, the way a child does,
and she heard it, and whirled and fetched a
shriek of joy, and made a jump for the kid and
snatched it and hugged it, and dropped it and
hugged Jim, and then snatched off a gold chain
and hung it around Jim's neck, and hugged him
again, and jerked up the child again, a-sobbing
and glorifying all the time; and Jim he shoved
for the ladder and up it, and in a minute we was
back up in the sky and the woman was staring
up, with the back of her head between her

*Jim slipped down and crept up easy, and she
made a jump for the child*

shoulders and the child with its arms locked around her neck. And there she stood, as long as we was in sight a-sailing away in the sky.

7: *Tom Respects the Flea*

"Noon!" says Tom, and so it was. His shadder was just a blot around his feet. We looked, and the Grinnage clock was so close to twelve the difference didn't amount to nothing. So Tom said London was right north of us or right south of us, one or t'other, and he reckoned by the weather and the sand and the camels it was north; and a good many miles north, too; as many as from New York to the city of Mexico, he guessed.

Jim said he reckoned a balloon was a good deal the fastest thing in the world, unless it might be some kinds of birds—a wild pigeon, maybe, or a railroad.

But Tom said he had read about railroads in England going nearly a hundred miles an hour for a little ways, and there never was a bird in the world that could do that—except one, and that was a flea.

"A flea? Why, Mars Tom, in de fust place he ain't a bird, strickly speakin'—"

"He ain't a bird, eh?   Well, then, what is he?"

"I don't rightly know, Mars Tom, but I speck he's only jist a' animal.   No, I reckon dat won't do, nuther, he ain't big enough for a' animal. He mus' be a bug.   Yassir, dat's what he is, he's a bug."

"I bet he ain't, but let it go.   What's your second place?"

"Well, in de second place, birds is creturs dat goes a long ways, but a flea don't."

"He don't, don't he?   Come, now, what is a long distance if you know?"

"Why, it's miles, and lots of 'em—anybody knows dat."

"Can't a man walk miles?"

"Yassir, he kin."

"As many as a railroad?"

"Yassir, if you give him time."

"Can't a flea?"

"Well—I s'pose so—ef you gives him heaps of time."

"Now you begin to see, don't you, that *distance* ain't the thing to judge by, at all; it's the time it takes to go the distance *in* that *counts,* ain't it?"

"Well, hit do look sorter so, but I wouldn't 'a' b'lieved it, Mars Tom."

"It's a matter of *proportion*, that's what it is; and when you come to gauge a thing's speed by its size, where's your bird and your man and your railroad 'longside of a flea? The fastest man can't run more than about ten miles in an hour—not much over ten thousand times his own length. But all the books says any common ordinary third-class flea can jump a hundred and fifty times his own length; yes, and he can make five jumps a second too—seven hundred and fifty times his own length, in one little second—for he don't fool away any time stopping and starting—he does them both at the same time; you'll see, if you try to put your finger on him. Now that's a common, ordinary, third-class flea's gait; but you take an Eyetalian *first*-class, that's been the pet of the nobility all his

life, and hasn't ever known what want or sickness or exposure was, and he can jump more
than three hundred times his own length, and
keep it up all day, five such jumps every second,
which is fifteen hundred times his own length.
Well, suppose a man could go fifteen hundred
times his own length in a second—say, a mile
and a half. It's ninety miles a minute; it's considerable more than five thousand miles an
hour. Where's your man *now?*—yes, and your
bird, and your railroad, and your balloon?
Laws, they don't amount to shucks 'longside of a
flea. A flea is just a comet b'iled down small."

Jim was a good deal astonished, and so was I.
Jim said:

"Is dem figgers jist edjackly true, en no jokin'
en no lies, Mars Tom?"

"Yes, they are; they're perfectly true."

"Well, den, honey, a body's got to respec' a
flea. I ain't had no respec' for um befo',
sca'sely, but dey ain't no gittin' roun' it, dey do
deserve it, dat's certain."

"Well, I bet they do. They've got ever so
much more sense, and brains, and brightness, in
proportion to their size, than any other cretur
in the world. A person can learn them 'most

anything; and they learn it quicker than any other cretur, too. They've been learnt to haul little carriages in harness, and go this way and that way and t'other way according to their orders; yes, and to march and drill like soldiers, doing it as exact, according to orders, as soldiers does it. They've been learnt to do all sorts of hard and troublesome things. S'pose you could cultivate a flea up to the size a man, and keep his natural smartness a-growing and a-growing right along up, bigger and bigger, and keener and keener, in the same proportion—where'd the human race be, do you reckon? That flea would be President of the United States, and you couldn't any more prevent it than you can prevent lightning."

"My lan', Mars Tom, I never knowed dey was so much *to* de beas'. No, sir, I never had no idea of it, and dat's de fac'."

"There's more to him, by a long sight, than there is to any other cretur, man or beast, in proportion to size. He's the interestingest of them all. People have so much to say about an ant's strength, and an elephant's, and a locomotive's. Shucks, they don't begin with a flea. He can lift two or three hundred times his own

weight. And none of them can come anywhere
near it. And, moreover, he has got notions of
his own, and is very particular, and you can't
fool him; his instinct, or his judgment, or whatever it is, is perfectly sound and clear, and don't
ever make a mistake. People think all humans
are alike to a flea. It ain't so. There's folks
that he won't go near, hungry or not hungry,
and I'm one of them. I've never had one of
them on me in my life."

"Mars Tom!"

"It's so; I ain't joking."

"Well, sah, I hain't ever heard de likes o' dat
befo'."

Jim couldn't believe it, and I couldn't; so we
had to drop down to the sand and git a supply
and see. Tom was right. They went for me
and Jim by the thousand, but not a one of them
lit on Tom. There warn't no explaining it, but
there it was and there warn't no getting around
it. He said it had always been just so, and he'd
just as soon be where there was a million of
them as not; they'd never touch him nor bother
him.

We went up to the cold weather to freeze 'em
out, and stayed a little spell, and then come back

to the comfortable weather and went lazying
along twenty or twenty-five miles an hour, the
way we'd been doing for the last few hours.
The reason was, that the longer we was in that
solemn, peaceful desert, the more the hurry and
fuss got kind of soothed down in us, and the
more happier and contented and satisfied we got
to feeling, and the more we got to liking the
desert, and then loving it. So we had cramped
the speed down, as I was saying, and was having
a most noble good lazy time, sometimes watching through the glasses, sometimes stretched out
on the lockers reading, sometimes taking a nap.

It didn't seem like we was the same lot that
was in such a state to find land and git ashore,
but it was. But we had got over that—clean
over it. We was used to the balloon now and
not afraid any more, and didn't want to be anywheres else. Why, it seemed just like home; it
'most seemed as if I had been born and raised in
it, and Jim and Tom said the same. And always
I had had hateful people around me, a-nagging
at me, and pestering of me, and scolding, and
finding fault, and fussing and bothering, and
sticking to me, and keeping after me, and making me do this, and making me do that and

t'other, and always selecting out the things I
didn't want to do, and then giving me Sam Hill
because I shirked and done something else, and
just aggravating the life out of a body all the
time; but up here in the sky it was so still and
sunshiny and lovely, and plenty to eat, and
plenty of sleep, and strange things to see, and no
nagging and no pestering, and no good people,
and just holiday all the time. Land, I warn't in
no hurry to git out and buck at civilization
again. Now, one of the worst things about civilization is, that anybody that gits a letter with
trouble in it comes and tells you all about it and
makes you feel bad, and the newspapers fetches
you the troubles of everybody all over the
world, and keeps you downhearted and dismal
'most all the time, and it's such a heavy load for
a person. I hate them newspapers; and I hate
letters; and if I had my way I wouldn't allow
nobody to load his troubles onto other folks he
ain't acquainted with, on t'other side of
the world, that way. Well, up in a balloon
there ain't any of that, and it's the darlingest
place there is.

We had supper, and that night was one of the
prettiest nights I ever see. The moon made it

just like daylight, only a heap softer; and once we see a lion standing all alone by himself, just all alone on the earth, it seemed like, and his shadder laid on the sand by him like a puddle of ink. That's the kind of moonlight to have.

Mainly we laid on our backs and talked; we didn't want to go to sleep. Tom said we was right in the midst of the *Arabian Nights* now. He said it was right along here that one of the cutest things in that book happened; so we looked down and watched while he told about it, because there ain't anything that is so interesting to look at as a place that a book has talked about. It was a tale about a camel-driver that had lost his camel, and he come along in the desert and met a man, and says:

"Have you run across a stray camel today?"

And the man says:

"Was he blind in his left eye?"

"Yes."

"Had he lost an upper front tooth?"

"Yes."

"Was his off hind leg lame?"

"Yes."

"Was he loaded with millet-seed on one side and honey on the other?"

"Yes, but you needn't go into no more details —that's the one, and I'm in a hurry. Where did you see him?"

"I hain't seen him at all," the man says.

"Hain't seen him at all? How can you describe him so close, then?"

"Because when a person knows how to use his eyes, everything has got a meaning to it; but most people's eyes ain't any good to them. I knowed a camel had been along, because I seen his track. I knowed he was lame in his off hind leg because he had favored that foot and trod light on it, and his track showed it. I knowed he was blind on his left side because he only nibbled the grass on the right side of the trail. I knowed he had lost an upper front tooth because where he bit into the sod his teeth-print showed it. The millet-seed sifted out on one side—the ants told me that; the honey leaked out on the other—the flies told me that. I know all about your camel, but I hain't seen him."

Jim says:

"Go on, Mars Tom, hit's a mighty good tale, and powerful interestin'."

"That's all," Tom says.

"All?" says Jim, astonished. "What 'come o' de camel?"

"I don't know."

"Mars Tom, don't de tale say?"

"No."

Jim puzzled a minute, then he says:

"Well! Ef dat ain't de beatenes' tale ever *I* struck. Jist gits to de place whah de intrust is gittin' red-hot, en down she breaks. Why, Mars Tom, dey ain't no *sense* in a tale dat acts like dat. Hain't you got no *idea* whether de man got de camel back er not?"

"No, I haven't."

I see myself there warn't no sense in the tale, to chop square off that way before it come to anything, but I warn't going to say so, because I could see Tom was souring up pretty fast over the way it flatted out and the way Jim had popped onto the weak place in it, and I don't think it's fair for everybody to pile onto a feller when he's down. But Tom he whirls on me and says:

"What do *you* think of the tale?"

Of course, then, I had to come out and make a clean breast and say it did seem to me, too, same as it did to Jim, that as long as the tale stopped square in the middle and never got to no place, it really warn't worth the trouble of telling.

Tom's chin dropped on his breast, and 'stead of being mad, as I reckoned he'd be, to hear me scoff at his tale that way, he seemed to be only sad; and he says:

"Some people can see, and some can't—just as that man said.   Let alone a camel, if a cyclone had gone by, *you* duffers wouldn't 'a' noticed the track."

I don't know what he meant by that, and he didn't say; it was just one of his irrulevances, I reckon—he was full of them, sometimes, when he was in a close place and couldn't see no other way out—but I didn't mind.   We'd spotted the soft place in that tale sharp enough, he couldn't git away from that little fact.   It graveled him like the nation, too, I reckon, much as he tried not to let on.

8: *The Disappearing Lake*

WE had an early breakfast in the morning, and
set looking down on the desert, and the weather
was ever so bammy and lovely, although
we warn't high up. You have to come down
lower and lower after sundown in the desert,
because it cools off so fast; and so, by the time it
is getting toward dawn, you are skimming along
only a little ways above the sand.

We was watching the shadder of the balloon
slide along the ground, and now and then gazing off across the desert to see if anything was
stirring, and then down on the shadder again,
when all of a sudden almost right under us we

see a lot of men and camels laying scattered about, perfectly quiet, like they was asleep.

We shut off the power, and backed up and stood over them, and then we see that they was all dead. It give us the cold shivers. And it made us hush down, too, and talk low, like people at a funeral. We dropped down slow and stopped, and me and Tom clumb down and went among them. There was men, and women, and children. They was dried by the sun, and dark and shriveled and leathery, like the pictures of mummies you see in books. And yet they looked just as human, you wouldn't 'a' believed it; just like they was asleep.

Some of the people and animals was partly covered with sand, but most of them not, for the sand was thin there, and the bed was gravel and hard. Most of the clothes had rotted away; and when you took hold of a rag, it tore with a touch, like spider-web. Tom reckoned they had been laying there for years.

Some of the men had rusty guns by them, some had swords on and had shawl belts with long, silver-mounted pistols stuck in them. All the camels had their loads on yet, but the packs had busted or rotted and spilt the freight out on

the ground.   We didn't reckon the swords was
any good to the dead people any more, so we
took one apiece, and some pistols.   We took a
small box, too, because it was so handsome and
inlaid so fine; and then we wanted to bury the
people; but there warn't no way to do it that we
could think of, and nothing to do it with but
sand, and that would blow away again, of
course.

Then we mounted high and sailed away, and
pretty soon that black spot on the sand was out
of sight, and we wouldn't ever see them poor
people again in this world.   We wondered, and
reasoned, and tried to guess how they come to
be there, and how it all happened to them, but
we couldn't make it out.   First we thought
maybe they got lost, and wandered around and
about till their food and water give out and they
starved to death; but Tom said no wild animals
nor vultures hadn't meddled with them, and so
that guess wouldn't do.   So at last we give it up,
and judged we wouldn't think about it no more,
because it made us low-spirited.

Then we opened the box, and it had gems
and jewels in it, quite a pile, and some little
veils of the kind the dead women had on, with

fringes made out of curious gold money that we
warn't acquainted with. We wondered if we
better go and try to find them again and give it
back; but Tom thought it over and said no, it
was a country that was full of robbers, and they
would come and steal it; and then the sin would
be on us for putting the temptation in their
way. So we went on; but I wished we had took
all they had, so there wouldn't 'a' been no temptation at all left.

We had had two hours of that blazing
weather down there, and was dreadful thirsty
when we got aboard again. We went straight
for the water, but it was spoiled and bitter, besides being pretty near hot enough to scald your
mouth. We couldn't drink it. It was Mississippi River water, the best in the world, and we
stirred up the mud in it to see if that would
help, but no, the mud wasn't any better than the
water.

Well, we hadn't been so very, very thirsty
before, while we was interested in the lost people, but we was now, and as soon as we found we
couldn't have a drink, we was more than thirty-
five times as thirsty as we was a quarter of a
minute before. Why, in a little while we

wanted to hold our mouths open and pant like a dog.

Tom said to keep a sharp lookout, all around, everywheres, because we'd got to find an oasis or there warn't no telling what would happen.   So we done it.   We kept the glasses gliding around all the time, till our arms got so tired we couldn't hold them any more.   Two hours— three hours—just gazing and gazing, and nothing but sand, sand, *sand,* and you could see the quivering heat-shimmer playing over it.   Dear, dear, a body don't know what real misery is till he is thirsty all the way through and is certain he ain't ever going to come to any water any more.   At last I couldn't stand it to look around on them baking plains; I laid down on the locker, and give it up.

But by and by Tom raised a whoop, and there she was!   A lake, wide and shiny, with pa'm trees leaning over it asleep, and their shadders in the water just as soft and delicate as ever you see.   I never see anything look so good.   It was a long ways off, but that warn't anything to us; we just slapped on a hundred-mile gait, and calculated to be there in seven minutes; but she stayed the same old distance away, all the time;

we couldn't seem to gain on her; yes, sir, just as far, and shiny, and like a dream; but we couldn't get no nearer; and at last, all of a sudden, she was gone!

Tom's eyes took a spread, and he says:

"Boys, it was a *my*ridge!"   Said it like he was glad.   I didn't see nothing to be glad about.   I says:

"Maybe.   I don't care nothing about its name, the thing I want to know is, what's become of it?"

Jim was trembling all over, and so scared he couldn't speak, but he wanted to ask that question himself if he could 'a' done it.   Tom says:

"What's *become* of it?   Why, you see yourself it's gone."

"Yes, I know; but where's it gone *to?*"

He looked me over and says:

"Well, now, Huck Finn, where *would* it go to!   Don't you know what a myridge is?"

"No, I don't.   What is it?"

"It ain't anything but imagination.   There ain't anything *to* it."

It warmed me up a little to hear him talk like that, and I says:

"What's the use you talking that kind of

stuff, Tom Sawyer? Didn't I see the lake?"

"Yes—you think you did."

"I don't think nothing about it, I *did* see it."

"I tell you you *didn't* see it either—because it warn't there to see."

It astonished Jim to hear him talk so, and he broke in and says, kind of pleading and distressed:

"Mars Tom, *please* don't say sich things in sich an awful time as dis. You ain't only reskin' yo' own self, but you's reskin' us—same way like Anna Nias en Siffira. De lake *wuz* dah—I seen it jis' as plain as I sees you en Huck dis minute."

I says:

"Why, he seen it himself! He was the very one that seen it first. *Now,* then!"

"Yes, Mars Tom, hit's so—you can't deny it. We all seen it, en dat *prove* it was dah."

"Proves it! *How* does it prove it?"

"Same way it does in de courts en everywheres, Mars Tom. One pusson might be drunk, or dreamy, or suthin', en he could be mistaken; en two might, maybe; but I tell you, sah, when three sees a thing, drunk or sober, it's *so*. Dey ain't no gettin' aroun' dat, en you knows it, Mars Tom."

"I don't know nothing of the kind. There used to be forty thousand million people that seen the sun move from one side of the sky to the other every day. Did that prove that the sun *done* it?"

" 'Course it did. En besides, dey warn't no 'casion to prove it. A body 'at's got any sense ain't gwine to doubt it. Dah she is now—a-sailin' thoo de sky, like she allays done."

Tom turned on me, then, and says:

"What do *you* say—is the sun standing still?"

"Tom Sawyer, what's the use to ask such a jackass question? Anybody that ain't blind can see it don't stand still."

"Well," he says, "I'm lost in the sky with no company but a passel of low-down animals that don't know no more than the head boss of a university did three or four hundred years ago."

It warn't fair play, and I let him know it. I says:

"Throwin' mud ain't arguin', Tom Sawyer."

"Oh, my goodness, oh, my goodness gracious, dah's de lake ag'in!" yelled Jim, just then.

"*Now*, Mars Tom, what you gwine to say?"

Yes, sir, there was the lake again, away yonder across the desert, perfectly plain, trees and all, just the same as it was before. I says:

"I reckon you're satisfied now, Tom Sawyer."

But he says, perfectly ca'm:

"Yes, satisfied there ain't no lake there."

Jim says:

"*Don't* talk so, Mars Tom—it sk'yers me to hear you. It's so hot, en you's so thirsty, dat you ain't in yo' right mine, Mars Tom. Oh, but don't she look good! 'clah I doan' know how I's gwine to wait tell we gits dah, I's *so* thirsty."

"Well, you'll have to wait; and it won't do you no good, either, because there ain't no lake there, I tell you."

I says:

"Jim, don't you take your eye off of it, and I won't, either."

" 'Deed I won't; en bless you, honey, I couldn't ef I wanted to."

We went a-tearing along toward it, piling the miles behind us like nothing, but never gaining an inch on it—and all of a sudden it was gone again! Jim staggered, and 'most fell down.

When he got his breath he says, gasping like a fish:

"Mars Tom, hit's a *ghos'*, dat's what it is, en I hopes to goodness we ain't gwine to see it no mo'. Dey's *been* a lake, en suthin's happened, en de lake's dead, en we's seen its ghos'; we's seen it twiste, en dat's proof. De desert's ha'nted, it's ha'nted, sho; oh, Mars Tom, le's git outen it; I'd ruther die den have de night ketch us in it ag'in en de ghos' er dat lake come a-mournin' aroun' us en we asleep en doan' know de danger we's in."

"Ghost, you gander! It ain't anything but air and heat and thirstiness pasted together by a person's imagination. If I—gimme the glass!"

He grabbed it and begun to gaze off to the right.

"It's a flock of birds," he says. "It's getting toward sundown, and they're making a bee-line across our track for somewheres. They mean business—maybe they're going for food or water, or both. Let her go to starboard!—Port your hellum! Hard down! There—ease up —steady, as you go."

We shut down some of the power, so as not to outspeed them, and took out after them. We went skimming along a quarter of a mile behind them, and when we had followed them an hour and a half and was getting pretty discouraged, and was thirsty clean to unendurableness, Tom says:

"Take the glass, one of you, and see what that is, away ahead of the birds."

Jim got the first glimpse, and slumped down on the locker sick. He was 'most crying, and says:

"She's dah ag'in, Mars Tom, she's dah ag'in, en I knows I's gwine to die, 'case when a body sees a ghos' de third time, dat's what it means. I wisht I'd never come in dis balloon, dat I does."

He wouldn't look no more, and what he said made me afraid, too, because I knowed it was true, for that has always been the way with ghosts; so then I wouldn't look any more, either. Both of us begged Tom to turn off and go some other way, but he wouldn't, and said we was ignorant superstitious blatherskites. Yes, and he'll git come up with, one of these days, I says to myself, insulting ghosts that way. They'll stand it for a while, maybe, but they won't stand it always, for anybody that knows about ghosts

knows how easy they are hurt, and how revenge-
ful they are.

So we was all quiet and still, Jim and me
being scared, and Tom busy. By and by Tom
fetched the balloon to a standstill, and says:

"*Now* get up and look, you sapheads."

We done it, and there was the sure-enough
water right under us!—clear, and blue, and
cool, and deep, and wavy with the breeze, the
loveliest sight that ever was. And all about it
was grassy banks, and flowers, and shady groves
of big trees, looped together with vines, and all
looking so peaceful and comfortable—enough
to make a body cry, it was so beautiful.

Jim *did* cry, and rip and dance and carry on,
he was so thankful and out of his mind for joy.
It was my watch, so I had to stay by the works,
but Tom and Jim clumb down and drunk a
barrel apiece, and fetched me up a lot, and I've
tasted a many a good thing in my life, but nothing that ever begun with that water.

Then they went down and had a swim, and
then Tom came up and spelled me, and me and
Jim had a swim, and then Jim spelled Tom, and
me and Tom had a foot-race and a boxing-mill,

Then we went down and had a swim

and I don't reckon I ever had such a good time in my life. It warn't so very hot, because it was close on to evening, and we hadn't any clothes on, anyway. Clothes is well enough in school, and in towns, and at balls, too, but there ain't no sense in them when there ain't no civilization nor other kinds of bothers and fussiness around.

"Lions a-comin'!—lions! Quick, Mars Tom! Jump for yo' life, Huck!"

Oh, and didn't we! We never stopped for clothes, but waltzed up the ladder just so. Jim lost his head straight off—he always done it whenever he got excited and scared; and so now, 'stead of just easing the ladder up from the ground a little, so the animals couldn't reach it, he turned on a raft of power, and we went whizzing up and was dangling in the sky before he got his wits together and seen what a foolish thing he was doing. Then he stopped her, but he had clean forgot what to do next; so there we was, so high that the lions looked like pups, and we was drifting off on the wind.

But Tom he shinned up and went for the works and begun to slant her down, and back toward the lake, where the animals was gathering like a camp-meeting, and I judged he had lost *his* head, too; for he knowed I was too scared to climb, and did he want to dump me among the tigers and things?

But no, his head was level; he knowed what he was about. He swooped down to within thirty or forty feet of the lake, and stopped right over the center, and sung out:

"Leggo, and drop!"

I done it, and shot down, feet first, and seemed to go about a mile toward the bottom; and when I come up, he says:

"Now lay on your back and float till you're rested and got your pluck back, then I'll dip the ladder in the water and you can climb aboard."

I done it. Now that was ever so smart in Tom, because if he had started off somewheres else to drop down on the sand, the menagerie would 'a' come along, too, and might 'a' kept us hunting a safe place till I got tuckered out and fell.

And all this time the lions and tigers was sorting out the clothes, and trying to divide them up so there would be some for all, but there was a misunderstanding about it some-wheres, on account of some of them trying to hog more than their share; so there was another insurrection, and you never see anything like it in the world. There must 'a' been fifty of them, all mixed up together, snorting and roaring and snapping and biting and tearing, legs and tails in the air, and you couldn't tell which was which, and the sand and fur a-flying. And when they got done, some was dead, and some was limping off crippled, and the rest was setting around on the battle-field, some of them licking their sore places and the others looking up at us and seemed to be kind of inviting us to come down and have some fun, but which we didn't want any.

As for the clothes, they warn't any, any more. Every last rag of them was inside of the animals; and not agreeing with them very well, I don't reckon, for there was considerable many brass buttons on them, and there was knives in the pockets too, and smoking-tobacco, and nails and chalk and marbles and fishhooks and things. But I wasn't caring. All that was bothering me was, that all we had now was the professor's clothes, a big enough assortment, but not suitable to go into company with, if we came across any, because the britches was as long as tunnels, and the coats and things according. Still, there was everything a tailor needed, and Jim was a kind of jack-legged tailor, and he allowed he could soon trim a suit or two down for us that would answer.

9: *Tom Discourses on the Desert*

STILL, we thought we would drop down there a minute, but on another errand. Most of the professor's cargo of food was put up in cans, in the new way that somebody had just invented; the rest was fresh. When you fetch Missouri beefsteak to the Great Sahara, you want to be particular and stay up in the coolish weather. So we reckoned we would drop down into the lion market and see how we could make out there.

We hauled in the ladder and dropped down till we was just above the reach of the animals, then we let down a rope with a slip-knot in it

and hauled up a dead lion, a small tender one,
then yanked up a cub tiger. We had to keep the
congregation off with the revolver, or they
would 'a' took a hand in the proceedings and
helped.

We carved off a supply from both, and saved
the skins, and hove the rest overboard. Then
we baited some of the professor's hooks with the
fresh meat and went a-fishing. We stood over
the lake just a convenient distance above the
water, and catched a lot of the nicest fish you
ever see. It was a most amazing good supper we
had; lion steak, tiger steak, fried fish, and hot
corn-pone. I don't want nothing better than
that.

We had some fruit to finish off with. We got
it out of the top of a monstrous tall tree. It was
a very slim tree that hadn't a branch on it from
the bottom plumb to the top, and there it
bursted out like a feather duster. It was a pa'm
tree, of course; anybody knows a pa'm tree the
minute he see it, by the pictures. We went for
cocoanuts in this one, but there warn't none.
There was only big loose bunches of things like
oversized grapes, and Tom allowed they was
dates, because he said they answered the

description in the *Arabian Nights* and the other books. Of course they mightn't be, and they might be poison; so we had to wait a spell, and watch and see if the birds et them. They done it; so we done it, too, and they was most amazing good.

By this time monstrous big birds begun to come and settle on the dead animals. They were plucky creturs; they would tackle one end of a lion that was being gnawed at the other end by another lion. If the lion drove the bird away, it didn't do no good; he was back again the minute the lion was busy.

The big birds come out of every part of the sky—you could make them out with the glass while they was still so far away you couldn't see them with your naked eye. Tom said the birds didn't find out the meat was there by the smell; they had to find it out by seeing it. Oh, but ain't that an eye for you! Tom said at the distance of five mile a patch of dead lions couldn't look any bigger than a person's finger-nail, and he couldn't imagine how the birds could notice such a little thing so far off.

It was strange and unnatural to see lion eat lion, and we thought maybe they warn't kin.

But Jim said that didn't make no difference. He said a hog was fond of her own children, and so was a spider, and he reckoned maybe a lion was pretty near as unprincipled, though maybe not quite. He thought likely a lion wouldn't eat his own father, if he knowed which was him, but reckoned he would eat his brother-in-law if he was uncommon hungry, and eat his mother-in-law any time. But *reckoning* don't settle nothing. You can reckon till the cows come home, but that don't fetch you to no decision. So we give it up and let it drop.

Generly it was very still in the desert nights, but this time there was music. A lot of other animals come to dinner; sneaking yelpers that Tom allowed was jackals, and roached-backed ones that he said was hyenas; and all the whole biling of them kept up a racket all the time. They made a picture in the moonlight that was more different than any picture I ever see. We had a line out and made fast to the top of a tree, and didn't stand no watch, but all turned in and slept; but I was up two or three times to look down at the animals and hear the music. It was like having a front seat at a menagerie for nothing, which I hadn't ever had before, and so it seemed foolish to sleep and not make the most of it; I mightn't ever have such a chance again.

We went a-fishing again in the early dawn, and then lazied around all day in the deep shade on an island, taking turn about to watch and see that none of the animals come a-snooping around there after erronorts for dinner. We was going to leave the next day, but couldn't, it was too lovely.

The day after, when we rose up toward the sky and sailed off eastward, we looked back and watched that place till it warn't nothing but just a speck in the desert, and I tell you it was like saying good-by to a friend that you ain't ever going to see any more.

Jim was thinking to himself, and at last he says: "Mars Tom, we's mos' to de end er de desert now, I speck."

"Why?"

"Well, hit stan' to reason we is. You knows how long we's been a-skimmin' over it. Mus' be mos' out o' san'. Hit's a wonder to me dat it's hilt out as long as it has."

"Shucks, there's plenty sand, you needn't worry."

"Oh, I ain't a-worryin', Mars Tom, only wonderin', dat's all. De Lord's got plenty san', I ain't doubtin' dat; but nemmine, He ain't gwyne to *was'e* it jist on dat account; en I allows dat dis desert's plenty big enough now, jist de way she is, en you can't spread her out no mo' 'dout was'in' san'."

"Oh, go 'long! we ain't much more than fairly *started* across this desert yet. The United States is a pretty big country, ain't it? Ain't it, Huck?"

"Yes," I says, "there ain't no bigger one, I don't reckon."

"Well," he says, "this desert is about the shape of the United States, and if you was to lay it down on top of the United States, it would cover the land of the free out of sight like a blanket. There'd be a little corner sticking out, up at Maine and away up northwest, and Florida sticking out like a turtle's tail, and that's all. We've took California away from the Mexicans two or three years ago, so that part of the Pacific coast is ours now, and if you laid the Great Sahara down with her edge on the Pacific, she would cover the United States and stick out past New York six hundred miles into the Atlantic Ocean."

I says:

"Good land! have you got the documents for that, Tom Sawyer?"

"Yes, and they're right here, and I've been studying them. You can look for yourself. From New York to the Pacific is 2,600 miles. From one end of the Great Desert to the other is 3,200. The United States contains 3,600,000 square miles, the desert contains 4,162,000. With the desert's bulk you could cover up every last inch of the United States, and in under, where the edges projected out, you could tuck England, Scotland, Ireland, France, Denmark, and all Germany. Yes, sir, you could hide the home of the brave and all of them countries clean out of sight under the Great Sahara, and you would still have 2,000 square miles of sand left."

"Well," I says, "it clean beats me. Why, Tom, it shows that the Lord took as much pains makin' this desert as makin' the United States and all them other countries."

Jim says: "Huck, dat don' stan' to reason. I reckon dis desert wa'n't made at all. Now you take en look at it like dis—you look at it, and see ef I's right.   What's a desert good for? 'Tain't good for nuthin'.   Dey ain't no way to make it pay.   Hain't dat so, Huck?"

"Yes, I reckon."

"Hain't it so, Mars Tom?"

"I guess so.   Go on."

"Ef a thing ain't no good, it's made in vain, ain't it?"

"Yes."

"*Now*, den!   Do de Lord make anything in vain?   You answer me dat."

"Well—no, He don't."

"Den how come He make a desert?"

"Well, go on.   How *did* He come to make it?"

"Mars Tom, *I* b'lieve it uz jes like when you's buildin' a house; dey's allays a lot o' truck en rubbish lef' over.   What does you do wid it? Doan' you take en k'yart it off en dump it into a ole vacant back lot? 'Course.   Now, den, it's my opinion hit was jest like dat—dat de Great Sahara warn't made at all, she jes' *happen'*."

I said it was a real good argument, and I believed it was the best one Jim ever made. Tom he said the same, but said the trouble

about arguments is, they ain't nothing but
theories, after all, and theories don't prove
nothing, they only give you a place to rest on, a
spell, when you are tuckered out butting
around and around trying to find out something
there ain't no way *to* find out.   And he says:

"There's another trouble about theories:
there's always a hole in them somewhere's, sure,
if you look close enough.   It's just so with this
one of Jim's.   Look what billions and billions of
stars there is.   How does it come that there was
just exactly enough star-stuff, and none left
over?   How does it come there ain't no sand-
pile up there?"

But Jim was fixed for him and says:

"What's de Milky Way?—dat's what *I* want
to know.   What's de Milky Way?   Answer me
dat!"

In my opinion it was just a sockdologer.   It's
only an opinion, it's only *my* opinion and others
may think different; but I said it then and I
stand to it now—it was a sockdologer.   And
moreover, besides, it landed Tom Sawyer.   He
couldn't say a word.   He had that stunned look
of a person that's been shot in the back with a
kag of nails.   All he said was, as for people like

me and Jim, he'd just as soon have intellectual intercourse with a catfish. But anybody can say that—and I notice they always do when somebody has fetched them a lifter. Tom Sawyer was tired of that end of the subject.

So we got back to talking about the size of the desert again, and the more we compared it with this and that and t'other thing, the more nobler and bigger and grander it got to look right along. And so, hunting among the figgers, Tom found, by and by, that it was just the same size as the Empire of China. Then he showed us the spread the Empire of China made on the map, and the room she took up in the world. Well, it was wonderful to think of, and I says:

"Why, I've heard talk about this desert plenty of times, but *I* never knowed before how important she was."

Then Tom says:

"Important! Sahara important! That's just the way with some people. If a thing's big, it's important. That's all the sense they've got. All they can see is *size*. Why, look at England. It's the most important country in the world; and yet you could put it in China's vest-pocket; and not only that, but you'd have the dickens's own time to find it again the next time you wanted it. And look at Russia. It spreads all around and everywhere, and yet ain't no more important in this world than Rhode Island is, and hasn't got half as much in it that's worth saving."

Away off now we see a little hill, a-standing up just on the edge of the world. Tom broke off his talk, and reached for a glass very much excited, and took a look, and says:

"That's it—it's the one I've been looking for, sure. If I'm right, it's the one the dervish took the man into and showed him all the treasures."

So we begun to gaze, and he begun to tell about it out of the *Arabian Nights*.

10: *The Treasure-Hill*

Tom said it happened like this:

A dervish was stumping it along through the desert, on foot, one blazing hot day, and he had come a thousand miles and was pretty poor, and hungry, and ornery and tired, and along about where we are now he run across a camel-driver with a hundred camels, and asked him for some a'ms. But the camel-driver he asked to be excused. The dervish said:

"Don't you own these camels?"

"Yes, they're mine."

"Are you in debt?"

"Who—me? No."

"Well, a man that owns a hundred camels and ain't in debt is rich—and not only rich, but very rich.   Ain't it so?"

The camel-driver owned up that it was so. Then the dervish says:

"God has made you rich, and He has made me poor.   He has His reasons, and they are wise, blessed be His name.   But He has willed that His rich shall help His poor, and you have turned away from me, your brother, in my need, and He will remember this, and you will lose by it."

That made the camel-driver feel shaky, but all the same he was born hoggish after money and didn't like to let go a cent; so he begun to whine and explain, and said times was hard, and although he had took a full freight down to Balsora and got a fat rate for it, he couldn't git no return freight, and so he warn't making no great things out of his trip.   So the dervish starts along again, and says:

"All right, if you want to take the risk; but I reckon you've made a mistake this time, and missed a chance."

Of course the camel-driver wanted to know what kind of a chance he had missed, because

maybe there was money in it; so he run after the
dervish, and begged him so hard and earnest to
take pity on him that at last the dervish gave in,
and says:

"Do you see that hill yonder? Well, in that
hill is all the treasures of the earth, and I was
looking around for a man with a particular
good kind heart and a noble, generous disposition, because if I could find just that man, I've
got a kind of a salve I could put on his eyes and
he could see the treasures and get them out."

So then the camel-driver was in a sweat; and
he cried, and begged, and took on, and went
down on his knees, and said he was just that
kind of a man, and said he could fetch a thousand people that would say he warn't ever de-
scribed so exact before.

"Well, then," says the dervish, "all right. If
we load the hundred camels, can I have half of
them?"

The driver was so glad he couldn't hardly
hold in, and says:

"Now you're shouting."

So they shook hands on the bargain, and the
dervish got out his box and rubbed the salve on
the driver's right eye, and the hill opened and

he went in, and there, sure enough, was piles and piles of gold and jewels sparkling like all the stars in heaven had fell down.

So him and the dervish laid into it, and they loaded every camel till he couldn't carry no more; then they said good-by, and each of them started off with his fifty. But pretty soon the camel-driver come a-running and overtook the dervish and says:

"You ain't in society, you know, and you don't really need all you've got. Won't you be good, and let me have ten of your camels?"

"Well," the dervish says, "I don't know but what you say is reasonable enough."

So he done it, and they separated, and the dervish started off again with his forty. But pretty soon here comes the camel-driver bawling after him again, and whines and slobbers around and begs another ten off of him, saying thirty camel-loads of treasures was enough to see a dervish through, because they live very simple, you know, and don't keep house, but board around and give their note.

But that warn't the end yet. That ornery hound kept coming and coming till he had begged back all the camels and had the whole hundred. Then he was satisfied, and ever so grateful, and said he wouldn't ever forgit the dervish as long as he lived, and nobody hadn't been so good to him before, and liberal. So they shook hands good-by, and separated and started off again.

But do you know, it warn't ten minutes till the camel-driver was unsatisfied again—he was the low-downest reptyle in seven counties—and he come a-running again. And this time the thing he wanted was to get the dervish to rub some of the salve on his other eye.

"Why?" said the dervish.

"Oh, you know," says the driver.

"Know what?"

"Well, you can't fool me," says the driver. "You're trying to keep back something from me, you know it mighty well. You know, I reckon, that if I had the salve on the other eye I could see a lot more things that's valuable. Come—please put it on."

The dervish says:

"I wasn't keeping anything back from you. I don't mind telling you what would happen if I put it on. You'd never see again. You'd be stone-blind the rest of your days."

But do you know that beat wouldn't believe him. No, he begged and begged, and whined and cried, till at last the dervish opened his box and told him to put it on, if he wanted to. So the man done it, and, sure enough, he was as blind as a bat in a minute.

Then the dervish laughed at him and mocked at him and made fun of him; and says:

"Good-by—a man that's blind hain't got no use for jewelry."

And he cleared out with the hundred camels, and left that man to wander around poor and miserable and friendless the rest of his days in the desert.

Jim said he'd bet it was a lesson to him.

"Yes," Tom says, "and like a considerable many lessons a body gets. They ain't no account, because the thing don't ever happen the same way again—and can't. The time Hen Scovil fell down the chimbly and crippled his back for life, everybody said it would be a lesson to him. What kind of a lesson? How was he going to use it? He couldn't climb chimblies no more, and he hadn't no more backs to break."

"All de same, Mars Tom, dey *is* sich a thing as

learnin' by expe'ence. De Good Book say de burnt chile shun de fire."

"Well, I ain't denying that a thing's a lesson if it's a thing that can happen twice just the same way. There's lots of such things, and *they* educate a person, that's what Uncle Abner always said; but there's forty *million* lots of the other kind—the kind that don't happen the same way twice—and they ain't no real use, they ain't no more instructive than the smallpox. When you've got it, it ain't no good to find out you ought to been vaccinated, and it ain't no good to git vaccinated afterward, because the smallpox don't come but once. But, on the other hand, Uncle Abner said that the person that had took a bull by the tail once had learnt sixty or seventy times as much as a person that hadn't, and said a person that started in to carry a cat home by the tail was gitting knowledge that was always going to be useful to him, and warn't ever going to grow dim or doubtful. But I can tell you, Jim, Uncle Abner was down on them people that's all the time trying to dig a lesson out of everything that happens, no matter whether—"

But Jim was asleep. Tom looked kind of ashamed, because you know a person always feels bad when he is talking uncommon fine and thinks the other person is admiring, and that other person goes to sleep that way. Of course he oughtn't to go to sleep, because it's shabby; but the finer a person talks the certainer it is to make you sleep, and so when you come to look at it it ain't nobody's fault in particular; both of them's to blame.

Jim begun to snore—soft and blubbery at first, then a long rasp, then a stronger one, then a half a dozen horrible ones, like the last water sucking down the plug-hole of a bathtub, then the same with more power to it, and some big coughs and snorts flung in, the way a cow does that is choking to death; and when the person has got to that point he is at his level best, and can wake up a man that is in the next block with a dipperful of loddanum in him, but can't wake himself up although all that awful noise of his'n ain't but three inches from his own ears. And that is the curiousest thing in the world, seems to me. But you rake a match to light the candle, and that little bit of a noise will fetch him. I wish I knowed what was the reason of that, but there don't seem to be no way to find out. Now there was Jim alarming the whole desert, and yanking the animals out, for miles and miles around, to see what in the nation was going on up there; there warn't nobody nor nothing that was as close to the noise as *he* was, and yet he was the only cretur that wasn't disturbed by it. We yelled at him and whooped at him, it never done no good; but the first time there come a little wee noise that wasn't of a usual kind, it woke him up. No, sir, I've thought it all over, and so has Tom, and there ain't no way to find out why a snorer can't hear himself snore.

Jim said he hadn't been asleep; he just shut his eyes so he could listen better.

Tom said nobody warn't accusing him.

That made him look like he wished he hadn't said anything. And he wanted to git away from the subject, I reckon, because he begun to abuse the camel-driver, just the way a person does when he has got catched in something and wants to take it out of somebody else. He let into the camel-driver the hardest he knowed how, and I had to agree with him; and he praised up the dervish the highest he could, and I had to agree with him there, too. But Tom says:

"I ain't so sure. You call that dervish so

dreadful liberal and good and unselfish, but I
don't quite see it. He didn't hunt up another
poor dervish, did he? No, he didn't. If he was
so unselfish, why didn't he go in there himself
and take a pocketful of jewels and go along and
be satisfied? No, sir, the person he was hunting
for was a man with a hundred camels. He
wanted to get away with all the treasure he
could."

"Why, Mars Tom, he was willin' to divide,
fair and square; he only struck for fifty camels."

"Because he knowed how he was going to git
all of them by and by."

"Mars Tom, he *tole* de man de truck would
make him bline."

"Yes, because he knowed the man's character.
It was just the kind of a man he was hunting
for—a man that never believes in anybody's
word or anybody's honorableness, because he
ain't got none of his own. I reckon there's lots
of people like that dervish. They swindle,
right and left, but they always make the other
person *seem* to swindle himself. They keep
inside of the letter of the law all the time, and
there ain't no way to git hold of them. *They*
don't put the salve on—oh, no, that would be

sin; but they know how to fool *you* into putting it on, then it's you that blinds yourself. I reckon the dervish and the camel-driver was just a pair—a fine, smart, brainy rascal, and a dull, coarse, ignorant one, but both of them rascals, just the same."

"Mars Tom, does you reckon dey's any o' dat kind o' salve in de worl' now?"

"Yes, Uncle Abner says there is. He says they've got it in New York, and they put it on country people's eyes and show them all the railroads in the world, and they go in and git them, and then when they rub the salve on the other eye the other man bids them good-by and goes off with their railroads. Here's the treasure-hill now. Lower away!"

We landed, but it warn't as interesting as I thought it was going to be, because we couldn't find the place where they went in to git the treasure. Still, it was plenty interesting enough, just to see the mere hill itself where such a wonderful thing happened. Jim said he wouldn't 'a' missed it for three dollars, and I felt the same way.

And to me and Jim, as wonderful a thing as any was the way Tom could come into a strange big country like this and go straight and find a little hump like that and tell it in a minute from a million other humps that was almost just like it, and nothing to help him but only his own learning and his own natural smartness. We talked and talked it over together, but couldn't make out how he done it. He had the best head on him I ever see; and all he lacked was age to make a name for himself equal to Captain Kidd or George Washington. I bet you it would 'a' crowded either of *them* to find that hill, with all their gifts, but it warn't nothing to Tom Sawyer; he went across Sahara and put his finger on it as easy as you could pick a darky out of a bunch of angels.

We found a pond of salt-water close by and scraped up a raft of salt around the edges, and loaded up the lion's skin and the tiger's so as they would keep till Jim could tan them.

11: *The Sandstorm*

WE went a-fooling along for a day or two, and then just as the full moon was touching the ground on the other side of the desert, we see a string of little black figgers moving across its big silver face. You could see them as plain as if they was painted on the moon with ink. It was another caravan. We cooled down our speed and tagged along after it, just to have company, though it warn't going our way. It was a rattler, that caravan, and a most bully sight to look at next morning when the sun come a-streaming across the desert and flung the long shadders of the camels on the gold sand like a thousand

grand-daddy-long-legses marching in procession. We never went very near it, because we
knowed better now than to act like that and
scare people's camels and break up their cara-
vans. It was the gayest outfit you ever see, for
rich clothes and nobby style. Some of the chiefs
rode on dromedaries, the first we ever see, and
very tall, and they go plunging along like they
was on stilts, and they rock the man that is on
them pretty violent and churn up his dinner
considerable, I bet you, but they make noble
good time, and a camel ain't nowheres with
them for speed.

The caravan camped, during the middle part
of the day, and then started again about the
middle of the afternoon. Before long the sun
begun to look very curious. First it kind of
turned to brass, and then to copper, and after
that it begun to look like a blood-red ball, and
the air got hot and close, and pretty soon all the
sky in the west darkened up and looked thick
and foggy, but fiery and dreadful—like it looks
through a piece of red glass, you know. We
looked down and see a big confusion going on in
the caravan, and a rushing every which way like
they was scared; and then they all flopped down

flat in the sand and laid there perfectly still.

Pretty soon we see something coming that stood up like an amazing wide wall, and reached from the desert up into the sky and hid the sun, and it was coming like the nation, too. Then a little faint breeze struck us, and then it come harder, and grains of sand begun to sift against our faces and sting like fire, and Tom sung out:

"It's a sandstorm—turn your backs to it!"

We done it; and in another minute it was blowing a gale, and the sand beat against us by the shovelful, and the air was so thick with it we couldn't see a thing. In five minutes the boat was level full, and we was setting on the lockers buried up to the chin in sand, and only our heads out and could hardly breathe.

Then the storm thinned, and we see that monstrous wall go a-sailing off across the desert, awful to look at, I tell you. We dug ourselves out and looked down, and where the caravan was before there wasn't anything but just the sand ocean now, and all still and quiet. All them people and camels was smothered and dead and buried—buried under ten foot of sand, we reckoned, and Tom allowed it might be years before the wind uncovered them, and

The sand beat against us by the shovelful

all that time their friends wouldn't ever know what become of that caravan. Tom said:

"*Now* we know what it was that happened to the people we got the swords and pistols from."

Yes, sir, that was just it. It was as plain as day now. They got buried in a sandstorm, and the wild animals couldn't get at them, and the wind never uncovered them again until they was dried to leather and warn't fit to eat. It seemed to me we had felt as sorry for them poor people as a person could for anybody, and as mournful, too, but we was mistaken; this last caravan's death went harder with us, a good deal harder. You see, the others was total strangers, and we never got to feeling acquainted with them at all, except, maybe, a little with the man that was watching the girl, but it was different with this last caravan. We was huvvering around them a whole night and 'most a whole day, and had got to feeling real friendly with them, and acquainted. I have found out that there ain't no surer way to find out whether you like people or hate them than to travel with them. Just so with these. We kind of liked them from the start, and traveling with them put on the finisher. The longer we traveled with them, and the more we got used to their ways, the better and better we liked them, and the gladder and gladder we was that we run across them. We had come to know some of them so well that we called them by name when we was talking about them, and soon got so familiar and sociable that we even dropped the Miss and Mister and just used their plain names without any handle, and it did not seem unpolite, but just the right thing. Of course, it wasn't their own names, but names we give them. There was Mr. Elexander Robinson and Miss Adaline Robinson, and Colonel Jacob McDougal and Miss Harryet McDougal, and Judge Jeremiah Butler and young Bushrod Butler, and these was big chiefs mostly that wore splendid great turbans and simmeters, and dressed like the Grand Mogul, and their families. But as soon as we come to know them good, and like them very much, it warn't Mister, nor Judge, nor nothing, any more, but only Elleck, and Addy, and Jake, and Hattie, and Jerry, and Buck, and so on.

And you know the more you join in with people in their joys and their sorrows, the more nearer and dearer they come to be to you. Now we warn't cold and indifferent, the way most travelers is, we was right down friendly and sociable, and took a chance in everything that was going, and the caravan could depend on us to be on hand every time, it didn't make no difference what it was.

When they camped, we camped right over them, ten or twelve hundred feet up in the air. When they et a meal, we et ourn, and it made it ever so much homeliker to have their company. When they had a wedding that night, and Buck and Addy got married, we got ourselves up in the very starchiest of the professor's duds for the blow-out, and when they danced we jined in and shook a foot up there.

But it is sorrow and trouble that brings you the nearest, and it was a funeral that done it with us. It was next morning, just in the still dawn. We didn't know the diseased, and he warn't in our set, but that never made no difference; he belonged to the caravan, and that was enough, and there warn't no more sincerer tears shed over him than the ones we dripped on him from up there eleven hundred foot on high.

Yes, parting with this caravan was much more bitterer than it was to part with them others, which was comparative strangers, and been dead so long, anyway. We had knowed these in their lives and was fond of them, too, and now to have death snatch them from right before our faces while we was looking, and leave us so lonesome and friendless in the middle of that big desert, it did hurt so, and we wished we mightn't ever make any more friends on that voyage if we was going to lose them again like that.

We couldn't keep from talking about them, and they was all the time coming up in our memory, and looking just the way they looked when we was all alive and happy together. We could see the line marching, and the shiny spearheads a-winking in the sun; we could see the dromedaries lumbering along; we could see the wedding and the funeral; and more oftener than anything else we could see them praying, because they don't allow nothing to prevent that; whenever the call come, several times a day, they would stop right there, and stand up and face to the east, and lift back their heads, and spread out their arms and begin, and four or five times they would go down on their knees, and then fall forward and touch their forehead to the ground.

Well, it warn't good to go on talking about them, lovely as they was in their life, and dear to us in their life and death both, because it didn't do no good, and made us too downhearted. Jim allowed he was going to live as good a life as he could, so he could see them again in a better world; and Tom kept still and didn't tell him they was only Mohammedans; it warn't no use to disappoint him, he was feeling bad enough just as it was.

When we woke up next morning we was feeling a little cheerfuler, and had had a most powerful good sleep, because sand is the comfortablest bed there is, and I don't see why people that can afford it don't have it more. And it's terrible good ballast, too; I never see the balloon so steady before.

Tom allowed we had twenty tons of it, and wondered what we better do with it; it was good sand, and it didn't seem good sense to throw it away. Jim says:

"Mars Tom, can't we tote it back home en sell it? How long'll it take?"

"Depends on the way we go."

"Well, sah, she's wuth a quarter of a dollar a load at home, en I reckon we's got as much as twenty loads, hain't we? How much would dat be?"

"Five dollars."

"By jings, Mars Tom, le's shove for home right on de spot! Hit's more'n a dollar en a half apiece, hain't it?"

"Yes."

"Well, ef dat ain't makin' money de easiest ever *I* struck! She jes' rained in—never cos' us a lick o' work. Le's mosey right along, Mars Tom."

But Tom was thinking and ciphering away so busy and excited he never heard him. Pretty soon he says:

"Five dollars—sho! Look here, this sand's worth—worth—why, it's worth no end of money."

"How is dat, Mars Tom? Go on, honey, go on!"

"Well, the minute people knows it's genuwyne sand from the genuwyne Desert of Sahara, they'll just be in a perfect state of mind to git hold of some of it to keep on the what-not in a vial with a label on it for a curiosity. All we got to do is to put it up in vials and float around all over the United States and peddle them out at ten cents apiece. We've got all of ten thousand dollars' worth of sand in this boat."

Me and Jim went all to pieces with joy, and begun to shout whoopjamboreehoo, and Tom says:

"And we can keep on coming back and fetching sand, and coming back and fetching more sand, and just keep it a-going till we've carted this whole desert over there and sold it out; and there ain't ever going to be any opposition, either, because we'll take out a patent."

"My goodness," I says, "we'll be as rich as Creosote, won't we, Tom?"

"Yes—Creesus, you mean. Why, that dervish was hunting in that little hill for the treasures of the earth, and didn't know he was walking over the real ones for a thousand miles. He was blinder than he made the driver."

"Mars Tom, how much is we gwyne to be worth?"

"Well, I don't know yet. It's got to be ciphered, and it ain't the easiest job to do, either, because it's over four million square miles of sand at ten cents a vial."

Jim was awful excited, but this faded it out considerable, and he shook his head and says:

"Mars Tom, we can't 'ford all dem vials—a king couldn't. We better not try to take de whole desert, Mars Tom, de vials gwyne to bust us, sho'."

Tom's excitement died out, too, now, and I reckoned it was on account of the vials, but it wasn't. He set there thinking, and got bluer and bluer, and at last he says:

"Boys, it won't work; we got to give it up."

"Why, Tom?"

"On account of the duties."

I couldn't make nothing out of that, neither could Jim. I says:

"What *is* our duty, Tom? Because if we can't git around it, why can't we just *do* it? People often has to."

But he says:

"Oh, it ain't that kind of duty. The kind I mean is a tax. Whenever you strike a frontier —that's the border of a country, you know— you find a custom-house there, and the gov'ment officers comes and rummages among your things and charges a big tax, which they call a duty because it's their duty to bust you if they can, and if you don't pay the duty they'll hog your sand. They call it confiscating, but that don't deceive nobody, it's just hogging, and that's all it is. Now if we try to carry this sand home the way we're pointed now, we got to climb fences till we git tired—just frontier after frontier—Egypt, Arabia, Hindustan, and so on, and they'll all whack on a duty, and so you see, easy enough, we *can't* go *that* road."

"Why, Tom," I says, "we can sail right over their old frontiers; how are *they* going to stop us?"

He looked sorrowful at me, and says, very grave: "Huck Finn, do you think that would be honest?"

I hate them kind of interruptions. I never said nothing, and he went on:

"Well, we're shut off the other way, too. If we go back the way we've come, there's the New York custom-house, and that is worse than all of them others put together, on account of the kind of cargo we've got."

"Why?"

"Well, they can't raise Sahara sand in America, of course, and when they can't raise a thing there, the duty is fourteen hundred thousand per cent on it if you try to fetch it in from where they do raise it."

"There ain't no sense in that, Tom Sawyer."

"Who said there *was?* What do you talk to me like that for, Huck Finn? You wait till I say a thing's got sense in it before you go to accusing me of saying it."

"All right, consider me crying about it, and sorry. Go on."

Jim says:

"Mars Tom, do dey jam dat duty onto everything we can't raise in America, en don't make no 'stinction 'twix' anything?"

"Yes, that's what they do."

"Mars Tom, ain't de blessin' o' de Lord de mos' valuable thing dey is?"

"Yes, it is."

"Don't de preacher stan' up in de pulpit en call it down on de people?"

"Yes."

"Whah do it come from?"

"From heaven."

"Yassir! you's jes' right, 'deed you is, honey —it come from heaven, en dat's a foreign country. *Now,* den! do dey put a tax on dat blessin'?"

"No, they don't."

" 'Course dey don't; en so it stan' to reason dat you's mistaken, Mars Tom. Dey wouldn't put de tax on po' truck like san', dat everybody ain't 'bleeged to have, en leave it off'n de bes' thing dey is, which nobody can't git along wid-out."

Tom Sawyer was stumped; he see Jim had got him where he couldn't budge. He tried to wiggle out by saying they had *forgot* to put on that tax, but they'd be sure to remember about it, next session of Congress, and then they'd put it on, but that was a poor lame come-off, and he knowed it. He said there warn't nothing foreign that warn't taxed but just that one, and so they couldn't be consistent without taxing it, and to be consistent was the first law of politics. So he stuck to it that they'd left it out unintentional and would be certain to do their best to fix it before they got caught and laughed at.

But I didn't feel no more interest in such things, as long as we couldn't git our sand through, and it made me low-spirited, and Jim the same. Tom he tried to cheer us up by saying he would think up another speculation for us that would be just as good as this one and

better, but it didn't do no good, we didn't believe there was any as big as this. It was mighty
hard; such a little while ago we was so rich, and
could 'a' bought a country and started a kingdom and been celebrated and happy, and now
we was so poor and ornery again, and had our
sand left on our hands. The sand was looking
so lovely before, just like gold and di'monds,
and the feel of it was so soft and so silky and
nice, but now I couldn't bear the sight of it, it
made me sick to look at it, and I knowed I
wouldn't ever feel comfortable again till we got
shut of it, and I didn't have it there no more to
remind us of what we had been and what we had
got degraded down to. The others was feeling
the same way about it that I was. I knowed it,
because they cheered up so, the minute I says
le's throw this truck overboard.

Well, it was going to be work, you know, and
pretty solid work, too; so Tom he divided it up
according to fairness and strength. He said me
and him would clear out a fifth apiece of the
sand, and Jim three-fifths. Jim he didn't quite
like that arrangement. He says:

" 'Course I's de stronges', en I's willin' to do a
share accordin', but by jings you's kinder pilin'

it onto ole Jim, Mars Tom, hain't you?"

"Well, I didn't think so, Jim, but you try your hand at fixing it, and let's see."

So Jim reckoned it wouldn't be no more than fair if me and Tom done a *tenth* apiece. Tom he turned his back to git room and be private, and then he smole a smile that spread around and covered the whole Sahara to the westward, back to the Atlantic edge of it where we come from. Then he turned around again and said it was a good enough arrangement, and we was satisfied if Jim was. Jim said he was.

So then Tom measured off our two-tenths in the bow and left the rest for Jim, and it surprised Jim a good deal to see how much difference there was and what a raging lot of sand his share come to, and said he was powerful glad now that he had spoke up in time and got the first arrangement altered, for he said that even the way it was now, there was more sand than enjoyment in his end of the contract, he believed.

Then we laid into it. It was mighty hot work, and tough; so hot we had to move up into cooler weather or we couldn't 'a' stood it. Me and Tom took turn about, and one worked

while t'other rested, but there warn't nobody to
spell poor old Jim, and he made all that part of
Africa damp, he sweated so. We couldn't work
good, we was so full of laugh, and Jim he kept
fretting and wanting to know what tickled us so,
and we had to keep making up things to account
for it, and they was pretty poor inventions, but
they done well enough, Jim didn't see through
them. At last when we got done we was 'most
dead, but not with work but with laughing. By
and by Jim was 'most dead, too, but it was with
work; then we took turns and spelled him, and
he was as thankful as he could be, and would set
on the gunnel and swab the sweat, and heave
and pant, and say how good we was to a poor old
darky, and he wouldn't ever forgit us. He was
always the gratefulest darky I ever see, for any
little thing you done for him. He was only
black outside; inside he was as white as you
be.

12: *Jim Standing Siege*

THE next few meals was pretty sandy, but that don't make no difference when you are hungry; and when you ain't it ain't no satisfaction to eat, anyway, and so a little grit in the meat ain't no particular drawback, as far as I can see.

Then we struck the east end of the desert at last, sailing on a northeast course. Away off on the edge of the sand, in a soft pinky light, we see three little sharp roofs like tents, and Tom says:

"It's the pyramids of Egypt."

It made my heart fairly jump. You see, I had seen a many and a many a picture of them, and heard tell about them a hundred times, and yet

to come on them all of a sudden, that way, and
find they was *real,* 'stead of imaginations, 'most
knocked the breath out of me with surprise.
It's a curious thing, that the more you hear
about a grand and big and bully thing or person, the more it kind of dreamies out, as you
may say, and gets to be a big dim wavery figger
made out of moonshine and nothing solid to it.
It's just so with George Washington, and the
same with them pyramids.

And moreover, besides the thing they always
said about them seemed to me to be stretchers.
There was a feller come to the Sunday-school
once, and had a picture of them, and made a
speech, and said the biggest pyramid covered
thirteen acres, and was 'most five hundred foot
high, just a steep mountain, all built out of
hunks of stone as big as a bureau, and laid up in
perfectly regular layers, like stair-steps.   Thirteen acres, you see, for just one building; it's a
farm.   If it hadn't been in Sunday-school, I
would 'a' judged it was a lie; and outside I was
certain of it.   And he said there was a hole in the
pyramid, and you could go in there with candles, and go ever so far up a long slanting tunnel, and come to a large room in the stomach of

that stone mountain, and there you would find a
big stone chest with a king in it, four thousand
years old. I said to myself, then, if that ain't a lie
I will eat that king if they will fetch him, for
even Methusalem warn't that old, and nobody
claims it.

As we come a little nearer we see the yaller
sand come to an end in a long straight edge like
a blanket, and onto it was joined, edge to edge, a
wide country of bright green, with a snaky
stripe crooking through it, and Tom said it was
the Nile.   It made my heart jump again, for the
Nile was another thing that wasn't real to me.
Now I can tell you one thing which is dead
certain: if you will fool along over three thousand miles of yaller sand, all glimmering with
heat so that it makes your eyes water to look at
it, and you've been a considerable part of a week
doing it, the green country will look so like
home and heaven to you that it will make your
eyes water *again*.

It was just so with me, and the same with
Jim.

And when Jim got so he could believe it *was*
the land of Egypt he was looking at, he wouldn't
enter it standing up, but got down on his knees

and took off his hat, because he said it wasn't fitten' for a humble poor darky to come any other way where such men had been as Moses and Joseph and Pharaoh and the other prophets. He was a Presbyterian, and had a most deep respect for Moses, which was a Presbyterian, too, he said. He was all stirred up, and says:

"Hit's de lan' of Egypt, de lan' of Egypt, en I's 'lowed to look at it wid my own eyes! En dah's de river dat was turn' to blood, en I's looking at de very same groun' whah de plagues was, and de lice, en de frogs, en de locus', en de hail, en whah dey marked de door-pos', en de angel o' de Lord come by in de darkness o' de night en slew de fust-born in all de lan' o' Egypt. Ole Jim ain't worthy to see dis day!"

And then he just broke down and cried, he was so thankful. So between him and Tom there was talk enough, Jim being excited because the land was so full of history—Joseph and his brethren, Moses in the bulrushers, Jacob coming down into Egypt to buy corn, the silver cup in the sack, and all them interesting things; and Tom just as excited too, because the land was so full of history that was in *his* line,

about Noureddin, and Bedreddin, and such like
monstrous giants, that made Jim's wool rise,
and a raft of other *Arabian Nights* folks, which
the half of them never done the things they let
on they done, I don't believe.

Then we struck a disappointment, for one of
them early morning fogs started up, and it
warn't no use to sail over the top of it, because
we would go by Egypt, sure, so we judged it was
best to set her by compass straight for the place
where the pyramids was gitting blurred and
blotted out, and then drop low and skin along
pretty close to the ground and keep a sharp
lookout. Tom took the hellum, I stood by to let
go the anchor, and Jim he straddled the bow to
dig through the fog with his eyes and watch out
for danger ahead. We went along a steady gait,
but not very fast, and the fog got solider and
solider, so solid that Jim looked dim and ragged
and smoky through it. It was awful still, and we
talked low and was anxious. Now and then Jim
would say:

"Highst her a p'int, Mars Tom, highst her!"
and up she would skip, a foot or two, and we
would slide right over a flat-roofed mud cabin,
with people that had been asleep on it just be-

ginning to turn out and gap and stretch; and once when a feller was clear up on his hind legs so he could gap and stretch better, we took him a blip in the back and knocked him off. By and by, after about an hour, and everything dead still and we a-straining our ears for sounds and holding our breath, the fog thinned a little, very sudden, and Jim sung out in an awful scare:

"Oh, for de lan's sake, set her back, Mars Tom, here's de biggest giant outen de '*Rabian Nights* a-comin' for us!" and he went over backwards in the boat.

Tom slammed on the back-action, and as we slowed to a standstill a man's face as big as our house at home looked in over the gunnel, same as a house looks out of its windows, and I laid down and died. I must 'a' been clear dead and gone for as much as a minute or more; then I come to, and Tom had hitched a boat-hook onto the lower lip of the giant and was holding the balloon steady with it whilst he canted his head back and got a good long look up at that awful face.

Jim was on his knees with his hands clasped, gazing up at the thing in a begging way, and working his lips, but not getting anything out.

I took only just a glimpse, and was fading out again, but Tom says:

"He ain't alive, you fools; it's the Sphinx!"

I never see Tom look so little and like a fly; but that was because the giant's head was so big and awful. Awful, yes, so it was, but not dreadful any more, because you could see it was a noble face, and kind of sad, and not thinking about you, but about other things and larger. It was stone, reddish stone, and its nose and ears battered, and that give it an abused look, and you felt sorrier for it for that.

We stood off a piece, and sailed around it and over it, and it was just grand. It was a man's head, or maybe a woman's, on a tiger's body a hundred and twenty-five foot long, and there was a dear little temple between its front paws. All but the head used to be under the sand, for hundreds of years, maybe thousands, but they had just lately dug the sand away and found that little temple. It took a power of sand to bury that cretur; 'most as much as it would to bury a steamboat, I reckon.

We landed Jim on top of the head, with an American flag to protect him, it being a foreign land; then we sailed off to this and that and t'other distance, to git what Tom called effects and perspectives and proportions, and Jim he done the best he could, striking all the different kinds of attitudes and positions he could study up, but standing on his head and working his legs the way a frog does was the best. The further we got away, the littler Jim got, and the grander the Sphinx got, till at last it was only a clothes-pin on a dome, you might say. That's the way perspective brings out the correct proportions, Tom said; he said Julus Cesar's slaves didn't know how big he was, they was too close to him.

Then we sailed off further and further, till we couldn't see Jim at all any more, and then that great figger was at its noblest, a-gazing out over the Nile Valley so still and solemn and lonesome, and all the little shabby huts and things that was scattered about it clean disappeared and gone, and nothing around it now but a soft wide spread of yaller velvet, which was the sand.

That was the right place to stop, and we done it. We set there a-looking and a-thinking for a half an hour, nobody a-saying anything, for it made us feel quiet and kind of solemn to remember it had been looking over that valley just that same way, and thinking its awful thoughts all to itself for thousands of years, and nobody can't find out what they are to this day.

At last I took up the glass and see some little black things a-capering around on that velvet carpet, and some more a-climbing up the cretur's back, and then I see two or three wee puffs of white smoke, and told Tom to look. He done it, and says:

"They're bugs. No—hold on; they—why, I believe they're men. Yes, it's men—men and horses both. They're hauling a long ladder up onto the Sphinx's back—now ain't that odd? And now they're trying to lean it up a—there's some more puffs of smoke—it's guns! Huck, they're after Jim."

We clapped on the power, and went for them a-biling. We was there in no time, and come a-whizzing down amongst them, and they broke and scattered every which way, and some that was climbing the ladder after Jim let go all holts and fell. We soared up and found him laying on top of the head panting and most tuckered out, partly from howling for help and partly from scare. He had been standing a siege a long time—a week, *he* said, but it warn't so, it only just seemed so to him because they was crowding him so. They had shot at him, and rained the bullets all around him, but he warn't hit, and when they found he wouldn't stand up and the bullets couldn't git at him when he was laying down, they went for the ladder, and then he knowed it was all up with him if we didn't come pretty quick. Tom was very indignant, and asked him why he didn't show the flag and command them to *git,* in the name of the United States. Jim said he done it, but they never paid no attention. Tom said he would have this thing looked into at Washington, and says:

"You'll see that they'll have to apologize for insulting the flag, and pay an indemnity, too, on top of it, even if they git off *that* easy."

Jim says:

"What's an indemnity, Mars Tom?"

"It's cash, that's what it is."

"Who gits it, Mars Tom?"

"Why, *we* do."

"En who gits de apology?"

"The United States. Or, we can take whichever we please. We can take the apology, if we want to, and let the gov'ment take the money."

"How much money will it be, Mars Tom?"

"Well, in an aggravated case like this one, it will be at least three dollars apiece, and I don't know but more."

"Well, den, we'll take de money, Mars Tom, blame de 'pology. Hain't dat yo' notion, too? En hain't it yourn, Huck?"

We talked it over a little and allowed that that was as good a way as any, so we agreed to take the money. It was a new business to me, and I asked Tom if countries always apologized when they had done wrong, and he says:

"Yes; the little ones does."

We was sailing around examining the pyramids, you know, and now we soared up and roosted on the flat top of the biggest one, and found it was just like what the man said in the Sunday-school. It was like four pairs of stairs that start broad at the bottom and slants up and comes together in a point at the top, only these stair-steps couldn't be clumb the way you climb other stairs; no, for each step was as high as your chin, and you have to be boosted up from behind. The two other pyramids warn't far away, and the people moving about on the sand be-

tween looked like bugs crawling, we was so high
above them.

Tom he couldn't hold himself he was so
worked up with gladness and astonishment to
be in such a celebrated place, and he just
dripped history from every pore, seemed to me.
He said he couldn't scarcely believe he was
standing on the very identical spot the prince
flew from on the Bronze Horse. It was in the
Arabian Night times, he said. Somebody give
the prince a bronze horse with a peg in its
shoulder, and he could git on him and fly
through the air like a bird, and go all over the
world, and steer it by turning the peg, and fly
high or low and land wherever he wanted to.

When he got done telling it there was one of
them uncomfortable silences that comes, you
know, when a person has been telling a
whopper and you feel sorry for him and wish
you could think of some way to change the subject and let him down easy, but git stuck and
don't see no way, and before you can pull your
mind together and *do* something, that silence
has got in and spared itself and done the business. I was embarrassed, Jim he was embarrassed, and neither of us couldn't say a word.

Well, Tom he glowered at me a minute, and says:

"Come, out with it. What do you think?"

I says:

"Tom Sawyer, *you* don't believe that, yourself."

"What's the reason I don't? What's to hender me?"

"There's one thing to hender you: it couldn't happen, that's all."

"What's the reason it couldn't happen?"

"You tell me the reason it *could* happen."

"This balloon is a good enough reason it could happen, I should reckon."

"*Why* is it?"

"*Why* is it? I never saw such an idiot. Ain't this balloon and the bronze horse the same thing under different names?"

"No, they're not. One is a balloon and the other's a horse. It's very different. Next you'll be saying a house and a cow is the same thing."

"By Jackson, Huck's got him ag'in! Dey ain't no wigglin' outer dat!"

"Shut your head, Jim; you don't know what you're talking about. And Huck don't. Look here, Huck, I'll make it plain to you, so you can understand. You see, it ain't the mere *form* that's got anything to do with their being similar or unsimilar, it's the *principle* involved; and the principle is the same in both. Don't you see, now?"

I turned it over in my mind, and says:

"Tom, it ain't no use. Principles is all very well, but they don't git around that one big fact, that the thing that a balloon can do ain't no sort of proof of what a horse can do."

"Shucks, Huck, you don't get the idea at all. Now look here a minute—it's perfectly plain. Don't we fly through the air?"

"Yes."

"Very well. Don't we fly high or fly low, just as we please?"

"Yes."

"Don't we steer whichever way we want to?"

"Yes."

"And don't we land when and where we please?"

"Yes."

"How do we move the balloon and steer it?"

"By touching the buttons."

"*Now* I reckon the thing is clear to you at last.

In the other case the moving and steering was done by turning a peg. We touch a button, the prince turned a peg. There ain't an atom of difference, you see. I knowed I could git it through your head if I stuck to it long enough."

He felt so happy he begun to whistle. But me and Jim was silent, so he broke off surprised, and says:

"Looky here, Huck Finn, don't you see it yet?"

I says:

"Tom Sawyer, I want to ask you some questions."

"Go ahead," he says, and I see Jim chirk up to listen.

"As I understand it, the whole thing is in the buttons and the peg—the rest ain't of no consequence. A button is one shape, a peg is another shape, but that ain't any matter?"

"No, that ain't any matter, as long as they've both got the same power."

"All right, then. What is the power that's in a candle and in a match?"

"It's the fire."

"It's the same in both, then?"

"Yes, just the same in both."

"All right. Suppose I set fire to a carpenter shop with a match, what will happen to that carpenter shop?"

"She'll burn up."

"And suppose I set fire to this pyramid with a candle—will she burn up?"

"Of course she won't."

"All right. Now the fire's the same, both times. *Why* does the shop burn, and the pyramid don't?"

"Because the pyramid *can't* burn."

"Ah! and *a horse can't fly!*"

"My lan', ef Huck ain't got him ag'in! Huck's landed him high en dry dis time, *I* tell you! Hit's de smartes' trap I ever see a body walk inter—en ef I—"

But Jim was so full of laugh he got to strangling and couldn't go on, and Tom was that mad to see how neat I had floored him, and turned his own argument ag'in him and knocked him all to rags and flinders with it, that all he could manage to say was that whenever he heard me and Jim try to argue it made him ashamed of the human race. I never said nothing; I was feeling pretty well satisfied. When I have got the best of a person that way, it ain't my way to go around crowing about it the way some people does, for I consider that if I was in his place I wouldn't wish him to crow over me. It's better to be generous, that's what I think.

13: *Going for Tom's Pipe*

By and by we left Jim to float around up there in the neighborhood of the pyramids, and we clumb down to the hole where you go into the tunnel, and went in with some Arabs and candles, and away in there in the middle of the pyramid we found a room and a big stone box in it where they used to keep that king, just as the man in the Sunday-school said; but he was gone, now; somebody had got him. But I didn't take no interest in the place, because there could be ghosts there, of course; not fresh ones, but I don't like no kind.

So then we come out and got some little don-keys and rode a piece, and then went in a boat another piece, and then more donkeys, and got to Cairo; and all the way the road was as smooth and beautiful a road as ever I see, and had tall date-pa'ms on both sides, and naked children everywhere, and the men was as red as copper, and fine and strong and handsome. And the city was a curiosity. Such narrow streets—why, they were just lanes, and crowded with people with turbans, and women with veils, and every-body rigged out in blazing bright clothes and all sorts of colors, and you wondered how the cam-els and the people got by each other in such narrow little cracks, but they done it—a perfect jam, you see, and everybody noisy. The stores warn't big enough to turn around in, but you didn't have to go in; the storekeeper sat tailor fashion on his counter, smoking his snaky long pipe, and had his things where he could reach them to sell, and he was just as good as in the street, for the camel-loads brushed him as they went by.

Now and then a grand person flew by in a carriage with fancy dressed men running and yelling in front of it and whacking anybody

*Everybody was rigged out in blazing bright
clothes and all sorts of colors*

with a long rod that didn't get out of the way.
And by and by along comes the Sultan riding
horseback at the head of a procession, and fairly
took your breath away, his clothes was so splendid; and everybody fell flat and laid on his
stomach while he went by.   I forgot, but a feller
helped me to remember.   He was one that had a
rod and run in front.

There was churches, but they don't know
enough to keep Sunday; they keep Friday and
break the Sabbath.   You have to take off your
shoes when you go in.   There was crowds of
men and boys in the church, setting in groups
on the stone floor and making no end of noise—
getting their lessons by heart, Tom said, out of
the Koran, which they think is a Bible, and
people that knows better knows enough to not
let on.   I never see such a big church in my life
before, and most awful high, it was; it made you
dizzy to look up; our village church at home
ain't a circumstance to it; if you was to put it in
there, people would think it was a dry-goods
box.

What I wanted to see was a dervish, because I
was interested in dervishes on account of the
one that played the trick on the camel-driver.

So we found a lot in a kind of a church, and they called themselves Whirling Dervishes; and they did whirl, too. I never see anything like it. They had tall sugar-loaf hats on, and linen petticoats; and they spun and spun and spun, round and round like tops, and the petticoats stood out on a slant, and it was the prettiest thing I ever see, and made me drunk to look at it. They was all Moslems, Tom said, and when I asked him what a Moslem was, he said it was a person that wasn't a Presbyterian. So there is plenty of them in Missouri, though I didn't know it before.

We didn't see half there was to see in Cairo, because Tom was in such a sweat to hunt out places that was celebrated in history. We had a most tiresome time to find the granary where Joseph stored up the grain before the famine, and when we found it it warn't worth much to look at, being such an old tumbledown wreck; but Tom was satisfied, and made more fuss over it than I would make if I stuck a nail in my foot. How he ever found that place was too many for me. We passed as much as forty just like it before we come to it, and any of them would 'a' done for me, but none but just the right one would suit him; I never see anybody so particular as Tom Sawyer. The minute he struck the right one he reconnized it as easy as I would reconnize my other shirt if I had one, but how he done it he couldn't any more tell than he could fly; he said so himself.

Then we hunted a long time for the house where the boy lived that learned the cadi how to try the case of the old olives and the new ones, and said it was out of the *Arabian Nights,* and he would tell me and Jim about it when he got time. Well, we hunted and hunted till I was ready to drop, and I wanted Tom to give it up and come next day and git somebody that knowed the town and could talk Missourian and could go straight to the place; but no, he wanted to find it himself, and nothing else would answer. So on we went. Then at last the remarkablest thing happened I ever see. The house was gone—gone hundreds of years ago—every last rag of it gone but just one mud brick. Now a person wouldn't ever believe that a backwoods Missouri boy that hadn't ever been in that town before could go and hunt that place over and find that brick, but Tom Sawyer done it. I know he done it, because I see him do it. I was right by his very side at the time, and see him see the brick and see him reconnize it. Well, I says to myself, how *does* he do it? Is it knowledge, or is it instink?

Now there's the facts, just as they happened: let everybody explain it their own way. I've ciphered over it a good deal, and it's my opinion that some of it is knowledge but the main bulk of it is instink. The reason is this: Tom put the brick in his pocket to give to a museum with his name on it and the facts when he went home, and I slipped it out and put another brick considerable like it in its place, and he didn't know the difference—but there was a difference, you see. I think that settles it—it's mostly instink, not knowledge. Instink tells him where the exact *place* is for the brick to be in, and so he reconnizes it by the place it's in, not by the look of the brick. If it was knowledge, not instink, he would know the brick again by the look of it the next time he seen it—which he didn't. So it shows that for all the brag you hear about knowledge being such a wonderful thing, instink is worth forty of it for real unerringness. Jim says the same.

When we got back Jim dropped down and

took us in, and there was a young man there
with a red skull-cap and tassel on and a beautiful silk jacket and baggy trousers with a shawl
around his waist and pistols in it that could talk
English and wanted to hire to us as guide and
take us to Mecca and Medina and Central
Africa and everywheres for a half a dollar a day
and his keep, and we hired him and left, and
piled on the power, and by the time we was
through dinner we was over the place where the
Israelites crossed the Red Sea when Pharaoh
tried to overtake them and was caught by the
waters. We stopped, then, and had a good look
at the place, and it done Jim good to see it. He
said he could see it all, now, just the way it
happened; he could see the Israelites walking
along between the walls of water, and the Egyp-
tians coming, from away off yonder, hurrying
all they could, and see them start in as the Israelites went out, and then when they was all in, see
the walls tumble together and drown the last
man of them. Then we piled on the power
again and rushed away and huvvered over
Mount Sinai, and saw the place where Moses
broke the tables of stone, and where the children of Israel camped in the plain and

worshiped the golden calf, and it was all just as interesting as could be, and the guide knowed every place as well as I knowed the village at home.

But we had an accident, now, and it fetched all the plans to a standstill. Tom's old ornery corn-cob pipe had got so old and swelled and warped that she couldn't hold together any longer, notwithstanding the strings and bandages, but caved in and went to pieces. Tom he didn't know *what* to do. The professor's pipe wouldn't answer; it warn't anything but a mershum, and a person that's got used to a cob pipe knows it lays a long ways over all the other pipes in this world, and you can't git him to smoke any other. He wouldn't take mine, I couldn't persuade him. So there he was.

He thought it over, and said we must scour around and see if we could roust out one in Egypt or Arabia or around in some of these countries, but the guide said no, it warn't no use, they didn't have them. So Tom was pretty glum for a little while, then he chirked up and said he'd got the idea and knowed what to do. He says:

"I've got another corn-cob pipe, and it's a

prime one, too, and nearly new.   It's laying on
the rafter that's right over the kitchen stove at
home in the village.   Jim, you and the guide
will go and get it, and me and Huck will camp
here on Mount Sinai till you come back."

"But, Mars Tom, we couldn't ever find de
village.   I could find de pipe, 'case I knows de
kitchen, but, my lan', *we* can't ever find de village, nur Sent Louis, nur none o' dem places.
We don't know de way, Mars Tom."

That was a fact, and it stumped Tom for a
minute.   Then he said:

"Looky here, it can be done, sure; and I'll tell
you how.   You set your compass and sail west as
straight as a dart, till you find the United States.
It ain't any trouble, because it's the first land
you'll strike the other side of the Atlantic.   If it's
daytime when you strike it, bulge right on,
straight west from the upper part of the Florida
coast, and in an hour and three-quarters you'll
hit the mouth of the Mississippi—at the speed
that I'm going to send you.   You'll be so high up
in the air that the earth will be curved considerable—sorter like a washbowl turned upside
down—and you'll see a raft of rivers crawling
around every which way, long before you get

there, and you can pick out the Mississippi without any trouble.   Then you can follow the river north nearly, an hour and three-quarters, till you see the Ohio come in; then you want to look sharp, because you're getting near.   Away up to your left you'll see another thread coming in— that's the Missouri and is a little above St. Louis. You'll come down low then, so as you can examine the villages as you spin along.   You'll pass about twenty-five in the next fifteen minutes, and you'll recognize ours when you see it—and if you don't you can yell down and ask."

"Ef it's dat easy, Mars Tom, I reckon we kin do it—yassir, I knows we kin."

The guide was sure of it, too, and thought that he could learn to stand his watch in a little while.

"Jim can learn you the whole thing in a half an hour," Tom said.   "This balloon's as easy to manage as a canoe."

Tom got out the chart and marked out the course and measured it, and says:

"To go back west is the shortest way, you see. It's only about seven thousand miles.   If you

went east, and so on around, it's over twice as
far." Then he says to the guide, "I want you
both to watch the telltale all through the
watches, and whenever it don't mark three hundred miles an hour, you go higher or drop lower
till you find a storm-current that's going your
way. There's a hundred miles an hour in this
old thing without any wind to help. There's
two-hundred-mile gales to be found, any time
you want to hunt for them."

"We'll hunt for them, sir."

"See that you do. Sometimes you may have
to go up a couple of miles, and it'll be p'ison
cold, but most of the time you'll find your storm
a good deal lower. If you can only strike a
cyclone—that's the ticket for you! You'll see
by the professor's books that they travel west in
these latitudes; and they travel low, too."

Then he ciphered on the time, and says:

"Seven thousand miles, three hundred miles
an hour—you can make the trip in a day—
twenty-four hours. This is Thursday; you'll be
back here Saturday afternoon. Come, now,
hustle out some blankets and food and books
and things for me and Huck, and you can start

right along.   There ain't no occasion to fool
around—I want a smoke, and the quicker you
fetch that pipe the better."

All hands jumped for the things, and in eight
minutes our things was out and the balloon
was ready for America.   So we shook hands
good-by, and Tom gave his last orders:

"It's ten minutes to 2 P.M. now, Mount Sinai
time.   In twenty-four hours you'll be home, and
it'll be six tomorrow morning, village time.
When you strike the village, land a little back of
the top of the hill, in the woods, out of sight;
then you rush down, Jim, and shove these letters in the post-office, and if you see anybody
stirring, pull your slouch down over your face so
they won't know you.   Then you go and slip in
the back way to the kitchen and git the pipe,
and lay this piece of paper on the kitchen table,
and put something on it to hold it, and then
slide out and git away, and don't let Aunt Polly
catch a sight of you, nor nobody else.   Then
you jump for the balloon and shove for Mount
Sinai three hundred miles an hour.   You won't
have lost more than an hour.   You'll start back
at 7 or 8 A.M., village time, and be here in twenty-

four hours, arriving at 2 or 3 P.M., Mount Sinai time."

Tom he read the piece of paper to us.   He had wrote on it:

"THURSDAY AFTERNOON. *Tom Sawyer the Erronort sends his love to Aunt Polly from Mount Sinai where the Ark was,*[1] *and so does Huck Finn, and she will get it tomorrow morning half-past six.*

"TOM SAWYER THE ERRONORT."

"That'll make her eyes bulge out and the tears come," he says.   Then he says:

"Stand by!   One—two—three—away you go!"

And away she *did* go!   Why, she seemed to whiz out of sight in a second.

Then we found a most comfortable cave that looked out over the whole big plain, and there we camped to wait for the pipe.

The balloon come back all right, and brung the pipe; but Aunt Polly had catched Jim when he was getting it, and anybody can guess what happened: she sent for Tom.   So Jim he says:

[1] This misplacing of the Ark is probably Huck's error, not Tom's.—M. T.

"Mars Tom, she's out on de porch wid her eye sot on de sky a-layin' for you, en she say she ain't gwyne to budge from dah tell she gits hold of you.   Dey's gwyne to be trouble, Mars Tom, 'deed dey is."

So then we shoved for home, and not feeling very gay, neither.

A Dog of Flanders

AND OTHER STORIES

The appealing story of an imaginative little boy, a loving old man, and a great faithful dog, all living together in poverty and love, has been a favorite for many years.

The "Nürnberg Stove," another of the stories in this book, is equally well loved by children everywhere. This tale centers around the magnificent stove of colored tile which warmed the hearts as well as the underfed little bodies of the Strehla children. How, in the end, the stove brought them all great happiness is a delightful and inspiring story.

Within the case were notes for two thousand francs

A Dog of Flanders

AND OTHER STORIES

By

LOUISE DE LA RAMÉE

(Ouida)

Illustrations by

MARIANO LEONE

Companion Library

GROSSET AND DUNLAP
PUBLISHERS
NEW YORK

CONTENTS

ILLUSTRATIONS

A DOG OF FLANDERS

*He kneeled down in the rank grass and surveyed the dog
with kindly eyes of pity*

A DOG OF FLANDERS

Nello and patrasche were left all alone in the world.

They were friends in a friendship closer than brotherhood. Nello was a little Ardennois—Patrasche was a big Fleming. They were both of the same age by length of years, yet one was still young, and the other was already old. They had dwelt together almost all their days: both were orphaned and destitute, and owed their lives to the same hand. It had been the beginning of the tie between them, their first bond of sympathy; and it had strengthened day by day, and had grown with their growth, firm and indissoluble, until they loved one another very greatly.

Their home was a little hut on the edge of a little village—a Flemish village a league from Antwerp, set amidst flat breadths of pasture and corn lands, with long lines of poplars and of alders bending in the breeze on the edge of the great canal which ran through it. It had about a score of houses and homesteads, with shutters of

bright green or sky-blue, and roofs rose-red or black and white, and walls whitewashed until they shone in the sun like snow. In the center of the village stood a windmill, placed on a little moss-grown slope: it was a landmark to all the level country round. It had once been painted scarlet, sails and all, but that had been in its infancy, half a century or more earlier, when it had ground wheat for the soldiers of Napoleon; and it was now a ruddy brown, tanned by wind and weather. It went queerly by fits and starts, as though rheumatic and stiff in the joints from age, but it served the whole neighborhood, which would have thought it almost as impious to carry grain elsewhere as to attend any other religious service than the mass that was performed at the altar of the little old gray church, with its conical steeple, which stood opposite to it, and whose single bell rang morning, noon, and night with that strange, subdued, hollow sadness which every bell that hangs in the Low Countries seems to gain as an integral part of its melody.

Within sound of the little melancholy clock almost from their birth upward, they had dwelt together, Nello and Patrasche, in the little hut on the edge of the village, with the cathedral spire of Antwerp rising in the northeast, beyond the great green plain of seeding grass and spreading corn that stretched away from them like a tideless, changeless sea. It was the hut of a very old man, of a very poor man—of old Jehan Daas, who in his time had been a soldier, and who remembered the wars that had trampled the country as oxen tread down the furrows, and who had brought from his service nothing except a wound, which had made him a cripple.

When old Jehan Daas had reached his full eighty, his daughter had died in the Ardennes, hard by Stavelot, and had left him in legacy her two-year-old son. The old man

could ill contrive to support himself, but he took up the additional burden uncomplainingly, and it soon became welcome and precious to him. Little Nello—which was but a pet diminutive for Nicolas—throve with him, and the old man and the little child lived in the poor little hut contentedly.

It was a very humble little mud hut indeed, but it was clean and white as a sea shell, and stood in a small plot of garden ground that yielded beans and herbs and pumpkins. They were very poor, terribly poor—many a day they had nothing at all to eat. They never by any chance had enough: to have had enough to eat would have been to have reached paradise at once. But the old man was very gentle and good to the boy, and the boy was a beautiful, innocent, truthful, tender-natured creature; and they were happy on a crust and a few leaves of cabbage, and asked no more of earth or heaven; save indeed that Patrasche should be always with them, since without Patrasche where would they have been?

For Patrasche was their alpha and omega; their treasury and granary; their store of gold and wand of wealth; their breadwinner and minister; their only friend and comforter. Patrasche dead or gone from them, they must have laid themselves down and died likewise. Patrasche was body, brains, hands, head, and feet to both of them: Patrasche was their very life, their very soul. For Jehan Daas was old and a cripple, and Nello was but a child; and Patrasche was their dog.

A dog of Flanders—yellow of hide, large of head and limb, with wolf-like ears that stood erect, and legs bowed and feet widened in the muscular development wrought in his breed by many generations of hard service. Patrasche came of a race which had toiled hard and cruelly from sire to son in Flanders many a century—slaves of slaves, dogs

of the people, beasts of the shafts and the harness, creatures that lived straining their sinews in the gall of the cart, and died breaking their hearts on the flints of the streets.

Patrasche had been born of parents who had labored hard all their days over the sharp-set stones of the various cities and the long, shadowless, weary roads of the two Flanders and of Brabant. He had been born to no other heritage than those of pain and of toil. He had been fed on curses and baptized with blows. Before he was fully grown he had known the bitter gall of the cart and the collar. Before he had entered his thirteenth month he had become the property of a hardware dealer, who was accustomed to wander over the land north and south, from the blue sea to the green mountains. They sold him for a small price, because he was too young.

This man was a drunkard and a brute. The life of Patrasche was a life of hell. His purchaser was a sullen, ill-living, brutal Brabantois, who heaped his cart full with pots and pans and flagons and buckets, and other wares of crockery and brass and tin, and left Patrasche to draw the load as best he might, whilst he himself lounged idly by the side in fat and sluggish ease, smoking his black pipe and stopping at every wine shop or café on the road.

Happily for Patrasche—or unhappily—he was very strong: he came of an iron race, long born and bred to such cruel travail; so that he did not die, but managed to drag on a wretched existence under the brutal burdens. One day, after two years of this long and deadly agony, Patrasche was going on as usual along one of the straight, dusty, unlovely roads that lead to the city of Rubens. It was full midsummer, and very warm. His cart was very heavy, piled high with goods in metal and in earthenware. His owner sauntered on without noticing him otherwise

than by the crack of the whip as it curled round his quivering loins. The Brabantois had paused to drink beer himself at every wayside house, but he had forbidden Patrasche to stop a moment for a draught from the canal. Going along thus, in the full sun, on a scorching highway, having eaten nothing for twenty-four hours, and, which was far worse to him, not having tasted water for near twelve, being blind with dust, sore with blows, and stupefied with the merciless weight which dragged upon his loins, Patrasche, for once, staggered and foamed a little at the mouth, and fell.

He fell in the middle of the white dusty road, in the full glare of the sun; he was sick unto death, and motionless. His master gave him the only medicine in his pharmacy—kicks and oaths and blows with a cudgel of oak, which had been often the only food and drink, the only wage and reward, ever offered to him. But Patrasche was beyond the reach of any torture or of any curses. Patrasche lay, dead to all appearances, down in the white powder of the summer dust. After a while, finding it useless to assail his ribs with punishment and his ears with maledictions, the Brabantois—deeming life gone in him, or going so nearly that his carcass was forever useless, unless indeed someone should strip it of the skin for gloves—cursed him fiercely in farewell, struck off the leathern bands of the harness, kicked his body heavily aside into the grass, and, groaning and muttering in savage wrath, pushed the cart lazily along the road uphill, and left the dying dog there for the ants to sting and for the crows to pick.

It was the last day before Kermesse away at Louvain, and the Brabantois was in haste to reach the fair and get a good place for his truck of brass wares. He was in fierce wrath, because Patrasche had been a strong and much-

enduring animal, and because he himself had now the hard task of pushing his charette all the way to Louvain. But to stay to look after Patrasche never entered his thoughts: the beast was dying and useless, and he would steal, to replace him, the first large dog that he found wandering alone out of sight of its master. Patrasche had cost him nothing, or next to nothing, and for two long, cruel years he had made him toil ceaselessly in his service from sunrise to sunset, through summer and winter, in fair weather and foul.

He had got a fair use and a good profit out of Patrasche: being human, he was wise, and left the dog to draw his last breath alone in the ditch, and have his bloodshot eyes plucked out as they might be by the birds, while he himself went on his way to beg and to steal, to eat and to drink, to dance and to sing, in the mirth at Louvain. A dying dog, a dog of the cart—why should he waste hours over its agonies at peril of losing a handful of copper coins, at peril of a shout of laughter?

Patrasche lay there, flung in the grass-green ditch. It was a busy road that day, and hundreds of people, on foot and on mules, in wagons or in carts, went by, tramping quickly and joyously on to Louvain. Some saw him, most did not even look: all passed on. A dead dog more or less—it was nothing in Brabant: it would be nothing anywhere in the world.

After a time, among the holiday makers, there came a little old man who was bent and lame, and very feeble. He was in no guise for feasting: he was very poorly and miserably clad, and he dragged his silent way slowly through the dust among the pleasure seekers. He looked at Patrasche, paused, wondered, turned aside, then kneeled down in the rank grass and weeds of the ditch, and surveyed the dog with kindly eyes of pity. There was

with him a little rosy, fair-haired, dark-eyed child of a few years old, who pattered in amidst the bushes, that were for him breast-high, and stood gazing with a pretty seriousness upon the poor, great, quiet beast.

Thus it was that these two first met—the little Nello and the big Patrasche.

The upshot of that day was, that old Jehan Daas, with much laborious effort, drew the sufferer homeward to his own little hut, which was a stone's throw off amidst the fields, and there tended him with so much care that the sickness, which had been a brain seizure, brought on by heat and thirst and exhaustion, with time and shade and rest passed away, and health and strength returned, and Patrasche staggered up again upon his four stout, tawny legs.

Now for many weeks he had been useless, powerless, sore, near to death; but all this time he had heard no rough word, had felt no harsh touch, but only the pitying murmurs of the little child's voice and the soothing caress of the old man's hand.

In his sickness they too had grown to care for him, this lonely old man and the little happy child. He had a corner of the hut, with a heap of dry grass for his bed; and they had learned to listen eagerly for his breathing in the dark night, to tell them that he lived; and when he first was well enough to essay a loud, hollow, broken bay, they laughed aloud, and almost wept together for joy at such a sign of his sure restoration; and little Nello, in delighted glee, hung round his rugged neck chains of marguerites, and kissed him with fresh and ruddy lips.

So then, when Patrasche arose, himself again, strong, big, gaunt, powerful, his great wistful eyes had a gentle astonishment in them that there were no curses to rouse him and no blows to drive him; and his heart awakened to

a mighty love, which never wavered once in its fidelity while life abode with him.

But Patrasche, being a dog, was grateful. Patrasche lay pondering long with grave, tender, musing brown eyes, watching the movements of his friends.

Now, the old soldier, Jehan Daas, could do nothing for his living but limp about a little with a small cart, with which he carried daily the milk cans of those happier neighbors who owned cattle away into the town of Antwerp. The villagers gave him the employment a little out of charity—more because it suited them well to send their milk into the town by so honest a carrier, and bide at home themselves to look after their gardens, their cows, their poultry, or their little fields. But it was becoming hard work for the old man. He was eighty-three, and Antwerp was a good league off, or more.

Patrasche watched the milk cans come and go that one day when he had got well and was lying in the sun with the wreath of marguerites round his tawny neck.

The next morning, Patrasche, before the old man had touched the cart, arose and walked to it and placed himself betwixt its handles, and testified as plainly as dumb show could do his desire and his ability to work in return for the bread of charity that he had eaten. Jehan Daas resisted long, for the old man was one of those who thought it a foul shame to bind dogs to labor for which Nature never formed them. But Patrasche would not be gainsaid: finding they did not harness him, he tried to draw the cart onward with his teeth.

At length Jehan Daas gave way, vanquished by the persistence and the gratitude of this creature whom he had succored. He fashioned his cart so that Patrasche could run in it, and this he did every morning of his life thenceforward.

When the winter came, Jehan Daas thanked the blessed fortune that had brought him to the dying dog in the ditch that fair-day of Louvain; for he was very old, and he grew feebler with each year, and he would ill have known how to pull his load of milk cans over the snows and through the deep ruts in the mud if it had not been for the strength and the industry of the animal he had befriended. As for Patrasche, it seemed heaven to him. After the frightful burdens that his old master had compelled him to strain under, at the call of the whip at every step, it seemed nothing to him but amusement to step out with this little light green cart, with its bright brass cans, by the side of the gentle old man who always paid him with a tender caress and with a kindly word. Besides, his work was over by three or four in the day, and after that time he was free to do as he would—to stretch himself, to sleep in the sun, to wander in the fields, to romp with the young child, or to play with his fellow dogs. Patrasche was very happy.

Fortunately for his peace, his former owner was killed in a drunken brawl at the Kermesse of Mechlin, and so sought not after him nor disturbed him in his new and well-loved home.

A few years later, old Jehan Daas, who had always been a cripple, became so paralyzed with rheumatism that it was impossible for him to go out with the cart any more. Then little Nello, being now grown to his sixth year of age, and knowing the town well from having accompanied his grandfather so many times, took his place beside the cart, and sold the milk and received the coins in exchange, and brought them back to their respective owners with a pretty grace and seriousness which charmed all who beheld him.

The little Ardennois was a beautiful child, with dark,

grave, tender eyes, and a lovely bloom upon his face, and fair locks that clustered to his throat; and many an artist sketched the group as it went by him—the green cart with the brass flagons of Teniers and Mieris and Van Tal, and the great tawny-colored, massive dog, with his belled harness that chimed cheerily as he went, and the small figure that ran beside him which had little white feet in great wooden shoes, and a soft, grave, innocent, happy face like the little fair children of Rubens.

Nello and Patrasche did the work so well and so joyfully together that Jehan Daas himself, when the summer came and he was better again, had no need to stir out, but could sit in the doorway in the sun and see them go forth through the garden wicket, and then doze and dream and pray a little, and then awake again as the clock tolled three and watch for their return. And on their return Patrasche would shake himself free of his harness with a bay of glee, and Nello would recount with pride the doings of the day; and they would all go in together to their meal of rye bread and milk or soup, and would see the shadows lengthen over the great plain, and see the twilight veil the fair cathedral spire; and then lie down together to sleep peacefully while the old man said a prayer.

So the days and the years went on, and the lives of Nello and Patrasche were very happy and innocent and healthful.

In the spring and summer especially were they glad. Flanders is not a lovely land, and around the burgh of Rubens it is perhaps least lovely of all. Corn and colza, pasture and plow, succeed each other on the characterless plain in wearying repetition, and save by some gaunt gray tower, with its peal of pathetic bells, or some figure coming athwart the fields, made picturesque by a gleaner's bundle

or a woodman's fagot, there is no change, no variety, no beauty anywhere; and he who has dwelt upon the mountains or amidst the forest feels oppressed as by imprisonment with the tedium and the needlessness of that vast and dreary level. But it is green and very fertile, and it has wide horizons that have a certain charm of their own even in their dullness and monotony; and among the rushes by the waterside the flowers grow, and the trees rise tall and fresh where the barges glide with their great hulks black against the sun, and their little green barrels and vari-colored flags gay against the leaves. Anyway, there is greenery and breadth of space enough to be as good as beauty to a child and a dog; and these two asked no better, when their work was done, than to lie buried in the lush grasses on the side of the canal, and watch the cumbrous vessels drifting by and bringing the crisp salt smell of the sea among the blossoming scents of the country summer.

True, in the winter it was harder, and they had to rise in the darkness and the bitter cold, and they had seldom as much as they could have eaten any day, and the hut was scarce better than a shed when the nights were cold, although it looked so pretty in warm weather, buried in a great kindly clambering vine, that never bore fruit, indeed, but which covered it with luxuriant green tracery all through the months of blossom and harvest. In winter the winds found many holes in the walls of the poor little hut, and the vine was black and leafless, and the bare lands looked very bleak and drear without, and sometimes within the floor was flooded and then frozen. In winter it was hard, and the snow numbed the little white limbs of Nello, and the icicles cut the brave untiring feet of Patrasche.

But even then they were never heard to lament, either

of them. The child's wooden shoes and the dog's four legs would trot manfully together over the frozen fields to the chime of the bells on the harness; and then sometimes, in the streets of Antwerp, some housewife would bring them a bowl of soup and a handful of bread, or some kindly trader would throw some billets of fuel into the little cart as it went homeward, or some woman in their own village would bid them keep some share of the milk they carried for their own food; and then they would run over the white lands, through the early darkness, bright and happy, and burst with a shout of joy into their home.

So, on the whole, it was well with them, very well; and Patrasche, meeting on the highway or in the public streets the many dogs who toiled from daybreak into nightfall, paid only with blows and curses, and loosened from the shafts with a kick to starve and freeze as best they might—Patrasche in his heart was very grateful to his fate, and thought it the fairest and the kindliest the world could hold. Though he was often very hungry indeed when he lay down at night; though he had to work in the heats of summer noons and the rasping chills of winter dawns; though his feet were often tender with wounds from the sharp edges of the jagged pavement; though he had to perform tasks beyond his strength and against his nature—yet he was grateful and content: he did his duty with each day, and the eyes that he loved smiled down on him. It was sufficient for Patrasche.

There was only one thing which caused Patrasche any uneasiness in his life, and it was this. Antwerp, as all the world knows, is full at every turn of old piles of stones dark and ancient and majestic, standing in crooked courts, jammed against gateways and taverns, rising by the water's edge, with bells ringing above them in the air,

and ever and again out of their arched doors a swell of music pealing. There they remain, the grand old sanctuaries of the past, shut in amidst the squalor, the hurry, the crowds, the unloveliness, and the commerce of the modern world, and all day long the clouds drift and the birds circle and the winds sigh around them, and beneath the earth at their feet there sleeps—RUBENS.

And the greatness of the mighty Master still rests upon Antwerp, and wherever we turn in its narrow streets his glory lies therein, so that all mean things are thereby transfigured; and as we pace slowly through the winding ways, and by the edge of the stagnant water, and through the noisome courts, his spirit abides with us, and the heroic beauty of his visions is about us, and the stones that once felt his footsteps and bore his shadow seem to arise and speak of him with living voices. For the city which is the tomb of Rubens still lives to us through him, and him alone.

It is so quiet there by that great white sepulcher—so quiet, save only when the organ peals and the choir cries aloud the Salve Regina or the Kyrie Eleison. Sure no artist ever had a greater gravestone than that pure marble sanctuary gives to him in the heart of his birthplace in the chancel of St. Jacques.

Without Rubens, what were Antwerp? A dirty, dusky, bustling mart, which no man would ever care to look upon save the traders who do business on its wharves. With Rubens, to the whole world of men it is a sacred name, a sacred soil, a Bethlehem where a god of Art saw light, a Golgotha where a god of Art lies dead.

O nations closely should you treasure your great men, for by them alone will the future know of you. Flanders in her generations has been wise. In his life she glorified

this greatest of her sons, and in his death she magnifies his name. But her wisdom is very rare.

Now, the trouble of Patrasche was this. Into these great, sad piles of stones, that reared their melancholy majesty above the crowded roofs, the child Nello would many and many a time enter, and disappear through their dark arched portals, whilst Patrasche, left without upon the pavement, would wearily and vainly ponder on what could be the charm which thus allured from him his inseparable and beloved companion. Once or twice he did essay to see for himself, clattering up the steps with his milk-cart behind him; but thereon he had been always sent back again summarily by a tall custodian in black clothes and silver chains of office; and fearful of bringing his little master into trouble, he desisted, and remained couched patiently before the churches until such time as the boy reappeared. It was not the fact of his going into them which disturbed Patrasche: he knew that people went to church: all the village went to the small, tumble-down, gray pile opposite the red windmill. What troubled him was that little Nello always looked strangely when he came out, always very flushed or very pale; and whenever he returned home after such visitations would sit silent and dreaming, not caring to play, but gazing out at the evening skies beyond the line of the canal, very subdued and almost sad.

What was it: wondered Patrasche. He thought it could not be good or natural for the little lad to be so grave, and in his dumb fashion he tried all he could to keep Nello by him in the sunny fields or in the busy market place. But to the churches Nello would go: most often of all would he go to the great cathedral; and Patrasche, left without on the stones by the iron fragments of Quentin Matsys's gate, would stretch himself and yawn

and sigh, and even howl now and then, all in vain, until
the doors closed and the child perforce came forth again,
and winding his arms about the dog's neck would kiss him
on his broad, tawny-colored forehead, and murmur
always the same words: "If I could only see them,
Patrasche!—if I could only see them!"

What were they? pondered Patrasche, looking up with
large, wistful, sympathetic eyes.

One day, when the custodian was out of the way and
the doors left ajar, he got in for a moment after his little
friend and saw. "They" were two great covered pictures
on either side of the choir.

Nello was kneeling, rapt as in an ecstasy, before the
altar picture of the Assumption, and when he noticed
Patrasche, and rose and drew the dog gently out into the
air, his face was wet with tears, and he looked up at the
veiled places as he passed them, and murmured to his
companion, "It is so terrible not to see them, Patrasche,
just because one is poor and cannot pay. He never meant
that the poor should not see them when he painted them, I
am sure. He would have had us see them any day, every
day: that I am sure. And they keep them shrouded
there—shrouded in the dark, the beautiful things!—and
they never feel the light, and no eyes look on them, unless
rich people come and pay. If I could only see them, I
would be content to die."

But he could not see them, and Patrasche could not
help him, for to gain the silver piece that the church
exacts as the price for looking on the glories of the
Elevation of the Cross and the Descent of the Cross was a
thing as utterly beyond the powers of either of them as it
would have been to scale the heights of the cathedral
spire. They had never so much as a sou to spare: if they
cleared enough to get a little wood for the stove, a little

broth for the pot, it was the utmost they could do. And yet the heart of the child was set in sore and endless longing upon beholding the greatness of the two veiled Rubens.

The whole soul of the little Ardennois thrilled and stirred with an absorbing passion for Art. Going on his ways through the old city in the early days before the sun or the people had risen, Nello, who looked only a little peasant boy, with a great dog drawing milk to sell from door to door, was in a heaven of dreams whereof Rubens was the god. Nello, cold and hungry, with stockingless feet in wooden shoes, and the winter winds blowing among his curls and lifting his poor thin garments, was in a rapture of meditation, wherein all that he saw was the beautiful fair face of the Mary of the Assumption, with the waves of her golden hair lying upon her shoulders, and the light of an eternal sun shining down upon her brow. Nello, reared in poverty, and buffeted by fortune, and untaught in letters and unheeded by men, had the compensation or the curse which is called Genius.

No one knew it. He as little as any. No one knew it. Only indeed Patrasche, who, being with him always, saw him draw with chalk upon the stones any and every thing that grew or breathed, heard him on his little bed of hay murmur all manner of timid, pathetic prayers to the spirit of the great Master; watched his gaze darken and his face radiate at the evening glow of sunset or the rosy rising of the dawn; and felt many and many a time the tears of a strange, nameless pain and joy, mingled together, fall hotly from the bright young eyes upon his own wrinkled yellow forehead.

"I should go to my grave quite content if I thought, Nello, that when thou growest a man thou couldst own this hut and the little plot of ground, and labor for thyself,

and be called Baas by thy neighbors," said the old man
Jehan many an hour from his bed. For to own a bit of
soil, and to be called Baas—master—by the hamlet
round, is to have achieved the highest ideal of a Flemish
peasant; and the old soldier, who had wandered over all
the earth in his youth, and had brought nothing back,
deemed in his old age that to live and die on one spot in
contented humility was the fairest fate he could desire for
his darling. But Nello said nothing.

The same leaven was working in him that in other
times begat Rubens and Jordaens and the Van Eycks, and
all their wondrous tribe, and in times more recent begat in
the green country of the Ardennes, where the Meuse
washes the old walls of Dijon, the great artist of the
Patroclus, whose genius is too near us for us aright to
measure its divinity.

Nello dreamed of other things in the future than of
tilling the little rood of earth, and living under the wattle
roof, and being called Baas by neighbors a little poorer or
a little less poor than himself. The cathedral spire, where
it rose beyond the fields in the ruddy evening skies or in
the dim, gray misty mornings, said other things to him
than this. But these he told only to Patrasche, whispering, childlike, his fancies in the dog's ear when they went
together at their work through the fogs of the daybreak,
or lay together at their rest among the rustling rushes by
the water's side.

For such dreams are not easily shaped into speech to
awake the slow sympathies of human auditors; and they
would only have sorely perplexed and troubled the poor
old man bedridden in his corner, who, for his part,
whenever he had trodden the streets of Antwerp, had
thought the daub of blue and red that they called a
Madonna, on the walls of the wine-shop where he drank

his sou's worth of black beer, quite as good as any of the famous altarpieces for which the stranger folk traveled far and wide into Flanders from every land on which the good sun shone.

There was only one other beside Patrasche to whom Nello could talk at all of his daring fantasies. This other was little Alois, who lived at the old red mill on the grassy mound, and whose father, the miller, was the best-to-do husbandman in all the village. Little Alois was only a pretty baby with soft, round, rosy features made lovely by those sweet dark eyes that the Spanish rule has left in so many a Flemish face, in testimony of the Alvan dominion, as Spanish art has left broadsown throughout the country majestic palaces and stately courts, gilded house fronts and sculptured lintels—histories in blazonry and poems in stone.

Little Alois was often with Nello and Patrasche. They played in the fields, they ran in the snow, they gathered the daisies and bilberries, they went up to the old gray church together, and they often sat together by the broad wood fire in the millhouse. Little Alois, indeed, was the richest child in the hamlet. She had neither brother nor sister; her blue serge dress had never a hole in it; at Kermesse she had as many gilded nuts and Agni Dei in sugar as her hands could hold; and when she went up for her first communion her flaxen curls were covered with a cap of richest Mechlin lace, which had been her mother's and her grandmother's before it came to her. Men spoke already, though she had but twelve years, of the good wife she would be for their sons to woo and win; but she herself was a little gay, simple child, in nowise conscious of her heritage, and she loved no playfellows so well as Jehan Daas's grandson and his dog.

One day her father, Baas Cogez, a good man, but

somewhat stern, came on a pretty group in the long meadow behind the mill, where the aftermath had that day been cut. It was his little daughter sitting amidst the hay with the great tawny head of Patrasche on her lap, many wreaths of poppies and blue cornflowers round them both: on a clean smooth slab of pine wood the boy Nello drew their likeness with a stick of charcoal.

The miller stood and looked at the portrait with tears in his eyes, it was so strangely like, and he loved his only child closely and well. Then he roughly chid the little girl for idling there while her mother needed her within, and sent her indoors crying and afraid: then, turning, he snatched the wood from Nello's hands. "Dost do much of such folly?" he asked, but there was a tremble in his voice.

Nello colored and hung his head. "I draw everything I see," he murmured.

The miller was silent: then he stretched his hand out with a franc in it. "It is folly, as I say, and evil waste of time: nevertheless, it is like Alois, and will please the housemother. Take this silver bit for it and leave it for me."

The color died out of the face of the young Ardennois; he lifted his head and put his hands behind his back. "Keep your money and the portrait both, Baas Cogez," he said, simply. "You have been often good to me." Then he called Patrasche to him, and walked away across the field.

"I could have seen them with that franc," he murmured to Patrasche, "but I could not sell her picture—not even for them."

Baas Cogez went into his millhouse sore troubled in his mind. "That lad must not be so much with Alois," he said to his wife that night. "Trouble may come of it

hereafter: he is fifteen now, and she is twelve; and the boy is comely of face and form."

"And he is a good lad and a loyal," said the housewife feasting her eyes on the piece of pine wood where it was throned above the chimney with a cuckoo clock in oak and a Calvary in wax.

"Yea, I do not gainsay that," said the miller, draining his pewter flagon.

"Then, if what you think of were ever to come to pass," said the wife, hesitatingly, "would it matter so much? She will have enough for both, and one cannot be better than happy."

"You are a woman, and therefore a fool," said the miller, harshly, striking his pipe on the table. "The lad is naught but a beggar, and, with these painter's fancies, worse than a beggar. Have a care that they are not together in the future, or I will send the child to the surer keeping of the nuns of the Sacred Heart."

The poor mother was terrified, and promised humbly to do his will. Not that she could bring herself altogether to separate the child from her favorite playmate, nor did the miller even desire that extreme of cruelty to a young lad who was guilty of nothing except poverty. But there were many ways in which little Alois was kept away from her chosen companion: and Nello, being a boy proud and quiet and sensitive, was quickly wounded, and ceased to turn his own steps and those of Patrasche, as he had been used to do with every moment of leisure, to the old red mill upon the slope. What his offense was he did not know: he supposed he had in some manner angered Baas Cogez by taking the portrait of Alois in the meadow; and when the child who loved him would run to him and nestle her hand in his, he would smile at her very sadly and say with tender concern for her before himself, "Nay,

*On a clean slab of pine wood, Nello drew their likeness
with a stick of charcoal*

Alois, do not anger your father. He thinks that I make you idle, dear, and he is not pleased that you should be with me. He is a good man and loves you well: we will not anger him, Alois."

But it was with a sad heart that he said it, and the earth did not look so bright to him as it had used to do when he went out at sunrise under the poplars down the straight roads with Patrasche. The old red mill had been a landmark to him, and he had been used to pause by it, going and coming, for a cheery greeting with its people as her little flaxen head rose above the low mill wicket, and her little rosy hands had held out a bone or a crust to Patrasche. Now the dog looked wistfully at a closed door, and the boy went on without pausing, with a pang at his heart, and the child sat within with tears dropping slowly on the knitting to which she was set on her little stool by the stove; and Baas Cogez, working among his sacks and his mill gear, would harden his will and say to himself, "It is best so. The lad is all but a beggar, and full of idle, dreaming fooleries. Who knows what mischief might not come of it in the future?" So he was wise in his generation, and would not have the door unbarred, except upon rare and formal occasions, which seemed to have neither warmth nor mirth in them to the two children, who had been accustomed so long to a daily gleeful, careless, happy interchange of greeting, speech, and pastime, with no other watcher of their sports or auditor of their fancies than Patrasche, sagely shaking the brazen bells of his collar and responding with all a dog's swift sympathies to their every change of mood.

All this while the little panel of pine wood remained over the chimney in the mill kitchen with the cuckoo clock and the waxen Calvary, and sometimes it seemed to

Nello a little hard that whilst his gift was accepted he himself should be denied.

But he did not complain: it was his habit to be quiet: old Jehan Daas had said ever to him, "We are poor: we must take what God sends—the ill with the good: the poor cannot choose."

To which the boy had always listened in silence, being reverent of his old grandfather; but nevertheless a certain vague, sweet hope, such as beguiles the children of genius, had whispered in his heart, "Yet the poor do choose sometimes—choose to be great, so that men cannot say them nay." And he thought so still in his innocence; and one day, when the little Alois, finding him by chance alone among the cornfields by the canal, ran to him and held him close, and sobbed piteously because the morrow would be her saint's day, and for the first time in all her life her parents had failed to bid him to the little supper and romp in the great barns with which her feast day was always celebrated, Nello had kissed her and murmured to her in firm faith, "It shall be different one day, Alois. One day that little bit of pine wood that your father has of mine shall be worth its weight in silver; and he will not shut the door against me then. Only love me always, dear little Alois, only love me always, and I will be great."

"And if I do not love you?" the pretty child asked, pouting a little through her tears, and moved by the instinctive coquetries of her sex.

Nello's eyes left her face and wandered to the distance, where in the red and gold of the Flemish night the cathedral spire rose. There was a smile on his face so sweet and yet so sad that little Alois was awed by it. "I will be great still," he said under his breath—"great still, or die, Alois."

"You do not love me," said the little spoilt child, pushing him away; but the boy shook his head and smiled, and went on his way through the tall yellow corn, seeing as in a vision some day in a fair future when he should come into that old familiar land and ask Alois of her people, and be not refused or denied, but received in honor, whilst the village folk should throng to look upon him and say in one another's ears, "Dost see him? He is a king among men, for he is a great artist and the world speaks his name; and yet he was only our poor little Nello, who was a beggar, as one may say, and only got his bread by the help of his dog." And he thought how he would fold his grandsire in furs and purples, and portray him as the old man is portrayed in the Family in the chapel of St. Jacques; and of how he would hang the throat of Patrasche with a collar of gold, and place him on his right hand, and say to the people, "This was once my only friend;" and of how he would build himself a great white marble palace, and make to himself luxuriant gardens of pleasure, on the slope looking outward to where the cathedral spire rose, and not dwell in it himself, but summon to it, as to a home, all men young and poor and friendless, but of the will to do mighty things; and of how he would say to them always, if they sought to bless his name, "Nay, do not thank me—thank Rubens. Without him, what should I have been?" And these dreams, beautiful, impossible, innocent, free of all selfishness, full of heroical worship, were so closely about him as he went that he was happy—happy even on this sad anniversary of Alois's saint's day, when he and Patrasche went home by themselves to the little dark hut and the meal of black bread, whilst in the millhouse all the children of the village sang and laughed, and ate the big round cakes of Dijon and the almond gingerbread of Brabant, and

danced in the great barn to the light of the stars and the music of flute and fiddle.

"Never mind, Patrasche," he said, with his arms round the dog's neck as they both sat in the door of the hut, where the sounds of the mirth at the mill came down to them on the night air—"never mind. It shall all be changed by and by."

He believed in the future: Patrasche, of more experience and of more philosophy, thought that the loss of the mill supper in the present was ill compensated by dreams of milk and honey in some vague hereafter. And Patrasche growled whenever he passed by Baas Cogez.

"This is Alois's name-day, is it not?" said the old man Daas that night from the corner where he was stretched upon his bed of sacking.

The boy gave a gesture of assent: he wished that the old man's memory had erred a little, instead of keeping such sure account.

"And why not there?" his grandfather pursued. "Thou hast never missed a year before, Nello."

"Thou art too sick to leave," murmured the lad, bending his handsome young head over the bed.

"Tut! tut! Mother Nulette would have come and sat with me, as she does scores of times. What is the cause, Nello?" the old man persisted. "Thou surely hast not had ill words with the little one?"

"Nay, grandfather—never," said the boy quickly, with a hot color in his bent face. "Simply and truly, Baas Cogez did not have me asked this year. He has taken some whim against me."

"But thou hast done nothing wrong?"

"That I know—nothing. I took the portrait of Alois on a piece of pine: that is all."

"Ah!" The old man was silent: the truth suggested

itself to him with the boy's innocent answer. He was tied to a bed of dried leaves in the corner of a wattle hut, but he had not wholly forgotten what the ways of the world were like.

He drew Nello's fair head fondly to his breast with a tenderer gesture. "Thou art very poor, my child," he said with a quiver the more in his aged, trembling voice—"so poor! It is very hard for thee."

"Nay, I am rich," murmured Nello; and in his innocence he thought so—rich with the imperishable powers that are mightier than the might of kings. And he went and stood by the door of the hut in the quiet autumn night, and watched the stars troop by and the tall poplars bend and shiver in the wind. All the casements of the millhouse were lighted, and every now and then the notes of the flute came to him. The tears fell down his cheeks, for he was but a child, yet he smiled, for he said to himself, "In the future!" He stayed there until all was quite still and dark, and then he and Patrasche went within and slept together, long and deeply, side by side.

Now he had a secret which only Patrasche knew. There was a little outhouse to the hut, which no one entered but himself—a dreary place, but with abundant clear light from the north. Here he had fashioned himself rudely an easel in rough lumber, and here on a great gray sea of stretched paper he had given shape to one of the innumerable fancies which possessed his brain. No one had ever taught him anything; colors he had no means to buy; he had gone without bread many a time to procure even the few rude vehicles that he had here; and it was only in black or white that he could fashion the things he saw. This great figure which he had drawn here in chalk was only an old man sitting on a fallen tree—only that. He had seen old Michel the woodman sitting so at evening

many a time. He had never had a soul to tell him of outline or perspective, of anatomy or of shadow, and yet he had given all the weary, worn-out age, all the sad, quiet patience, all the rugged, careworn pathos of his original, and given them so that the old lonely figure was a poem, sitting there, meditative and alone, on the dead tree, with the darkness of the descending night behind him.

It was rude of course, in a way, and had many faults, no doubt; and yet it was real, true in nature, true in art and very mournful, and in a manner beautiful.

Patrasche had lain quiet countless hours watching its gradual creation after the labor of each day was done, and he knew that Nello had a hope—vain and wild perhaps, but strongly cherished—of sending this great drawing to compete for a prize of two hundred francs a year which it was announced in Antwerp would be open to every lad of talent, scholar or peasant, under eighteen, who would attempt to win it with some unaided work of chalk or pencil. Three of the foremost artists in the town of Rubens were to be the judges and elect the victor according to his merits.

All the spring and summer and autumn Nello had been at work upon this treasure, which, if triumphant, would build him his first step toward independence and the mysteries of the art which he blindly, ignorantly, and yet passionately adored.

He said nothing to any one: his grandfather would not have understood, and little Alois was lost to him. Only to Patrasche he told all, and whispered, "Rubens would give it me, I think, if he knew."

Patrasche thought so too, for he knew that Rubens had loved dogs or he had never painted them with such exquisite fidelity; and men who loved dogs were, as Patrasche knew, always pitiful.

The drawings were to go in on the first day of December, and the decision be given on the twenty-fourth, so that he who should win might rejoice with all his people at the Christmas season.

In the twilight of a bitter wintry day, and with a beating heart, now quick with hope, now faint with fear Nello placed the great picture on his little green milk cart, and took it with the help of Patrasche, into the town, and there left it, as enjoined, at the doors of a public building.

"Perhaps it is worth nothing at all.   How can I tell?" he thought, with the heartsickness of a great timidity.   Now that he had left it there, it seemed to him so hazardous, so vain, so foolish, to dream that he, a little lad with bare feet, who barely knew his letters, could do anything at which great painters, real artists, could ever deign to look. Yet he took heart as he went by the cathedral: the lordly form of Rubens seemed to rise from the fog and the darkness, and to loom in its magnificence before him, whilst the lips, with their kindly smile, seemed to him to murmur, "Nay, have courage!   It was not by a weak heart and by faint fears that I wrote my name for all time upon Antwerp."

Nello ran home through the cold night, comforted. He had done his best: the rest must be as God willed, he thought, in that innocent, unquestioning faith which had been taught him in the little gray chapel among the willows and the poplar trees.

The winter was very sharp already.   That night, after they reached the hut, snow fell; and fell for very many days after that, so that the paths and the divisions in the fields were all obliterated, and all the smaller streams were frozen over, and the cold was intense upon the plains.   Then, indeed, it became hard work to go round for the milk while the world was all dark, and carry it

through the darkness to the silent town. Hard work, especially for Patrasche, for the passage of the years, that were only bringing Nello a stronger youth, were bringing him old age, and his joints were stiff and his bones ached often. But he would never give up his share of the labor. Nello would fain have spared him and drawn the cart himself, but Patrasche would not allow it. All he would ever permit or accept was the help of a thrust from behind to the truck as it lumbered along through the ice ruts. Patrasche had lived in harness, and he was proud of it. He suffered a great deal sometimes from frost, and the terrible roads, and the rheumatic pains of his limbs, but he only drew his breath hard and bent his stout neck, and trod onward with steady patience.

"Rest thee at home, Patrasche—it is time thou didst rest—and I can quite well push in the cart by myself," urged Nello many a morning; but Patrasche, who understood him aright, would no more have consented to stay at home than a veteran soldier to shirk when the charge was sounding; and every day he would rise and place himself in his shafts, and plod along over the snow through the fields that his four round feet had left their print upon so many, many years.

"One must never rest till one dies," thought Patrasche; and sometimes it seemed to him that that time of rest for him was not very far off. His sight was less clear than it had been, and it gave him pain to rise after the night's sleep, though he would never lie a moment in his straw when once the bell of the chapel tolling five let him know that the daybreak of labor had begun.

"My poor Patrasche, we shall soon lie quiet together, you and I," said old Jehan Daas, stretching out to stroke the head of Patrasche with the old withered hand which had always shared with him its one poor crust of bread;

and the hearts of the old man and the old dog ached together with one thought: When they were gone, who would care for their darling?

One afternoon, as they came back from Antwerp over the snow, which had become hard and smooth as marble over all the Flemish plains, they found dropped in the road a pretty little puppet, a tambourine-player, all scarlet and gold, about six inches high, and, unlike greater personages when Fortune lets them drop, quite unspoiled and unhurt by its fall. It was a pretty toy. Nello tried to find its owner, and, failing, thought that it was just the thing to please Alois.

It was quite night when he passed the millhouse: he knew the little window of her room. It could be no harm, he thought, if he gave her his little piece of treasure-trove, they had been playfellows so long. There was a shed with a sloping roof beneath her casement: he climbed it and tapped softly at the lattice: there was a little light within. The child opened it and looked out half frightened.

Nello put the tambourine-player into her hands. "Here is a doll I found in the snow, Alois. Take it," he whispered—"take it, and God bless thee, dear!"

He slid down from the shed roof before she had time to thank him, and ran off through the darkness.

That night there was a fire at the mill. Outbuildings and much corn were destroyed although the mill itself and the dwelling house were unharmed. All the village was out in terror, and engines came tearing through the snow from Antwerp. The miller was insured, and would lose nothing: nevertheless, he was in furious wrath, and declared aloud that the fire was due to no accident, but to some foul intent.

Nello, awakened from his sleep, ran to help with the

"*Here is a doll I found in the snow, Alois*"

rest: Baas Cogez thrust him angrily aside. "Thou wert loitering here after dark," he said roughly. "I believe that thou dost know more of the fire than any one."

Nello heard him in silence, stupefied, not supposing that any one could say such things except in jest, and not comprehending how any one could pass a jest at such a time.

Nevertheless, the miller said the brutal thing openly to many of his neighbors in the day that followed; and though no serious charge was ever preferred against the lad, it got bruited about that Nello had been seen in the mill yard after dark on some unspoken errand, and that he bore Baas Cogez a grudge for forbidding his intercourse with little Alois; and so the hamlet, which followed the sayings of its richest landowner servilely, and whose families all hoped to secure the riches of Alois in some future time for their sons, took the hint to give grave looks and cold words to old Jehan Daas's grandson. No one said anything to him openly, but all the village agreed together to humor the miller's prejudice, and at the cottages and farms where Nello and Patrasche called every morning for the milk for Antwerp, downcast glances and brief phrases replaced to them the broad smiles and cheerful greetings to which they had been always used. No one really credited the miller's absurd suspicion, nor the outrageous accusations born of them, but the people were all very poor and very ignorant, and the one rich man of the place had pronounced against him. Nello, in his innocence and his friendlessness, had no strength to stem the popular tide.

"Thou art very cruel to the lad," the miller's wife dared to say, weeping, to her lord. "Sure he is an innocent lad and a faithful, and would never dream of any such wickedness, however sore his heart might be."

But Baas Cogez being an obstinate man, having once

said a thing held to it doggedly, though in his innermost soul he knew well the injustice that he was committing.

Meanwhile, Nello endured the injury done against him with a certain proud patience that disdained to complain: he only gave way a little when he was quite alone with old Patrasche. Besides, he thought, "If it should win! They will be sorry then, perhaps."

Still, to a boy not quite sixteen, and who had dwelt in one little world all his short life, and in his childhood had been caressed and applauded on all sides, it was a hard trial to have the whole of that little world turn against him for naught. Especially hard in that bleak, snow-bound, famine-stricken wintertime, when the only light and warmth there could be found abode beside the village hearths and in the kindly greetings of neighbors. In the wintertime all drew nearer to each other, all to all, except to Nello and Patrasche, with whom none now would have anything to do, and who were left to care as they might with the old paralyzed, bedridden man in the little cabin, whose fire was often low, and whose board was often without bread, for there was a buyer from Antwerp who had taken to drive his mule in of a day for the milk of the various dairies, and there were only three or four of the people who had refused his terms of purchase and remained faithful to the little green cart. So that the burden which Patrasche drew had become very light, and the centime pieces in Nello's pouch had become, alas! very small likewise.

The dog would stop, as usual, at all the familiar gates which were now closed to him, and look up at them with wistful, mute appeal; and it cost the neighbors a pang to shut their doors and their hearts, and let Patrasche draw his cart on again, empty. Nevertheless, they did it, for they desired to please Baas Cogez.

Noël was close at hand.

The weather was very wild and cold. The snow was six feet deep, and the ice was firm enough to bear oxen and men upon it everywhere. At this season the little village was always gay and cheerful. At the poorest dwelling there were possets and cakes, joking and dancing, sugared saints and gilded Jésus. The merry Flemish bells jingled everywhere on the horses; everywhere within doors some well-filled soup-pot sang and smoked over the stove; and everywhere over the snow without laughing maidens pattered in bright kerchiefs and stout kirtles, going to and from the mass. Only in the little hut it was very dark and very cold.

Nello and Patrasche were left utterly alone, for one night in the week before the Christmas Day, Death entered there, and took away from life forever old Jehan Daas, who had never known of life aught save its poverty and its pains. He had long been half dead, incapable of any movement except a feeble gesture, and powerless for anything beyond a gentle word; and yet his loss fell on them both with a great horror in it: they mourned him passionately. He had passed away from them in his sleep, and when in the gray dawn they learned their bereavement, unutterable solitude and desolation seemed to close around them. He had long been only a poor, feeble, paralyzed old man, who could not raise a hand in their defense, but he had loved them well: his smile had always welcomed their return. They mourned for him unceasingly, refusing to be comforted, as in the white winter day they followed the deal shell that held his body to the nameless grave by the little gray church. They were his only mourners, these two whom he had left friendless upon earth—the young boy and the old dog.

"Surely, he will relent now and let the poor lad come

hither?" thought the miller's wife, glancing at her husband where he smoked by the hearth.

Baas Cogez knew her thought, but he hardened his heart, and would not unbar his door as the little, humble funeral went by. "The boy is a beggar," he said to himself: "he shall not be about Alois."

The woman dared not say anything aloud, but when the grave was closed and the mourners had gone, she put a wreath of immortelles into Alois's hands and bade her go and lay it reverently on the dark, unmarked mound where the snow was displaced.

Nello and Patrasche went home with broken hearts. But even of that poor, melancholy, cheerless home they were denied the consolation. There was a month's rent overdue for their little home, and when Nello had paid the last sad service to the dead he had not a coin left. He went and begged grace of the owner of the hut, a cobbler who went every Sunday night to drink his pint of wine and smoke with Baas Cogez. The cobbler would grant no mercy. He was a harsh, miserly man, and loved money. He claimed in default of his rent every stick and stone, every pot and pan, in the hut, and bade Nello and Patrasche be out of it on the morrow.

Now, the cabin was lowly enough, and in some sense miserable enough, and yet their hearts clove to it with a great affection. They had been so happy there, and in the summer, with its clambering vine and its flowering beans, it was so pretty and bright in the midst of the sun-lighted fields! There life in it had been full of labor and privation, and yet they had been so well content, so gay of heart, running together to meet the old man's never-failing smile of welcome!

All night long the boy and the dog sat by the fireless hearth in the darkness, drawn close together for warmth

and sorrow. Their bodies were insensible to the cold, but their hearts seemed frozen in them.

When the morning broke over the white, chill earth it was the morning of Christmas Eve. With a shudder, Nello clasped close to him his only friend, while his tears fell hot and fast on the dog's frank forehead. "Let us go, Patrasche—dear, dear Patrasche," he murmured. "We will not wait to be kicked out: let us go."

Patrasche had no will but his, and they went sadly, side by side, out from the little place which was so dear to them both, and in which every humble, homely thing was to them precious and beloved. Patrasche drooped his head wearily as he passed by his own green cart: it was no longer his—it had to go with the rest to pay the rent, and his brass harness lay idle and glittering on the snow. The dog could have lain down beside it and died for very heartsickness as he went, but whilst the lad lived and needed him Patrasche would not yield and give way.

They took the old accustomed road into Antwerp. The day had yet scarce more than dawned, most of the shutters were still closed, but some of the villagers were about. They took no notice whilst the dog and the boy passed by them. At one door Nello paused and looked wistfully within: his grandfather had done many a kindly turn in neighbor's service to the people who dwelt there.

"Would you give Patrasche a crust?" he said, timidly. "He is old, and he has had nothing since last forenoon."

The woman shut the door hastily, murmuring some vague saying about wheat and rye being very dear that season. The boy and the dog went on again wearily: they asked no more. By slow and painful ways they reached Antwerp as the chimes tolled ten.

"If I had anything about me I could sell to get him

bread!" thought Nello, but he had nothing except the wisp of linen and serge that covered him, and his pair of wooden shoes.

Patrasche understood, and nestled his nose into the lad's hand, as though to pray him not to be disquieted for any woe or want of his.

The winner of the drawing-prize was to be proclaimed at noon, and to the public building where he had left his treasure Nello made his way. On the steps and in the entrance-hall there was a crowd of youths—some of his age, some older, all with parents or relatives or friends. His heart was sick with fear as he went among them, holding Patrasche close to him. The great bells of the city clashed out the hour of noon with brazen clamor. The doors of the inner hall were opened; the eager, panting throng rushed in: it was known that the selected picture would be raised above the rest upon a wooden dais.

A mist obscured Nello's sight, his head swam, his limbs almost failed him. When his vision cleared he saw the drawing raised on high: it was not his own! A slow, sonorous voice was proclaiming aloud that victory had been adjudged to Stephan Kiesslinger, born in the burgh of Antwerp, son of a wharfinger in that town.

When Nello recovered his consciousness he was lying on the stones without, and Patrasche was trying with every art he knew to call him back to life. In the distance a throng of the youths of Antwerp were shouting around their successful comrade, and escorting him with acclamations to his home upon the quay.

The boy staggered to his feet and drew the dog into his embrace. "It is all over, dear Patrasche," he murmured—"all over!"

He rallied himself as best he could, for he was weak

from fasting, and retraced his steps to the village. Patrasche paced by his side with his head drooping and his old limbs feeble from hunger and sorrow.

The snow was falling fast: a keen hurricane blew from the north: it was bitter as death on the plains. It took them long to traverse the familiar path, and the bells were sounding four of the clock as they approached the hamlet. Suddenly Patrasche paused, arrested by a scent in the snow, scratched, whined, and drew out with his teeth a small case of brown leather. He held it up to Nello in the darkness. Where they were there stood a little Calvary, and a lamp burned dully under the cross: the boy mechanically turned the case to the light: on it was the name of Baas Cogez, and within it were notes for two thousand francs.

The sight roused the lad a little from his stupor. He thrust it in his shirt, and stroked Patrasche and drew him onward. The dog looked up wistfully in his face.

Nello made straight for the millhouse, and went to the house door and struck on its panels. The miller's wife opened it weeping, with little Alois clinging close to her skirts. "Is it thee, thou poor lad?" she said kindly through her tears. "Get thee gone ere the Baas see thee. We are in sore trouble to-night. He is out seeking for a power of money that he has let fall riding homeward, and in this snow he never will find it; and God knows it will go nigh to ruin us. It is Heaven's own judgment for the things we have done to thee."

Nello put the note-case in her hand and called Patrasche within the house. "Patrasche found the money to-night," he said quickly. "Tell Baas Cogez so: I think he will not deny the dog shelter and food in his old age. Keep him from pursuing me, and I pray of you to be good to him."

Ere either woman or dog knew what he meant he had stooped and kissed Patrasche: then closed the door hurriedly, and disappeared in the gloom of the fast-falling night.

The woman and the child stood speechless with joy and fear: Patrasche vainly spent the fury of his anguish against the iron-bound oak of the barred house-door. They did not dare unbar the door and let him forth: they tried all they could to solace him. They brought him sweet cakes and juicy meats; they tempted him with the best they had; they tried to lure him to abide by the warmth of the hearth, but to no avail. Patrasche refused to be comforted or to stir from the barred portal.

It was six o'clock when from an opposite entrance the miller at last came, jaded and broken, into his wife's presence. "It is lost forever," he said with an ashen cheek and a quiver in his stern voice. "We have looked with lanterns everywhere: it is gone—the little maiden's portion and all!"

His wife put the money into his hand, and told him how it had come to her. The strong man sank trembling into a seat and covered his face, ashamed and almost afraid. "I have been cruel to the lad," he muttered at length: "I deserved not to have good at his hands."

Little Alois, taking courage, crept close to her father and nestled against him her fair curly head. "Nello may come here again, father?" she whispered. "He may come to-morrow as he used to do?"

The miller pressed her in his arms: his hard, sunburned face was very pale and his mouth trembled. "Surely, surely," he answered his child. "He shall bide here on Christmas Day, and any other day he will. God helping me, I will make amends to the boy—I will make amends."

Little Alois kissed him in gratitude and joy, then slid from his knees and ran to where the dog kept watch by the door. "And to-night I may feast Patrasche?" she cried in a child's thoughtless glee.

Her father bent his head gravely: "Ay, ay: let the dog have the best;" for the stern old man was moved and shaken to his heart's depths.

It was Christmas Eve, and the mill-house was filled with oak logs and squares of turf, with cream and honey, with meat and bread, and the rafters were hung with wreaths of evergreen, and the Calvary and the cuckoo clock looked out from a mass of holly. There were little paper lanterns, too, for Alois, and toys of various fashions and sweetmeats in bright-pictured papers. There were light and warmth and abundance everywhere, and the child would fain have made the dog a guest honored and feasted.

But Patrasche would neither lie in the warmth nor share in the cheer. Famished he was and very cold, but without Nello he would partake neither of comfort nor food. Against all temptation he was proof, and close against the door he leaned always, watching only for a means of escape.

"He wants the lad," said Baas Cogez. "Good dog! good dog! I will go over to the lad the first thing at day-dawn." For no one but Patrasche knew that Nello had left the hut, and no one but Patrasche divined that Nello had gone to face starvation and misery alone.

The mill kitchen was very warm: great logs crackled and flamed on the hearth; neighbors came in for a glass of wine and a slice of the fat goose baking for supper. Alois, gleeful and sure of her playmate back on the morrow, bounded and sang and tossed back her yellow hair. Baas Cogez, in the fullness of his heart, smiled on

her through moistened eyes, and spoke of the way in which he would befriend her favorite companion; the housemother sat with calm, contented face at the spinning wheel; the cuckoo in the clock chirped mirthful hours. Amidst it all Patrasche was bidden with a thousand words of welcome to tarry there a cherished guest. But neither peace nor plenty could allure him where Nello was not.

When the supper smoked on the board, and the voices were loudest and gladdest, and the Christ-child brought choicest gifts to Alois, Patrasche, watching always an occasion, glided out when the door was unlatched by a careless newcomer, and as swiftly as his weak and tired limbs would bear him sped over the snow in the bitter, black night. He had only one thought—to follow Nello. A human friend might have paused for the pleasant meal, the cheery warmth, the cosy slumber; but that was not the friendship of Patrasche. He remembered a bygone time, when an old man and a little child had found him sick unto death in the wayside ditch.

Snow had fallen freshly all the evening long; it was now nearly ten; the trail of the boy's footsteps was almost obliterated. It took Patrasche long to discover any scent. When at last he found it, it was lost again quickly, and again lost and again recovered, a hundred times or more.

The night was very wild. The lamps under the wayside crosses were blown out; the roads were sheets of ice; the impenetrable darkness hid every trace of habitations; there was no living thing abroad. All the cattle were housed, and in all the huts and homesteads men and women rejoiced and feasted. There was only Patrasche out in the cruel cold—old and famished and full of pain, but with the strength and the patience of a great love to sustain him in his search.

The trail of Nello's steps, faint and obscure as it was under the new snow, went straightly along the accustomed tracks into Antwerp. It was past midnight when Patrasche traced it over the boundaries of the town and into the narrow, tortuous, gloomy streets. It was all quite dark in the town, save where some light gleamed ruddily through the crevices of house-shutters or some group went homeward with lanterns chanting drinking songs. The streets were all white with ice: the high walls and roofs loomed black against them. There was scarce a sound save the riot of the winds down the passages as they tossed the creaking signs and shook the tall lamp-irons.

So many passers-by had trodden through and through the snow, so many diverse paths had crossed and recrossed each other, that the dog had a hard task to retain any hold on the track he followed. But he kept on his way, though the cold pierced him to the bone, and the jagged ice cut his feet, and the hunger in his body gnawed like a rat's teeth. He kept on his way, a poor gaunt, shivering thing, and by long patience traced the steps he loved into the very heart of the burgh and up to the steps of the great cathedral.

"He is gone to the things that he loved," thought Patrasche: he could not understand, but he was full of sorrow and of pity for the art-passion that to him was so incomprehensible and yet so sacred.

The portals of the cathedral were unclosed after the midnight mass. Some heedlessness in the custodians, too eager to go home and feast or sleep, or too drowsy to know whether they turned the keys aright, had left one of the doors unlocked. By that accident the footfalls Patrasche sought had passed through into the building, leaving the white marks of snow upon the dark stone floor. By that slender white thread, frozen as it fell, he

was guided through the intense silence, through the immensity of the vaulted space—guided straight to the gates of the chancel, and, stretched there upon the stones, he found Nello. He crept up and touched the face of the boy. "Didst thou dream that I should be faithless and forsake thee? I—a dog?" said that mute carcass.

The lad raised himself with a low cry and clasped him close. "Let us lie down and die together," he murmured. "Men have no need of us, and we are all alone."

In answer, Patrasche crept closer yet, and laid his head upon the young boy's breast. The great tears stood in his brown, sad eyes: not for himself—for himself he was happy.

They lay close together in the piercing cold. The blasts that blew over the Flemish dikes from the northern seas were like waves of ice, which froze every living thing they touched. The interior of the immense vault of stone in which they were was even more bitterly chill than the snow-covered plains without. Now and then a bat moved in the shadows—now and then a gleam of light came on the ranks of carven figures. Under the Rubens they lay together quite still, and soothed almost into a dreaming slumber by the numbing narcotic of the cold. Together they dreamed of the old glad days when they had chased each other through the flowering grasses of the summer meadows, or sat hidden in the tall bulrushes by the water's side, watching the boats go seaward in the sun.

Suddenly through the darkness a great white radiance streamed through the vastness of the aisles; the moon, that was at her height, had broken through the clouds, the snow had ceased to fall, the light reflected from the snow without was clear as the light of dawn. It fell through the arches full upon the two pictures above, from which the boy on his entrance had flung back the veil: the Elevation

The lad raised himself with a low cry and clasped him close

and the Descent of the Cross were for one instant
visible.

Nello rose to his feet and stretched his arms to them;
the tears of a passionate ecstasy glistened on the paleness
of his face. "I have seen them at last!" he cried aloud.
"O God, it is enough!"

His limbs failed under him, and he sank upon his
knees, still gazing upward at the majesty that he adored.
For a few brief moments the light illumined the divine
visions that had been denied to him so long—light clear
and sweet and strong as though it streamed from the
throne of Heaven. Then suddenly it passed away: once
more a great darkness covered the face of Christ.

The arms of the boy drew close again the body of the
dog. "We shall see His face—*there*," he murmured;
"and He will not part us, I think."

On the morrow, by the chancel of the cathedral, the
people of Antwerp found them both. They were both
dead: the cold of the night had frozen into stillness alike
the young life and the old. When the Christmas morning
broke and the priests came to the temple, they saw them
lying thus on the stones together. Above, the veils were
drawn back from the great visions of Rubens, and the
fresh rays of the sunrise touched the thorn-crowned head
of the Christ.

As the day grew on there came an old, hard-featured
man who wept as women weep. "I was cruel to the lad,"
he muttered, "and now I would have made amends—yea,
to the half of my substance—and he should have been to
me as a son."

There came also, as the day grew apace, a painter who
had fame in the world, and who was liberal of hand and of
spirit. "I seek one who should have had the prize
yesterday had worth won," he said to the people—"a boy

of rare promise and genius. An old wood-cutter on a fallen tree at eventide—that was all his theme. But there was greatness for the future in it. I would fain find him, and take him with me and teach him Art."

And a little child with curling fair hair, sobbing bitterly as she clung to her father's arm, cried aloud, "Oh, Nello, come! We have all ready for thee. The Christ-child's hands are full of gifts, and the old piper will play for us; and the mother says thou shalt stay by the hearth and burn nuts with us all the Noël week long—yes, even to the Feast of the Kings! And Patrasche will be so happy! Oh, Nello, wake and come!"

But the young pale face, turned upward to the light of the great Rubens with a smile upon its mouth, answered them all, "It is too late."

For the sweet, sonorous bells went ringing through the frost, and the sunlight shone upon the plains of snow, and the populace trooped gay and glad through the streets, but Nello and Patrasche no more asked charity at their hands. All they needed now Antwerp gave unbidden.

Death had been more pitiful to them than longer life would have been. It had taken the one in the loyalty of love, and the other in the innocence of faith, from a world which for love has no recompense and for faith no fulfillment.

All their lives they had been together, and in their deaths they were not divided: for when they were found the arms of the boy were folded too closely around the dog to be severed without violence, and the people of their little village, contrite and ashamed, implored a special grace for them, and, making them one grave, laid them to rest there side by side—forever!

THE NÜRNBERG STOVE

"I shall soon be home with dear Hirschvogel!"

THE NÜRNBERG STOVE

AUGUST lived in a little town called Hall. Hall is a favorite name for several towns in Austria and in Germany; but this one especial little Hall, in the Upper Innthal, is one of the most charming Old-World places that I know, and August for his part did not know any other. It has the green meadows and the great mountains all about it, and the gray-green glacier-fed water rushes by it.

It has paved streets and enchanting little shops that have all latticed panes and iron gratings to them; it has a very grand old Gothic church that has the noblest blendings of light and shadow, and marble tombs of dead knights, and a look of infinite strength and repose as a church should have.

Then there is the Muntze Tower, black and white, rising out of greenery and looking down on a long wooden bridge and the broad rapid river; and there is an old schloss which has been made into a guardhouse, with

battlements and frescoes and heraldic devices in gold and colors, and a man-at-arms carved in stone standing life-size in his niche and bearing his date 1530.

A little farther on, but close at hand, is a cloister with beautiful marble columns and tombs, and a colossal wood-carved Calvary, and beside that a small and very rich chapel: indeed, so full is the little town of the undisturbed past, that to walk in it is like opening a missal of the Middle Ages, all emblazoned and illuminated with saints and warriors, and it is so clean, and so still, and so noble, by reason of its monuments and its historic color, that I marvel much no one has ever cared to sing its praises. The old pious heroic life of an age at once more restful and more brave than ours still leaves its spirit there, and then there is the girdle of the mountains all around, and that alone means strength, peace, majesty.

In this little town a few years ago August Strehla lived with his people in the stone-paved irregular square where the grand church stands.

He was a small boy of nine years at that time—a chubby-faced little man with rosy cheeks, big hazel eyes, and clusters of curls the brown of ripe nuts. His mother was dead, his father was poor, and there were many mouths at home to feed. In this country the winters are long and very cold, the whole land lies wrapped in snow for many months, and this night that he was trotting home, with a jug of beer in his numb red hands, was terribly cold and dreary. The good burghers of Hall had shut their double shutters, and the few lamps there were flickered dully behind their quaint, old-fashioned iron casings. The mountains indeed were beautiful, all snow-white under the stars that are so big in frost. Hardly anyone was astir; a few good souls wending home from vespers, a tired post-boy who blew a shrill blast from his

tasseled horn, as he pulled up his sledge before a hostelry, and little August hugging his jug of beer to his ragged sheepskin coat, were all who were abroad, for the snow fell heavily and the good folks of Hall go early to their beds. He could not run, or he would have spilled the beer; he was half frozen and a little frightened, but he kept up his courage by saying over and over again to himself, "I shall soon be at home with dear Hirschvogel."

He went on through the streets, past the stone man-at-arms of the guardhouse, and so into the place where the great church was, and where near it stood his father Karl Strehla's house, with a sculptured Bethlehem over the doorway, and the Pilgrimage of the Three Kings painted on its wall. He had been sent on a long errand outside the gates in the afternoon, over the frozen fields and the broad white snow, and had been belated, and had thought he had heard the wolves behind him at every step, and had reached the town in a great state of terror, thankful with all his little panting heart to see the oil-lamp burning under the first house-shrine. But he had not forgotten to call for the beer, and he carried it carefully now, though his hands were so numb that he was afraid they would let the jug down every moment.

The snow outlined with white every gable and cornice of the beautiful old wooden houses; the moonlight shone on the gilded signs, the lambs, the grapes, the eagles, and all the quaint devices that hung before the doors; covered lamps burned before the Nativities and Crucifixions painted on the walls or let into the woodwork; here and there, where a shutter had not been closed, a ruddy firelight lit up a homely interior, with the noisy band of children clustering round the housemother and a big brown loaf, or some gossips spinning and listening to the cobbler's or the barber's story of a neighbor, while the oil

wicks glimmered, and the hearthlogs blazed, and the chestnuts sputtered in their iron roasting-pot.

Little August saw all these things as he saw everything with his two big bright eyes that had such curious lights and shadows in them; but he went heedfully on his way for the sake of the beer which a single slip of the foot would make him spill.

At his knock and call the solid oak door, four centuries old if one, flew open, and the boy darted in with his beer, and shouted, with all the force of mirthful lungs, "Oh, dear Hirschvogel, but for the thought of you I should have died!"

It was a large barren room into which he rushed with so much pleasure, and the bricks were bare and uneven. It had a walnut-wood press, handsome and very old, a broad deal table, and several wooden stools for all its furniture; but at the top of the chamber, sending out warmth and color together as the lamp shed its rays upon it, was a tower of porcelain, burnished with all the hues of a king's peacock and a queen's jewels, and surmounted with armed figures, and shields, and flowers of heraldry, and a great golden crown upon the highest summit of all.

It was a stove of 1532, and on it were the letters H. R. H., for it was in every portion the handiwork of the great potter of Nürnberg, Augustin Hirschvogel, who put his mark thus, as all the world knows.

The stove no doubt had stood in palaces and been made for princes, had warmed the crimson stockings of cardinals and the gold-broidered shoes of archduchesses, had glowed in presence-chambers and lent its carbon to help kindle sharp brains in anxious councils of state; no one knew what it had seen or done or been fashioned for: but it was a right royal thing. Yet perhaps it had never

been more useful than it was now in this poor desolate room, sending down heat and comfort into the troop of children tumbled together on a wolf-skin at its feet, who received frozen August among them with loud shouts of joy.

"Oh, dear Hirschvogel, I am so cold, so cold!" said August, kissing its gilded lion's claws. "Is father not in, Dorothea?"

"No, dear. He is late."

Dorothea was a girl of seventeen, dark-haired and serious, and with a sweet sad face, for she had had many cares laid on her shoulders, even whilst still a mere baby. She was the eldest of the Strehla family; and there were ten of them in all.

Next to her there came Jan and Karl and Otho, big lads, gaining a little for their own living; and then came August, who went up in the summer to the high alps with the farmers' cattle, but in winter could do nothing to fill his own little platter and pot; and then all the little ones, who could only open their mouths to be fed like young birds,—Albrecht and Hilda, and Waldo and Christof, and last of all little three-year-old Ermengilda, with eyes like forget-me-nots, whose birth had cost them the life of their mother.

They were of that mixed race, half Austrian, half Italian, so common in the Tyrol; some of the children were white and golden as lilies, others were brown and brilliant as fresh-fallen chestnuts.

The father was a good man, but weak and weary with so many to find for and so little to do it with. He worked at the salt furnaces, and by that gained a few florins; people said he would have worked better and kept his family more easily if he had not loved his pipe and a draft of ale too well; but this had only been said of him after his

wife's death, when trouble and perplexity had begun to dull a brain never too vigorous, and to enfeeble further a character already too yielding. As it was, the wolf often bayed at the door of the Strehla household, without a wolf from the mountains coming down.

Dorothea was one of those maidens who almost work miracles, so far can their industry and care and intelligence make a home sweet and wholesome and a single loaf seem to swell into twenty. The children were always clean and happy, and the table was seldom without its big pot of soup once a day. Still, very poor they were, and Dorothea's heart ached with shame, for she knew that their father's debts were many for flour and meat and clothing.

Of fuel to feed the big stove they had always enough without cost, for their mother's father was alive, and sold wood and fir cones and coke, and never grudged them to his grandchildren, though he grumbled at Strehla's improvidence and hapless, dreamy ways.

"Father says we are never to wait for him: we will have supper, now you have come home, dear," said Dorothea, who, however she might fret her soul in secret as she knitted their hose and mended their shirts, never let her anxieties cast a gloom on the children; only to August she did speak a little sometimes, because he was so thoughtful and so tender of her always, and knew as well as she did that there were troubles about money—though these troubles were vague to them both, and the debtors were patient and kindly, being neighbors all in the old twisting streets between the guardhouse and the river.

Supper was a huge bowl of soup, with big slices of brown bread swimming in it and some onions bobbing up and down: the bowl was soon emptied by ten wooden spoons, and then the three eldest boys slipped off to bed,

being tired with their rough bodily labor in the snow all day, and Dorothea drew her spinning wheel by the stove and set it whirring, and the little ones got August down upon the old worn wolf-skin and clamored to him for a picture or a story. For August was the artist of the family.

He had a piece of planed deal that his father had given him, and some sticks of charcoal, and he would draw a hundred things he had seen in the day, sweeping each out with his elbow when the children had seen enough of it and sketching another in its stead—faces and dogs' heads, and men in sledges, and old women in their furs, and pine trees, and cocks and hens, and all sorts of animals, and now and then—very reverently—a Madonna and Child. It was all very rough, for there was no one to teach him anything. But it was all lifelike, and kept the whole troop of children shrieking with laughter, or watching breathless, with wide-open, wondering, awed eyes.

They were all so happy: what did they care for the snow outside? Their little bodies were warm, and their hearts merry; even Dorothea, troubled about the bread for the morrow, laughed as she spun; and August, with all his soul in his work, and little rosy Ermengilda's cheek on his shoulder, glowing after his frozen afternoon, cried out loud, smiling, as he looked up at the stove that was shedding its heat down on them all—

"Oh, dear Hirschvogel! you are almost as great and good as the sun! No, you are greater and better, I think, because he goes away nobody knows where all these long, dark, cold hours, and does not care how people die for want of him; but you—you are always ready: just a little bit of wood to feed you, and you will make a summer for us all the winter through!"

The grand old stove seemed to smile through all its

iridescent surface at the praises of the child. No doubt the stove, though it had known three centuries and more, had known but very little gratitude.

It was one of those magnificent stoves in enameled faïence which so excited the jealousy of the other potters of Nürnberg that in a body they demanded of the magistracy that Augustin Hirschvogel should be forbidden to make any more of them—the magistracy, happily, proving of a broader mind, and having no sympathy with the wish of the artisans to cripple their greater fellow.

It was of great height and breadth, with all the majolica luster which Hirschvogel learned to give to his enamels when he was making love to the young Venetian girl whom he afterwards married. There was the statue of a king at each corner, modeled with as much force and splendor as his friend Albrecht Dürer could have given unto them on copperplate or canvas. The body of the stove itself was divided into panels, which had the Ages of Man painted on them in polychrome; the borders of the panels had roses and holly and laurel and other foliage, and German mottoes in black letter of odd Old-World moralizing, such as the old Teutons, and the Dutch after them, love to have on their chimneyplaces and their drinking cups, their dishes and flagons. The whole was burnished with gilding in many parts, and was radiant everywhere with that brilliant coloring of which the Hirschvogel family, painters on glass and great in chemistry as they were, were all masters.

The stove was a very grand thing, as I say: possibly Hirschvogel had made it for some mighty lord of the Tyrol at that time when he was an imperial guest at Innspruck and fashioned so many things for the Schloss Amras and beautiful Philippine Welser, the burgher's daughter, who gained an archduke's heart by her beauty

and the right to wear his honors by her wit. Nothing was known of the stove at this latter day in Hall. The grandfather Strehla, who had been a mastermason, had dug it up out of some ruins where he was building, and, finding it without a flaw, had taken it home, and only thought it worth finding because it was such a good one to burn. That was now sixty years past, and ever since then the stove had stood in the big desolate empty room, warming three generations of the Strehla family, and having seen nothing prettier perhaps in all its many years than the children tumbled now in a cluster like gathered flowers at its feet. For the Strehla children, born to nothing else, were all born with beauty: white or brown, they were equally lovely to look upon, and when they went into the church to mass, with their curling locks and their clasped hands, they stood under the grim statues like cherubs flown down off some fresco.

"Tell us a story, August," they cried, in chorus, when they had seen charcoal pictures till they were tired; and August did as he did every night, pretty nearly—looked up at the stove and told them what he imagined of the many adventures and joys and sorrows of the human being who figured on the panels from his cradle to his grave.

To the children the stove was a household god. In summer they laid a mat of fresh moss all round it, and dressed it up with green boughs and the numberless beautiful wild flowers of the Tyrol country. In winter all their joys centered in it, and scampering home from school over the ice and snow they were happy, knowing that they would soon be cracking nuts or roasting chestnuts in the broad ardent glow of its noble tower, which rose eight feet high above them with all its spires and pinnacles and crowns.

Once a traveling peddler had told them that the letters on it meant Augustin Hirschvogel, and that Hirschvogel had been a great German potter and painter, like his father before him, in the art-sanctified city of Nürnberg, and had made many such stoves, that were all miracles of beauty and of workmanship, putting all his heart and his soul and his faith into his labors, as the men of those earlier ages did, and thinking but little of gold or praise.

An old trader too, who sold curiosities not far from the church, had told August a little more about the brave family of Hirschvogel, whose houses can be seen in Nürnberg to this day; of old Veit, the first of them, who painted the Gothic windows of St. Sebald with the marriage of the Margravine; of his sons and of his grandsons, potters, painters, engravers all, and chief of them great Augustin, the Luca della Robbia of the North. And August's imagination, always quick, had made a living personage out of these few records, and saw Hirschvogel as though he were in the flesh walking up and down the Maximilian-Strass in his visit to Innspruck, and maturing beautiful things in his brain as he stood on the bridge and gazed on the emerald-green flood of the Inn.

So the stove had got to be called Hirschvogel in the family, as if it were a living creature, and little August was very proud because he had been named after that famous old dead German who had had the genius to make so glorious a thing. All the children loved the stove, but with August the love of it was a passion; and in his secret heart he used to say to himself, "When I am a man, I will make just such things too, and then I will set Hirschvogel in a beautiful room in a house that I will build myself in Innspruck just outside the gates, where the chestnuts are, by the river: that is what I will do when I am a man."

For August, a salt-baker's son, and a little cowkeeper
when he was anything, was a dreamer of dreams, and
when he was upon the high alps with his cattle, with the
stillness and the sky around him, was quite certain that he
would live for greater things than driving the herds up
when the spring-tide came among the blue sea of gen-
tians, or toiling down in the town with wood and with
timber as his father and grandfather did every day of their
lives. He was a strong and healthy little fellow, fed on the
free mountain air, and he was very happy, and loved his
family devotedly, and was as active as a squirrel and as
playful as a hare; but he kept his thoughts to himself, and
some of them went a very long way for a little boy who
was only one among many, and to whom nobody had ever
paid any attention except to teach him his letters and tell
him to fear God. August in winter was only a little
hungry schoolboy, trotting to be catechised by the priest,
or to bring the loaves from the bakehouse, or to carry his
father's boots to the cobbler; and in summer he was only
one of hundreds of cowboys, who drove the poor,
half-blind, blinking, stumbling cattle, ringing their throat-
bells, out into the sweet intoxication of the sudden
sunlight, and lived up with them in the heights among the
Alpine roses, with only the clouds and the snow summits
near. But he was always thinking, thinking, thinking, for
all that; and under his little sheepskin winter coat and his
rough hempen summer shirt, his heart had as much
courage in it as Hofer's ever had—great Hofer, who is a
household word in all the Innthal, and whom August
always reverently remembered when he went to the city of
Innspruck and ran out by the foaming watermill and
under the wooded height of Berg Isel.

August lay now in the warmth of the stove and told the
children stories, his own little brown face growing red

with excitement as his imagination glowed to fever heat. That human being on the panels, who was drawn there as a baby in a cradle, as a boy playing among flowers, as a lover sighing under a casement, as a soldier in the midst of strife, as a father with children round him, as a weary, old, blind man on crutches, and, lastly, as a ransomed soul raised up by angels, had always had the most intense interest for August, and he had made, not one history for him, but a thousand; he seldom told them the same tale twice. He had never seen a storybook in his life; his primer and his massbook were all the volumes he had. But nature had given him Fancy, and she is a good fairy that makes up for the want of very many things! Only, alas! her wings are so very soon broken, poor thing, and then she is of no use at all.

"It is time for you all to go to bed, children," said Dorothea, looking up from her spinning. "Father is very late tonight. You must not sit up for him."

"Oh, five minutes more, dear Dorothea!" they pleaded, and little rosy and golden Ermengilda climbed up into her lap. "Hirschvogel is so warm, the beds are never so warm as he. Cannot you tell us another tale, August?"

"No," cried August, whose face had lost its light, now that his story had come to an end, and who sat serious, with his hands clasped on his knees, gazing onto the luminous arabesques of the stove.

"It is only a week to Christmas," he said suddenly.

"Grandmother's big cakes!" chuckled little Christof, who was five years old, and thought Christmas meant a big cake and nothing else.

"What will Santa Claus find for 'Gilda if she be good?" murmured Dorothea over the child's sunny head; for, however hard poverty might pinch, it could never pinch so tightly that Dorothea would not find some wooden toy

and some rosy apples to put in her little sister's socks.

"Father Max has promised me a big goose, because I saved the calf's life in June," said August. It was the twentieth time he had told them so that month, he was so proud of it.

"And Aunt Maïla will be sure to send us wine and honey and a barrel of flour; she always does," said Albrecht. Their aunt Maïla had a châlet and a little farm over on the green slopes towards Dorp Ampas.

"I shall go up into the woods and get Hirschvogel's crown," said August; they always crowned Hirschvogel for Christmas with pine boughs and ivy and mountain berries. The heat soon withered the crown; but it was part of the religion of the day to them, as much so as it was to cross themselves in church and raise their voices in the "O Salutaris Hostia."

And they fell chatting of all they would do on the Christ-night, and one little voice piped loud against another's, and they were as happy as though their stockings would be full of golden purses and jeweled toys, and the big goose in the soup pot seemed to them such a meal as kings would envy.

In the midst of their chatter and laughter a blast of frozen air and a spray of driven snow struck like ice through the room, and reached them even in the warmth of the old wolf skins and the great stove. It was the door which had opened and let in the cold; it was their father who had come home.

The younger children ran joyous to meet him. Dorothea pushed the one wooden armchair of the room to the stove, and August flew to set the jug of beer on a little round table, and fill a long clay pipe; for their father was good to them all, and seldom raised his voice in anger, and they had been trained by the mother they had loved to

dutifulness and obedience and a watchful affection.

Tonight Karl Strehla responded very wearily to the young ones' welcome, and came to the wooden chair with a tired step and sat down heavily, not noticing either pipe or beer.

"Are you not well, dear father?" his daughter asked.

"I am well enough," he answered dully, and sat there with his head bent, letting the lighted pipe grow cold.

He was a fair, tall man, gray before his time, and bowed with labor.

"Take the children to bed," he said suddenly, at last, and Dorothea obeyed. August stayed behind, curled before the stove; at nine years old, and when one earns money in the summer from the farmers, one is not altogether a child any more, at least in one's own estimation.

August did not heed his father's silence: he was used to it. Karl Strehla was a man of few words, and, being of weakly health, was usually too tired at the end of the day to do more than drink his beer and sleep. August lay on the wolf skin, dreamy and comfortable, looking up through his drooping eyelids at the golden coronets on the crest of the great stove, and wondering for the millionth time whom it had been made for, and what grand places and scenes it had known.

Dorothea came down from putting the little ones in their beds; the cuckoo clock in the corner struck eight; she looked to her father and the untouched pipe, then sat down to her spinning, saying nothing. She thought he had been drinking in some tavern; it had been often so with him of late.

There was a long silence; the cuckoo called the quarter twice; August dropped asleep, his curls falling over his face; Dorothea's wheel hummed like a cat.

Suddenly Karl Strehla struck his hand on the table, sending the pipe on the ground.

"I have sold Hirschvogel," he said, and his voice was husky and ashamed in his throat. The spinning wheel stopped. August sprang erect out of his sleep.

"Sold Hirschvogel!" If their father had dashed the holy crucifix on the floor at their feet and spat on it, they could not have shuddered under the horror of a greater blasphemy.

"I have sold Hirschvogel!" said Karl Strehla, in the same husky, dogged voice. "I have sold it to a traveling trader in such things for two hundred florins. What would you?—I owe double that. He saw it this morning when you were all out. He will pack it and take it to Munich tomorrow."

Dorothea gave a low shrill cry:

"Oh, father!—the children—in midwinter!"

She turned white as the snow without; her words died away in her throat.

August stood, half blind with sleep, staring with dazed eyes as his cattle stared at the sun when they came out from their winter's prison.

"It is not true! It is not true!" he muttered. "You are jesting, father?"

Strehla broke into a dreary laugh.

"It is true. Would you like to know what is true, too?—that the bread you eat, and the meat you put in this pot, and the roof you have over your heads, are none of them paid for, have been none of them paid for for months and months: if it had not been for your grandfather I should have been in prison all summer and autumn, and he is out of patience and will do no more now. There is no work to be had; the masters go to younger men: they say I work ill; it may be so. Who can

keep his head above water with ten hungry children dragging him down? When your mother lived, it was different. Boy, you stare at me as if I were a mad dog! You have made a god of yon china thing. Well—it goes: goes tomorrow. Two hundred florins, that is something. It will keep me out of prison for a little, and with the spring things may turn——"

August stood like a creature paralyzed. His eyes were wide open, fastened on his father's with terror and incredulous horror; his face had grown as white as his sister's; his chest heaved with tearless sobs.

"It is not true! It is not true!" he echoed stupidly. It seemed to him that the very skies must fall, and the earth perish, if they could take away Hirschvogel. They might as soon talk of tearing down God's sun out of the heavens.

"You will find it true," said his father doggedly, and angered because he was in his own soul bitterly ashamed to have bartered away the heirloom and treasure of his race and the comfort and health-giver of his young children. "You will find it true. The dealer has paid me half the money tonight, and will pay me the other half tomorrow when he packs it up and takes it away to Munich. No doubt it is worth a great deal more—at least I suppose so, as he gives that—but beggars cannot be choosers. The little black stove in the kitchen will warm you all just as well. Who would keep a gilded, painted thing in a poor house like this, when one can make two hundred florins by it? Dorothea, you never sobbed more when your mother died. What is it, when all is said?—a bit of hardware much too grand looking for such a room as this. If all the Strehlas had not been born fools it would have been sold a century ago, when it was dug up out of the ground. 'It is a stove for a museum,' the trader

said when he saw it. 'To a museum let it go.' "

August gave a shrill shriek like a hare's when it is caught for its death, and threw himself on his knees at his father's feet.

"Oh, father, father!" he cried, convulsively, his hands closing on Strehla's knees, and his uplifted face blanched and distorted with terror. "Oh, father, dear father, you cannot mean what you say? Send *it* away—our life, our sun, our joy, our comfort? We shall all die in the dark and the cold. Sell *me* rather. Sell me to any trade or any pain you like; I will not mind. But Hirschvogel!—it is like selling the very cross off the altar! You must be in jest. You could not do such a thing—you could not!— you have always been gentle and good, and who have sat in the warmth here year after year with our mother. It is not a piece of hardware, as you say; it is a living thing, for a great man's thoughts and fancies have put life into it, and it loves us though we are only poor little children, and we love it with all our hearts and souls, and up in heaven I am sure the dead Hirschvogel knows! Oh, listen; I will go and try and get work tomorrow! I will ask them to let me cut ice or make the paths through the snow. There must be something I could do, and I will beg the people we owe money to to wait; they are all neighbors, they will be patient. But sell Hirschvogel!—oh, never! never! never! Give the florins back to the vile man. Tell him it would be like selling the shroud out of mother's coffin, or the golden curls off Ermengilda's head! Oh, father, dear father! do hear me, for pity's sake!"

Strehla was moved by the boy's anguish. He loved his children, though he was often weary of them, and their pain was pain to him. But besides emotion, and stronger than emotion, was the anger that August roused in him: he hated and despised himself for the barter of the

heirloom of his race, and every word of the child stung him with a stinging sense of shame.

And he spoke in his wrath rather than in his sorrow.

"You are a little fool," he said harshly, as they had never heard him speak. "You rave like a play-actor. Get up and go to bed. The stove is sold. There is no more to be said. Children like you have nothing to do with such matters. The stove is sold, and goes to Munich tomorrow. What is it to you? Be thankful I can get bread for you. Get on your legs, I say, and go to bed."

Strehla took up the jug of ale as he paused, and drained it slowly as a man who had no cares.

August sprang to his feet and threw his hair back off his face; the blood rushed into his cheeks, making them scarlet; his great soft eyes flamed alight with furious passion.

"You *dare* not!" he cried aloud, "you dare not sell it, I say; It is not yours alone; it is ours——"

Strehla flung the emptied jug on the bricks with a force that shivered it to atoms, and, rising to his feet, struck his son a blow that felled him to the floor. It was the first time in all his life that he had ever raised his hand against any one of his children.

Then he took the oil lamp that stood at his elbow and stumbled off to his own chamber with a cloud before his eyes.

"What has happened?" said August, a little while later, as he opened his eyes and saw Dorothea weeping above him on the wolf skin before the stove. He had been struck backward, his head had fallen on the hard bricks where the wolf skin did not reach. He sat up a moment, with his face bent upon his hands.

"I remember now," he said, very low, under his breath.

Dorothea showered kisses on him, while her tears fell like rain.

"But, oh, dear, how could you speak so to father?" she murmured. "It was very wrong."

"No, I was right," said August, and his little mouth, that hitherto had only curled in laughter, curved downward with a fixed and bitter seriousness. "How dare he? How dare he?" he muttered, with his head sunk in his hands. "It is not his alone. It belongs to us all. It is as much yours and mine as it is his."

Dorothea could only sob in answer. She was too frightened to speak. The authority of their parents in the house had never in her remembrance been questioned.

"Are you hurt by the fall, dear August?" she murmured, at length, for he looked to her so pale and strange.

"Yes—no. I do not know. What does it matter?"

He sat up upon the wolf skin with passionate pain upon his face; all his soul was in rebellion, and he was only a child and was powerless.

"It is a sin; it is a theft; it is an infamy," he said slowly, his eyes fastened on the gilded feet of Hirschvogel.

"Oh, August, do not say such things of father!" sobbed his sister. "Whatever he does, *we* ought to think it right."

August laughed aloud.

"Is it right that he should spend his money in drink?— that he should let orders lie unexecuted?—that he should do his work so ill that no one cares to employ him?—that he should live on Grandfather's charity, and then dare sell a thing that is ours every whit as much as it is his? To sell

Hirschvogel! Oh, dear God! I would sooner sell my soul!"

"August!" cried Dorothea, with piteous entreaty. He terrified her, she could not recognize her little, gay, gentle brother in those fierce and blasphemous words.

August laughed aloud again; then all at once his laughter broke down into bitterest weeping. He threw himself forward on the stove, covering it with kisses, and sobbing as though his heart would burst from his bosom.

What could he do? Nothing, nothing, nothing!

"August, dear August," whispred Dorothea, piteously, and trembling all over—for she was a very gentle girl, and fierce feeling terrified her—"August, do not lie there. Come to bed: it is quite late. In the morning you will be calmer. It is horrible indeed, and we shall die of cold, at least the little ones; but if it be father's will——"

"Let me alone," said August, through his teeth, striving to still the storm of sobs that shook him from head to foot. "Let me alone. In the morning!—how can you speak of the morning?"

"Come to bed, dear," sighed his sister. "Oh, August, do not lie and look like that! you frighten me. Do come to bed."

"I shall stay here."

"Here! all night!"

"They might take it in the night. Besides, to leave it *now!*"

"But it is cold! the fire is out."

"It will never be warm any more, nor shall we."

All his childhood had gone out of him, all his gleeful, careless, sunny temper had gone with it; he spoke sullenly and wearily, choking down the great sobs in his chest. To him it was as if the end of the world had come.

His sister lingered by him while striving to persuade

him to his place in the little crowded bedchamber with Albrecht and Waldo and Christof. But it was in vain. "I shall stay here," was all he answered her. And he stayed—all the night long.

The lamps went out; the rats came and ran across the floor; as the hours crept on through midnight and past, the cold intensified and the air of the room grew like ice. August did not move; he lay with his face downward on the golden and rainbow-hued pedestal of the household treasure, which henceforth was to be cold for evermore, an exiled thing in a foreign city in a far-off land.

While yet it was dark his three elder brothers came down the stairs and let themselves out, each bearing his lantern and going to his work in stoneyard and timber yard and at the salt works. They did not notice him; they did not know what had happened.

A little later his sister came down with a light in her hand to make ready the house ere morning should break.

She stole up to him and laid her hand on his shoulder timidly.

"Dear August, you must be frozen. August, do look up! do speak!"

August raised his eyes with a wild, feverish, sullen look in them that she had never seen there. His face was ashen white: his lips were like fire. He had not slept all night; but his passionate sobs had given way to delirious waking dreams and numb senseless trances, which had alternated one on another all through the freezing, lonely, horrible hours.

"It will never be warm again," he muttered, "never again!"

Dorothea clasped him with trembling hands.

"August! do you not know me?" she cried, in an agony.

"I am Dorothea. Wake up, dear—wake up! It is morning, only so dark!"

August shuddered all over.

"The morning!" he echoed.

He slowly rose up onto his feet.

"I will go to Grandfather," he said, very low. "He is always good: perhaps he could save it."

Loud blows with the heavy iron knocker of the house door drowned his words. A strange voice called aloud through the keyhole—

"Let me in! Quick!—there is no time to lose! More snow like this, and the roads will all be blocked. Let me in! Do you hear? I am come to take the great stove."

August sprang erect, his fists doubled, his eyes blazing.

"You shall never touch it!" he screamed, "you shall never touch it!"

"Who shall prevent us?" laughed a big man, who was a Bavarian, amused at the fierce little figure fronting him.

"I!" said August. "You shall never have it! You shall kill me first!"

"Strehla," said the big man, as August's father entered the room, "you have got a little mad dog here: muzzle him."

One way and another they did muzzle him. He fought like a little demon, and hit out right and left, and one of his blows gave the Bavarian a black eye. But he was soon mastered by four grown men, and his father flung him with no light hand out from the door of the back entrance, and the buyers of the stately and beautiful stove set to work to pack it heedfully and carry it away.

When Dorothea stole out to look for August, he was

nowhere in sight. She went back to little 'Gilda, who was ailing, and sobbed over the child, while the others stood looking on, dimly understanding that with Hirschvogel was going all the warmth of their bodies, all the light of their hearth.

Even their father now was sorry and ashamed; but two hundred florins seemed a big sum to him, and, after all, he thought the children could warm themselves quite as well at the black iron stove in the kitchen. Besides, whether he regretted it now or not, the work of the Nürnberg potter was sold irrevocably, and he had to stand still and see the men from Munich wrap it in manifold wrappings and bear it out into the snowy air to where an ox-cart stood in waiting for it.

In another moment Hirschvogel was gone—gone forever and aye.

August had stood still for a time, leaning, sick and faint from the violence that had been used to him, against the back wall of the house. The wall looked on a court where a well was, and the backs of other houses, and beyond them the spire of the Muntze Tower and the peaks of the mountains.

Into the court an old neighbor hobbled for water, and, seeing the boy, said to him—

"Child, is it true your father is selling the big painted stove?"

August nodded, then burst into a passion of tears.

"Well, for sure he is a fool," said the neighbor. "Heaven forgive me for calling him so before his own child! But the stove was worth a mint of money. I do remember in my young days, in old Anton's time (that was your great-grandfather, my lad), a stranger from Vienna saw it, and said it was worth its weight in gold."

August's sobs went on their broken, impetuous course. "I loved it! I loved it!" he moaned. "I do not care what its value was. I loved it. *I loved it!'*

"You little simpleton!" said the old man kindly. "But you are wiser than your father, when all's said. If sell it he must, he should have taken it to good Herr Steiner over at Sprüz, who would have given him honest value. But no doubt they took him over his beer—ay, ay! but if I were you I would do better than cry. I would go after it."

August raised his head, the tears raining down his cheeks.

"Go after it when you are bigger," said the neighbor, with a good-natured wish to cheer him up a little. "The world is a small thing after all: I was a traveling clockmaker once upon a time, and I know that your stove will be safe enough whoever gets it; anything that can be sold for a round sum is always wrapped up in cotton wool by everybody. Ay, ay, don't cry so much; you will see your stove again some day."

Then the old man hobbled away to draw his brazen pail full of water at the well.

August remained leaning against the wall; his head was buzzing and his heart fluttering with the new idea which had presented itself to his mind. "Go after it," the old man had said. He thought, "Why not go with it?" He loved it better than anyone, even better than Dorothea; and he shrank from the thought of meeting his father again, his father who had sold Hirschvogel.

He was by this time in that state of exaltation in which the impossible looks quite natural and commonplace. His tears were still wet on his pale cheeks, but they had ceased to fall. He ran out of the courtyard by a little gate, and across to the huge Gothic porch of the church.

From there he could watch unseen his father's house door, at which were always hanging some blue-and-gray pitchers, such as are common and so picturesque in Austria, for a part of the house was let to a man who dealt in pottery.

He hid himself in the grand portico, which he had so often passed through to go to mass or complin within, and presently his heart gave a great leap, for he saw the straw-enwrapped stove brought out and laid with infinite care on the bullock-dray. Two of the Bavarian men mounted beside it, and the sleigh-wagon slowly crept over the snow of the place—snow crisp and hard as stone. The noble old minster looked its grandest and most solemn, with its dark-gray stone and its vast archways, and its porch that was itself as big as many a church, and its strange gargoyles and lamp-irons black against the snow on its roof and on the pavement; but for once August had no eyes for it: he only watched for his old friend. Then he, a little unnoticeable figure enough, like a score of other boys in Hall, crept, unseen by any of his brothers or sisters, out of the porch and over the shelving uneven square, and followed in the wake of the dray.

Its course lay towards the station of the railway, which is close to the salt-works, whose smoke at times sullies this part of clean little Hall, though it does not do very much damage. From Hall the iron road runs northward through glorious country to Salzburg, Vienna, Prague, Buda, and southward over the Brenner into Italy. Was Hirschvogel going north or south? This at least he would soon know.

August had often hung about the little station, watching the trains come and go and dive into the heart of the hills and vanish. No one said anything to him for idling about; people are kindhearted and easy of temper in this

pleasant land, and children and dogs are both happy there. He heard the Bavarians arguing and vociferating a great deal, and learned that they meant to go too and wanted to go with the great stove itself. But this they could not do, for neither could the stove go by passenger train nor they themselves go in a goods train. So at length they insured their precious burden for a large sum, and consented to send it by a luggage train which was to pass through Hall in half an hour. The swift trains seldom deign to notice the existence of Hall at all.

August heard, and a desperate resolve made itself up in his little mind. Where Hirschvogel went would he go. He gave one terrible thought to Dorothea—poor, gentle Dorothea—sitting in the cold at home, then set to work to execute his project. How he managed it he never knew very clearly himself, but certain it is that when the goods train from the north, that had come all the way from Linz on the Danube, moved out of Hall, August was hidden behind the stove in the great covered truck, and wedged, unseen and undreamt of by any human creature, amidst the cases of wood carving, of clocks and clockwork, of Vienna toys, of Turkish carpets, of Russian skins, of Hungarian wines, which shared the same abode as did his swathed and bound Hirschvogel. No doubt he was very naughty, but it never occurred to him that he was so: his whole mind and soul were absorbed in the one entrancing idea, to follow his beloved friend and fire-king.

It was very dark in the closed truck, which had only a little window above the door; and it was crowded, and had a strong smell in it from the Russian hides and the hams that were in it. But August was not frightened; he was close to Hirschvogel, and presently he meant to be closer still; for he meant to do nothing less than get inside Hirschvogel itself. Being a shrewd little boy, and having

had by great luck two silver groschen in his breeches-pocket, which he had earned the day before by chopping wood, he had bought some bread and sausage at the station of a woman there who knew him, and who thought he was going out to his uncle Joachim's châlet above Jenbach. This he had with him, and this he ate in the darkness and the lumbering, pounding, thundering noise which made him giddy, as never had he been in a train of any kind before. Still he ate, having had no breakfast, and being a child, and half a German, and not knowing at all how or when he ever would eat again.

When he had eaten, not as much as he wanted, but as much as he thought was prudent (for who could say when he would be able to buy anything more?), he set to work like a little mouse to make a hole in the withes of straw and hay which enveloped the stove. If it had been put in a packing case he would have been defeated at the onset. As it was, he gnawed, and nibbled, and pulled, and pushed, just as a mouse would have done, making his hole where he guessed that the opening of the stove was—the opening through which he had so often thrust the big oak logs to feed it. No one disturbed him; the heavy train went lumbering on and on, and he saw nothing at all of the beautiful mountains, and shining waters, and great forests through which he was being carried. He was hard at work getting through the straw and hay and twisted ropes; and get through them at last he did, and found the door of the stove, which he knew so well, and which was quite large enough for a child of his age to slip through, and it was this which he had counted upon doing.

Slip through he did, as he had often done at home for fun, and curled himself up to see if he could remain there during many hours. He found that he could; air came in through the brass fretwork of the stove; and with admi-

rable caution in such a little fellow he leaned out, drew the hay and straw together, and rearranged the ropes, so that no one could ever have dreamed a little mouse had been at them. Then he curled himself up again, this time more like a dormouse than anything else; and, being safe inside his dear Hirschvogel and intensely cold, he went fast asleep as if he were in his own bed at home with Albrecht and Christof on either side of him. The train lumbered on, stopping often and long, as the habit of goods trains is, sweeping the snow away with its cow-switcher, and rumbling through the deep heart of the mountains, with its lamps aglow like the eyes of a dog in a night of frost.

The train rolled on in its heavy, slow fashion, and the child slept soundly for a long while. When he did awake, it was quite dark outside in the land; he could not see, and of course he was in absolute darkness; and for a while he was sorely frightened, and trembled terribly, and sobbed in a quiet, heartbroken fashion, thinking of them all at home. Poor Dorothea! How anxious she would be! How she would run over the town and walk up to Grandfather's at Dorf Ampas, and perhaps even send over to Jenbach, thinking he had taken refuge with Uncle Joachim! His conscience smote him for the sorrow he must be even then causing to his gentle sister; but it never occurred to him to try and go back. If he once were to lose sight of Hirschvogel how could he ever hope to find it again? How could he ever know whither it had gone—north, south, east, or west? The old neighbor had said that the world was small; but August knew at least that it must have a great many places in it: that he had seen himself on the maps on his schoolhouse walls. Almost any other little boy would, I think, have been frightened out of his wits at the position in which he found himself;

but August was brave, and he had a firm belief that God and Hirschvogel would take care of him. The master potter of Nürnberg was always present to his mind, a kindly, benign, and gracious spirit, dwelling manifestly in that porcelain tower whereof he had been the maker.

A droll fancy, you say? But every child with a soul in him has quite as quaint fancies as this one of August's.

So he got over his terror and his sobbing both, though he was so utterly in the dark. He did not feel cramped at all, because the stove was so large, and air he had in plenty, as it came through the fretwork running round the top. He was hungry again, and again nibbled with prudence at his loaf and his sausage. He could not at all tell the hour. Every time the train stopped and he heard the banging, stamping, shouting, and jangling of chains that went on, his heart seemed to jump up into his mouth. If they should find him out! Sometimes porters came and took away this case and the other, a sack here, a bale there, now a big bag, now a dead chamois. Every time the men trampled near him, and swore at each other, and banged this and that to and fro, he was so frightened that his very breath seemed to stop. When they came to lift the stove out, would they find him? And if they did find him, would they kill him? That was what he kept thinking of all the way, all through the dark hours, which seemed without end.

Goods trains are usually very slow because of the stops, and are many days doing what a quick train does in a few hours. This one was quicker than most, because it was bearing goods to the King of Bavaria; still it took all the short winter's day and the long winter's night and half another day to go over ground that the mail trains cover in a forenoon. It passed great armored Kuffstein stand-ing across the beautiful and solemn gorge, denying the

right of way to all the foes of Austria. It passed twelve hours later, after lying by in out-of-the-way stations, pretty Rosenheim, that marks the border of Bavaria. And here the Nürnberg stove, with August inside it, was lifted out heedfully and set under a covered way. When it was lifted out, the boy had hard work to keep in his screams; he was tossed to and fro as the men lifted the huge thing, and the earthenware walls of his beloved fire-king were not cushions of down. However, though they swore and grumbled at the weight of it, they never suspected that a living child was inside it, and they carried it out onto the platform and set it down under the roof of the goods shed. There it passed the rest of the night and all the next morning, and August was all the while within.

The winds of early winter sweep bitterly over Rosenheim, and all the vast Bavarian plain was one white sheet of snow. If there had not been whole armies of men at work always clearing the iron rails of the snow, no trains could ever have run at all. Happily for August, the thick wrappings in which the stove was enveloped and the stoutness of its own make screened him from the cold, of which, else, he must have died—frozen. He had still some of his loaf, and a little—a very little—of his sausage. What he did begin to suffer from was thirst; and this frightened him almost more than anything else, for Dorothea had read aloud to them one night a story of the tortures some wrecked men had endured because they could not find any water but the salt sea. It was many hours since he had last taken a drink from the wooden spout of their old pump, which brought them the sparkling, ice-cold water of the hills.

But, fortunately for him, the stove, having been marked and registered as "fragile and valuable," was not

treated quite like a mere bale of goods, and the Rosenheim station master, who knew its consignees, resolved to
send it on by a passenger train that would leave there at
daybreak. And when this train went out, in it, among
piles of luggage belonging to other travelers, to Vienna,
Prague, Budapest, Salzburg, was August, still undiscov-
ered, still doubled up like a mole in the winter under the
grass. Those words, "fragile and valuable," had made
the men lift Hirschvogel gently and with care. He had
begun to get used to his prison, and a little used to the
incessant pounding and jumbling and rattling and shaking with which modern travel is always accompanied,
though modern invention does deem itself so mightily
clever. All in the dark he was, and he was terribly
thirsty; but he kept feeling the earthenware sides of the
Nürnberg giant and saying, softly, "Take care of me; oh,
take care of me, dear Hirschvogel!"

He did not say, "Take me back;" for, now that he was
fairly out in the world, he wished to see a little of it. He
began to think that they must have been all over the world
in all this time that the rolling and roaring and hissing and
jangling had been about his ears shut up in the dark. He
began to remember the tales that had been told in Yule
round the fire at his grandfather's good house at Dorf, of
gnomes and elves and subterranean terrors, and the Erl
King riding on the black horse of night, and—and—and
he began to sob and to tremble again, and this time did
scream outright. But the steam was screaming itself so
loudly that no one, had there been anyone nigh, would
have heard him; and in another minute or so the train
stopped with a jar and a jerk, and he in his cage could
hear men crying aloud, "München! München!"

Then he knew enough of geography to know that he
was in the heart of Bavaria. He had had an uncle killed

in the Bayerischenwald by the Bavarian forest guards, when in the excitement of hunting a black bear he had overpassed the limits of the Tyrol frontier.

That fate of his kinsman, a gallant young chamois hunter who had taught him to handle a trigger and load a muzzle, made the very name of Bavaria a terror to August.

"It is Bavaria! It is Bavaria!" he sobbed to the stove; but the stove said nothing to him; it had no fire in it. A stove can no more speak without fire than a man can see without light. Give it fire, and it will sing to you, tell tales to you, offer you in return all the sympathy you ask.

"It is Bavaria!" sobbed August; for it is always a name of dread augury to the Tyroleans, by reason of those bitter struggles and midnight shots and untimely deaths which come from those meetings of jäger and hunter in the Bayerischenwald. But the train stopped: Munich was reached, and August, hot and cold by turns, and shaking like a little aspen leaf, felt himself once more carried out on the shoulders of men, rolled along on a truck, and finally set down, where he knew not, only he knew he was thirsty—so thirsty! If only he could have reached his hand out and scooped up a little snow!

He thought he had been moved on this truck many miles, but in truth the stove had been only taken from the railway station to a shop in the Marienplatz. Fortunately, the stove was always set upright on its four gilded feet, a junction to that effect having been affixed to its written label, and on its gilded feet it stood now in the small dark curiosity shop of one Hans Rhilfer.

"I shall not unpack it till Anton comes," he heard a man's voice say; and then he heard a key grate in a lock, and by the unbroken stillness that ensued he concluded he was alone, and ventured to peep through the straw and

hay. What he saw was a small square room filled with pots and pans, pictures, carvings, old blue jugs, old steel armor, shields, daggers, Chinese idols, Vienna china, Turkish rugs, and all the art lumber and fabricated rubbish of a *bric-à-brac* dealer's. It seemed a wonderful place to him; but, oh! was there one drop of water in it all? That was his single thought; for his tongue was parching, and his throat felt on fire, and his chest began to be dry and choked as with dust. There was not a drop of water, but there was a lattice window grated, and beyond the window was a wide stone ledge covered with snow. August cast one look at the locked door, darted out of his hiding place, ran and opened the window, crammed the snow into his mouth again and again, and then flew back into the stove, drew the hay and straw over the place he entered by, tied the cords, and shut the brass door down on himself. He had brought some big icicles in with him, and by them his thirst was finally, if only temporarily, quenched. Then he sat still in the bottom of the stove, listening intently, wide awake, and once more recovering his natural boldness.

The thought of Dorothea kept nipping his heart and his conscience with a hard squeeze now and then, but he thought to himself, "If I can take her back Hirschvogel, then how pleased she will be, and how little 'Gilda will clap her hands!" He was not at all selfish in his love for Hirschvogel: he wanted it for them all at home quite as much as for himself. There was at the bottom of his mind a kind of ache of shame that his father—his own father—should have stripped their hearth and sold their honor thus.

A robin had been perched upon a stone griffin sculptured on a house-eave near. August had felt for the crumbs of his loaf in his pocket, and had thrown them to

the little bird sitting so easily on the frozen snow.

In the darkness where he was he now heard a little song, made faint by the stove wall and the window-glass that was between him and it, but still distinct and exquisitely sweet. It was the robin, singing after feeding on the crumbs. August, as he heard, burst into tears. He thought of Dorothea, who every morning threw out some grain or some bread on the snow before the church. "What use is it going *there*," she said, "if we forget the sweetest creatures God has made?" Poor Dorothea! Poor, good, tender, much-burdened little soul! He thought of her till his tears ran like rain.

Yet it never once occurred to him to dream of going home. Hirschvogel was here.

Presently the key turned in the lock of the door, he heard heavy footsteps and the voice of the man who had said to his father, "You have a little mad dog; muzzle him!" The voice said, "Ay, ay, you have called me a fool many times. Now you shall see what I have gotten for two hundred dirty florins. *Potztausend!* never did *you* do such a stroke of work."

Then the other voice grumbled and swore, and the steps of the two men approached more closely, and the heart of the child went pit-a-pat, pit-a-pat, as a mouse's does when it is on the top of a cheese and hears a housemaid's broom sweeping near. They began to strip the stove of its wrappings: that he could tell by the noise they made with the hay and the straw. Soon they had stripped it wholly: that, too, he knew by the oaths and exclamations of wonder and surprise and rapture which broke from the man who had not seen it before.

"A right royal thing! A wonderful and never-to-be-rivaled thing! Grander than the great stove of Hohen-Salzburg! Sublime! Magnificent! Matchless!"

So the epithets ran on in thick guttural voices, diffusing a smell of lager beer so strong as they spoke that it reached August crouching in his stronghold. If they should open the door of the stove! That was his frantic fear. If they should open it, it would be all over with him. They would drag him out; most likely they would kill him, he thought, as his mother's young brother had been killed in the Wald.

The perspiration rolled off his forehead in his agony; but he had control enough over himself to keep quiet, and after standing by the Nürnberg master's work for nigh an hour, praising, marveling, expatiating in the lengthy German tongue, the men moved to a little distance and began talking of sums of money and divided profits, of which discourse he could make out no meaning. All he could make out was that the name of the king—the king—the king came over very often in their arguments. He fancied at times they quarrelled, for they swore lustily and their voices rose hoarse and high; but after a while they seemed to pacify each other and agree to something, and were in great glee, and so in these merry spirits came and slapped the luminous sides of stately Hirschvogel, and shouted to it—

"Old Mumchance, you have brought us rare good luck! To think you were smoking in a silly fool of a salt-baker's kitchen all these years!"

Then inside the stove August jumped up, with flaming cheeks and clinching hands, and was almost on the point of shouting out to them that they were the thieves and should say no evil of his father, when he remembered, just in time, that to breathe a word or make a sound was to bring ruin on himself and sever him forever from Hirschvogel. So he kept quite still, and the men barred the shutters of the little lattice and went out by the door,

double locking it after them. He had made out from their talk that they were going to show Hirschvogel to some great person: therefore he kept quite still and dared not move.

Muffled sounds came to him through the shutters from the streets below—the rolling of wheels, the clanging of church bells, and bursts of that military music which is so seldom silent in the streets of Munich. An hour perhaps passed by; sounds of steps on the stairs kept him in perpetual apprehension. In the intensity of his anxiety, he forgot that he was hungry and many miles away from cheerful, Old World little Hall, lying by the clear gray river water, with the ramparts of the mountains all around.

Presently the door opened again sharply. He could hear the two dealers' voices murmuring unctuous words, in which "honor," "gratitude," and many fine long noble titles played the chief parts. The voice of another person, more clear and refined than theirs, answered them curtly, and then, close by the Nürnberg stove and the boy's ear, ejaculated a single *"Wunderschön!"* August almost lost his terror for himself in his thrill of pride at his beloved Hirschvogel being thus admired in the great city. He thought the master-potter must be glad too.

"Wunderschön!" ejaculated the stranger a second time, and then examined the stove in all its parts, read all its mottoes, gazed long on all its devices.

"It must have been made for the Emperor Maximilian," he said at last; and the poor little boy, meanwhile, within, was "hugged up into nothing," as you children say, dreading that every moment he would open the stove. And open it truly he did, and examined the brasswork of the door; but inside it was so dark that crouching August passed unnoticed, screwed up into a ball like a hedgehog

as he was. The gentleman shut the door at length, without having seen anything strange inside it; and then he talked long and low with the tradesmen, and, as his accent was different from that which August was used to, the child could distinguish little that he said, except the name of the king and the word "gulden" again and again. After a while he went away, one of the dealers accompanying him, one of them lingering behind to bar up the shutters. Then this one also withdrew again, double locking the door.

The poor little hedgehog uncurled itself and dared to breathe aloud.

What time was it?

Late in the day, he thought, for to accompany the stranger they had lighted a lamp; he had heard the scratch of the match, and through the brass fretwork had seen the lines of light.

He would have to pass the night here, that was certain. He and Hirschvogel were locked in, but at least they were together. If only he could have had something to eat! He thought with a pang of how at this hour at home they ate the sweet soup, sometimes with apples in it from Aunt Maïla's farm orchard, and sang together, and listened to Dorothea's reading of little tales, and basked in the glow and delight that had beamed on them from the great Nürnberg fire-king.

"Oh, poor, poor little 'Gilda! What is she doing without dear Hirschvogel?" he thought. Poor little 'Gilda! she had only now the black iron stove of the ugly little kitchen. Oh, how cruel of father!

August could not bear to hear the dealers blame or laugh at his father, but he did feel that it had been so, so cruel to sell Hirschvogel. The mere memory of all those long winter evenings, when they had all closed round it,

and roasted chestnuts or crabapples in it, and listened to the howling of the wind and the deep sound of the church bells, and tried very much to make each other believe that the wolves still came down from the mountains into the streets of Hall, and were that very minute growling at the house door—all this memory coming on him with the sound of the city bells, and the knowledge that night drew near upon him so completely, being added to his hunger and his fear, so overcame him that he burst out crying for the fiftieth time since he had been inside the stove, and felt that he would starve to death, and wondered dreamily if Hirschvogel would care. Yes, he was sure Hirschvogel would care. Had he not decked it all summer long with alpine roses and edelweiss and heaths and made it sweet with thyme and honeysuckle and great garden lilies? Had he ever forgotten when Santa Claus came to make it its crown of holly and ivy and wreathe it all around?

"Oh, shelter me; save me; take care of me!" he prayed to the old fire-king, and forgot, poor little man, that he had come on this wild-goose chase northward to save and take care of Hirschvogel!

After a time he dropped asleep, as children can do when they weep, and little robust hill-born boys most surely do, be they where they may. It was not very cold in this lumber-room; it was tightly shut up, and very full of things, and at the back of it were the hot pipes of an adjacent house, where a great deal of fuel was burnt. Moreover, August's clothes were warm ones and his blood was young. So he was not cold, though Munich is terribly cold in the nights of December; and he slept on and on—which was a comfort to him, for he forgot his woes, and his perils, and his hunger, for a time.

Midnight was once more chiming from all the brazen tongues of the city when he awoke, and, all being still

around him, ventured to put his head out of the brass door of the stove to see why such a strange bright light was round him.

It was a very strange and brilliant light indeed; and yet, what is perhaps still stranger, it did not frighten or amaze him, nor did what he saw alarm him either, and yet I think it would have done you or me. For what he saw was nothing less than all the *bric-à-brac* in motion.

A big jug, an Apostel-Krug, of Kruessen, was solemnly dancing a minuet with a plump Faenza jar. A tall Dutch clock was going through a gavotte with a spindle-legged ancient chair. A very droll porcelain figure of Littenhausen was bowing to a very stiff soldier in *terre cuite* of Ulm. An old violin of Cremona was playing itself, and a queer little shrill plaintive music that thought itself merry came from a painted spinnet covered with faded roses. Some gilt Spanish leather had got up on the wall and laughed. A Dresden mirror was tripping about, crowned with flowers, and a Japanese bonze was riding along on a griffin. A slim Venetian rapier had come to blows with a stout Ferrara saber, all about a little pale-faced chit of a damsel in white Nymphenburg china. And a portly Franconian pitcher in *grès gris* was calling aloud, "Oh, these Italians! always at feud!" But nobody listened to him at all. A great number of little Dresden cups and saucers were all skipping and waltzing; the teapots, with their broad round faces, were spinning their own lids like teetotums. The high-backed gilded chairs were having a game of cards together; and a little Saxe poodle, with a blue ribbon at its throat, was running from one to another, whilst a yellow cat of Cornelis Lachtleven's rode about on a Delft horse in blue pottery of 1489. Meanwhile the brilliant light shed on the scene came from three silver candelabra, though they had no candles set up in them. And, what is

the greatest miracle of all, August looked on at these mad freaks and felt no sensation of wonder! He only, as he heard the violin and the spinnet playing, felt an irresistible desire to dance too.

No doubt his face said what he wished; for a lovely little lady, all in pink and gold and white, with powdered hair, and high-heeled shoes, and all made of the very finest and fairest Meissen china, tripped up to him, and smiled, and gave him her hand and led him out to a minuet. And he danced it perfectly—poor little August in his thick, clumsy shoes and his thick, clumsy sheepskin jacket, and his rough homespun linen, and his broad Tyrolean hat! He must have danced it perfectly, this dance of kings and queens in days when crowns were duly honored, for the lovely lady always smiled benignly and never scolded him at all, and danced so divinely herself to the stately measures the spinnet was playing that August could not take his eyes off her till, their minuet ended, she sat down on her own white-and-gold bracket.

"I am the Princess of Saxe-Royale," she said to him, with a benignant smile; "and you have got through that minuet very fairly."

Then he ventured to say to her—

"Madame my princess, could you tell me kindly why some of the figures and furniture dance and speak, and some lie up in a corner like lumber? It does make me curious. Is it rude to ask?"

For it greatly puzzled him why, when some of the *bric-à-brac* was all full of life and motion, some was quite still and had not a single thrill in it.

"My dear child," said the powdered lady, "is it possible that you do not know the reason? Why, those silent, dull things are *imitation!*"

This she said with so much decision that she evidently considered it a condensed but complete answer.

"Imitation?" repeated August, timidly, not understanding.

"Of course! Lies, falsehoods, fabrications!" said the princess in pink shoes, very vivaciously. "They only *pretend* to be what we *are!* They never wake up:how can they? No imitation ever had any soul in it yet."

"Oh!" said August humbly, not even sure that he understood entirely yet. He looked at Hirschvogel; surely it had a royal soul within it: would it not wake up and speak? Oh dear! how he longed to hear the voice of his fire-king! And he began to forget that he stood by a lady who sat upon a pedestal of gold-and-white china, with the year 1746 cut on it, and the Meissen mark.

"What will you be when you are a man?" said the little lady sharply, for her black eyes were quick though her red lips were smiling. "Will you work for the *Königliche Porcellan-Manufactur,* like my great dead Kandler?"

"I have never thought," said August, stammering, "at least—that is—I do wish—I do hope to be a painter, as was Master Augustin Hirschvogel at Nürnberg."

"Bravo!" said all the real *bric-à-brac* in one breath, and the two Italian rapiers left off their fighting to cry, *"Benone!"* For there is not a bit of true *bric-à-brac* in all Europe that does not know the names of the mighty masters.

August felt quite pleased to have won so much applause, and grew as red as the lady's shoes with bashful contentment.

"I knew all the Hirschvögel, from old Veit downwards," said a fat *grès de Flandre* beer jug: "I myself was made at Nürnberg." And he bowed to the great stove

very politely, taking off his own silver hat—I mean lid—
with a courtly sweep that he could scarcely have learned
from burgomasters. The stove, however, was silent, and
a sickening suspicion (for what is such heartbreak as a
suspicion of what we love?) came through the mind of
August: *Was Hirschvogel only imitation?*

"No, no, no, no!" he said to himself stoutly: though
Hirschvogel never stirred, never spoke, yet would he keep
all faith in it. After all their happy years together, after
all the nights of warmth and joy he owed it, should he
doubt his own friend and hero, whose gilt lion's feet he
had kissed in his babyhood? "No, no, no, no!" he said,
again, with so much emphasis that the Lady of Meissen
looked sharply again at him.

"No," she said, with pretty disdain, "no, believe me,
they may 'pretend' forever. They can never look like us!
They imitate even our marks, but never can they look like
the real thing, never can they *chassent de race.*"

"How should they?" said a bronze statuette of
Vischer's. "They daub themselves green with verdigris,
or sit out in the rain to get rusted; but green and rust are
not *patina;* only the ages can give that!"

"And *my* imitations are all in primary colors, staring
colors, hot as the colors of a hostelry's signboard!" said
the Lady of Meissen, with a shiver.

"Well, there is a *grès de Flandre* over there, who
pretends to be a Hans Kraut, as I am," said the jug with
the silver hat, pointing with his handle to a jug that lay
prone on its side in a corner. "He has copied me as
exactly as it is given to moderns to copy us. Almost he
might be mistaken for me. But yet what a difference
there is! How crude are his blues! how evidently done
over the glaze are his black letters! He has tried to give
himself my very twist; but what a lamentable exaggera-

tion of that playful deviation in my lines which in his
becomes actual deformity!"

"And look at that," said the gilt Cordovan leather with
a contemptuous glance at a broad piece of gilded leather
spread out on a table. "They will sell him cheek by jowl
with me, and give him my name; but look! *I* am overlaid
with pure gold beaten thin as a film and laid on me in
absolute honesty by worthy Diego de las Gorgias, worker
in leather of lovely Cordova in the blessed reign of Fer-
dinand the Most Christian. *His* gilding is one part gold to
eleven other parts of brass and rubbish, and it has been
laid on him with a brush—*a brush!*—pah! of course he
will be as black as a crock in a few years' time, while I am
as bright as when I first was made, and, unless I am burnt
as my Cordova burnt its heretics, I shall shine on forever."

"They carve pearwood because it is so soft, and dye it
brown, and call it *me!*" said an old oak cabinet, with a
chuckle.

"That is not so painful; it does not vulgarize you so
much as the cups they paint today and christen after *me!*"
said a Carl Theodor cup subdued in hue, yet gorgeous as a
jewel.

"Nothing can be so annoying as to see common gim-
cracks aping *me!*" interposed the princess in the pink
shoes.

"They even steal my motto, though it is Scripture," said
a *Trauerkrug* of Regensburg in black-and-white.

"And my own dots they put on plain English china
creatures!" sighed the little white maid of Nymphenburg.

"And they sell hundreds and thousands of common
china plates, calling them after me, and baking my saints
and my legends in a muffle of today; it is blasphemy!" said

a stout plate of Gubbio, which in its year of birth had seen the face of Maestro Giorgio.

"That is what is so terrible in these *bric-à-brac* places," said the princess of Meissen. "It brings one in contact with such low, imitative creatures; one really is safe nowhere nowadays unless under glass at the Louvre or South Kensington."

"And they get even there," sighed the *grès de Flandre*. "A terrible thing happened to a dear friend of mine, a *terre cuite* of Blasius (you know the *terres cuites* of Blasius date from 1560). Well, he was put under glass in a museum that shall be nameless, and he found himself set next to his own imitation born and baked yesterday at Frankfort, and what think you the miserable creature said to him, with a grin? 'Old Pipeclay,'—that is what he called my friend—'the fellow that bought *me* got just as much commission on me as the fellow that bought *you,* and that was all that *he* thought about. You know it is only the public money that goes!' And the horrid creature grinned again till he actually cracked himself. There is a Providence above all things, even museums."

"Providence might have interfered before, and saved the public money," said the little Meissen lady.

"After all, does it matter?" said a Dutch jar of Haarlem. "All the shamming in the world will not *make* them us!"

"One does not like to be vulgarized," said the Lady of Meissen angrily.

"My maker, the Krabbetje,* did not trouble his head about that," said the Haarlem jar proudly. "The Krabbetje made me for the kitchen, the bright, clean,

---

* Jan Asselyn, called Krabbetje, the little Crab, born 1610, master-potter of Delft and Haarlem.

snow-white Dutch kitchen, well nigh three centuries ago, and now I am thought worthy the palace; yet I wish I were at home; yet, I wish I could see the good Dutch vrouw, and the shining canals, and the great green meadows dotted with the kine."

"Ah! if we could all go back to our makers!" sighed the Gubbio plate, thinking of the Giorgio Andreoli and the glad and gracious days of the Renaissance: and somehow the words touched the frolicsome souls of the dancing jars, the spinning teapots, the chairs that were playing cards; and the violin stopped its merry music with a sob, and the spinnet sighed—thinking of dead hands.

Even the little Saxe poodle howled for a master forever lost; and only the swords went on quarreling, and made such a clattering noise that the Japanese bonze rode at them on his monster and knocked them both right over, and they lay straight and still, looking foolish, and the little Nymphenburg maid, though she was crying, smiled and almost laughed.

Then from where the great stove stood there came a solemn voice.

All eyes turned upon Hirschvogel, and the heart of its little human comrade gave a great jump of joy.

"My friends," said that clear voice from the turret of Nürnberg faïence, "I have listened to all you have said. There is too much talking among the Mortalities whom one of themselves has called the Windbags. Let not us be like them. I hear among men so much vain speech, so much precious breath and precious time wasted in empty boasts, foolish anger, useless reiteration, blatant argument, ignoble mouthings, that I have learned to deem speech a curse, laid on man to weaken and envenom all his undertakings. For over two hundred years I have never spoken myself: you, I hear, are not so reticent. I

only speak now because one of you said a beautiful thing that touched me. If we all might but go back to our makers! Ah, yes! if we might! We were made in days when even men were true creatures, and so we, the work of their hands, were true too. We, the begotten of ancient days, derive all the value in us from the fact that our makers wrought at us with zeal, with piety, with integrity, with faith—not to win fortunes or to glut a market, but to do nobly an honest thing and create for the honor of the Arts and God.

"I see there is here amidst you a little human thing who loves me, and in his own ignorant childish way loves Art. Now, I want him forever to remember this night and these words; to remember that we are what we are, and precious in the eyes of the world, because centuries ago those who were of single mind and of pure hand so created us, scorning sham and haste and counterfeit. Well do I recollect my master, Augustin Hirschvogel. He led a wise and blameless life, and wrought in loyalty and love, and made his time beautiful thereby, like one of his own rich, many-colored church casements, that told holy tales as the sun streamed through them. Ah, yes, my friends, to go back to our masters!—that would be the best that could befall us. But they are gone, and even the perishable labors of their lives outlive them. For many, many years I, once honored of emperors, dwelt in a humble house and warmed in successive winters three generations of little, cold, hungry children. When I warmed them they forgot that they were hungry; they laughed and told tales, and slept at last about my feet. Then I knew that humble as had become my lot it was one that my master would have wished for me, and I was content. Sometimes a tired woman would creep up to me, and smile because she was near me, and point out my golden crown

or my ruddy fruit to a baby in her arms. That was better than to stand in a great hall of a great city, cold and empty, even though wise men came to gaze and throngs of fools gaped, passing with flattering words. Where I go now I know not; but since I go from that humble house where they loved me, I shall be sad and alone. They pass so soon—those fleeting mortal lives! Only we endure— we, the things that the human brain creates. We can but bless them a little as they glide by: if we have done that, we have done what our masters wished. So in us our masters, being dead, yet may speak and live."

Then the voice sank away in silence, and a strange golden light that had shone on the great stove faded away; so also the light died down in the silver candelabra. A soft, pathetic melody stole gently through the room. It came from the old, old spinnet that was covered with the faded roses.

Then that sad, sighing music of a bygone day died too; the clocks of the city struck six of the morning; day was rising over the Bayerischenwald. August awoke with a great start, and found himself lying on the bare bricks of the floor of the chamber, and all the *bric-à-brac* was lying quite still all around. The pretty Lady of Meissen was motionless on her porcelain bracket, and the little Saxe poodle was quiet at her side.

August rose slowly to his feet. He was very cold, but he was not sensible of it or of the hunger that was gnawing his little empty entrails. He was absorbed in the wondrous sight, in the wondrous sounds, that he had seen and heard.

All was dark around him. Was it still midnight or had morning come? Morning, surely; for against the barred shutters he heard the tiny song of the robin.

Tramp, tramp, too, came a heavy step up the stair. He

had but a moment in which to scramble back into the interior of the great stove, when the door opened and the two dealers entered, bringing burning candles with them to see their way.

August was scarcely conscious of danger more than he was of cold or hunger. A marvelous sense of courage, of security, of happiness, was about him, like strong and gentle arms enfolding him and lifting him upwards—upwards—upwards! Hirschvogel would defend him.

The dealers undid the shutters, scaring the redbreast away, and then tramped about in their heavy boots and chattered in contented voices, and began to wrap up the stove once more in all its straw and hay and cordage.

It never once occurred to them to glance inside. Why should they look inside a stove that they had bought and were about to sell again for all its glorious beauty of exterior?

The child did not feel afraid. A great exaltation had come to him: he was like one lifted up by his angels.

Presently the two traders called up their porters, and the stove, heedfully swathed and wrapped and tended as though it were some sick prince going on a journey, was borne on the shoulders of six stout Bavarians down the stairs and out of the door into the Marienplatz. Even behind all those wrappings August felt the icy bite of the intense cold of the outer air at dawn of a winter's day in Munich. The men moved the stove with exceeding gentleness and care, so that he had often been far more roughly shaken in his big brothers' arms than he was in his journey now; and though both hunger and thirst made themselves felt, being foes that will take no denial, he was still in that state of nervous exaltation which deadens all physical suffering and is at once a cordial and an opiate. He had heard Hirschvogel speak; that was enough.

It never once occurred to him to dream of going home

The stout carriers tramped through the city, six of them, with the Nürnberg fire-castle on their brawny shoulders, and went right across Munich to the railway station, and August in the dark recognized all the ugly, jangling, pounding, roaring, hissing railway noises, and thought, despite his courage and excitement, "Will it be a *very* long journey?" For his stomach had at times an odd sinking sensation, and his head sadly often felt light and swimming. If it was a very, very long journey he felt half afraid that he would be dead or something bad before the end, and Hirschvogel would be so lonely: that was what he thought most about; not much about himself, and not much about Dorothea and the house at home. He was "high strung to high emprise," and could not look behind him.

Whether for a long or a short journey, whether for weal or woe, the stove with August still within it was once more hoisted up into a great van: but this time it was not all alone, and the two dealers as well as the six porters were all with it.

He in his darkness knew that, for he heard their voices. The train glided away over the Bavarian plain southward; and he heard the men say something of Berg and the Wurm-See, but their German was strange to him, and he could not make out what these names meant.

The train rolled on, with all its fume and fuss, and roar of steam, and stench of oil and burning coal. It had to go quietly and slowly on account of the snow which was falling, and which had fallen all night.

"He might have waited till he came to the city," grumbled one man to another. "What weather to stay on at Berg!"

But who he was that stayed on at Berg, August could not make out at all.

Though the men grumbled about the state of the roads and the season, they were hilarious and well content, for they laughed often, and, when they swore, did so good-humoredly, and promised their porters fine presents at New Year; and August, like a shrewd little boy as he was, who even in the secluded Innthal had learned that money is the chief mover of men's mirth, thought to himself, with a terrible pang—

"They have sold Hirschvogel for some great sum! They have sold him already!"

Then his heart grew faint and sick within him, for he knew very well that he must soon die, shut up without food and water thus; and what new owner of the great fireplace would ever permit him to dwell in it?

"Never mind, I *will* die," thought he, "and Hirschvogel will know it."

Perhaps you think him a very foolish little fellow, but I do not.

It is good to be loyal and ready to endure to the end.

It is but an hour and a quarter that the train usually takes to pass from Munich to the Wurm-See or Lake of Starnberg; but this morning the journey was much slower, because the way was encumbered by snow. When it did reach Possenhofen and stop, and the Nürnberg stove was lifted out once more, August could see through the fretwork of the brass door, as the stove stood upright facing the lake, that this Wurm-See was a calm and noble piece of water, of great width, with low wooded banks and distant mountains, a peaceful, serene place, full of rest.

It was now near ten o'clock. The sun had come forth; there was a clear gray sky hereabouts; the snow was not falling, though it lay white and smooth everywhere, down to the edge of the water, which before long would itself be ice.

Before he had time to get more than a glimpse of the green gliding surface, the stove was again lifted up and placed on a large boat that was in waiting—one of those very long and huge boats which the women in these parts use as laundries, and the men as timber rafts. The stove, with much labor and much expenditure of time and care, was hoisted into this, and August would have grown sick and giddy with the heaving and falling if his big brothers had not long used him to such tossing about, so that he was as much at ease head, as feet, downward. The stove once in it safely with its guardians, the big boat moved across the lake to Leoni. How a little hamlet on a Bavarian lake got that Tuscan-sounding name I cannot tell; but Leoni it is. The big boat was a long time crossing: the lake here is about three miles broad, and these heavy barges are unwieldy and heavy to move, even though they are towed and tugged at from the shore.

"If we should be too late!" the two dealers muttered to each other, in agitation and alarm. "He said eleven o'clock."

"Who was he?" thought August. "The buyer, of course, of Hirschvogel." The slow passage across the Wurm-See was accomplished at length: the lake was placid; there was a sweet calm in the air and on the water; there was a great deal of snow in the sky, though the sun was shining and gave a solemn hush to the atmosphere. Boats and one little steamer were going up and down; in the clear frosty light the distant mountains of Zillerthal and the Algau Alps were visible; market people, cloaked and furred, went by on the water or on the banks; the deep woods of the shores were black and gray and brown. Poor August could see nothing of a scene that would have delighted him; as the stove was now set, he could only see the old worm-eaten wood of the huge barge.

Presently they touched the pier at Leoni.

"Now men, for a stout mile and a half! You shall drink your reward at Christmas time," said one of the dealers to his porters, who, stout, strong men as they were, showed a disposition to grumble at their task. Encouraged by large promises, they shouldered sullenly the Nürnberg stove, grumbling again at its preposterous weight, but little dreaming that they carried within it a small, panting, trembling boy; for August began to tremble now that he was about to see the future owner of Hirschvogel.

"If he look a good, kind man," he thought, "I will beg him to let me stay with it."

The porters began their toilsome journey, and moved off from the village pier. He could see nothing, for the brass door was over his head, and all that gleamed through it was the clear gray sky. He had been tilted onto his back, and if he had not been a little mountaineer, used to hanging head downwards over crevasses, and, moreover, seasoned to rough treatment by the hunters and guides of the hills and the salt-workers in the town, he would have been made ill and sick by the bruising and shaking and many changes of position to which he had been subjected.

The way the men took was a mile and a half in length, but the road was heavy with snow, and the burden they bore was heavier still. The dealers cheered them on, swore at them and praised them in one breath; besought them and reiterated their splendid promises, for a clock was striking eleven, and they had been ordered to reach their destination at that hour, and, though the air was so cold, the heat drops rolled off their foreheads as they walked, they were so frightened at being late. But the porters would not budge a foot quicker than they chose,

and as they were not poor four-footed carriers their employers dared not thrash them, though most willingly would they have done so.

The road seemed terribly long to the anxious tradesmen, to the plodding porters, to the poor little man inside the stove, as he kept sinking and rising, sinking and rising, with each of their steps.

Where they were going he had no idea, only after a very long time he lost the sense of the fresh icy wind blowing on his face through the brass work above, and felt by their movements beneath him that they were mounting steps or stairs. Then he heard a great many different voices, but he could not understand what was being said. He felt that his bearers paused some time, then moved on and on again. Their feet went so softly he thought they must be moving on carpet, and as he felt a warm air come to him he concluded that he was in some heated chambers, for he was a clever little fellow, and could put two and two together, though he was so hungry and so thirsty and his empty stomach felt so strangely. They must have gone, he thought, through some very great number of rooms, for they walked so long on and on, on and on. At last the stove was set down again, and, happily for him, set so that his feet were downward.

What he fancied was that he was in some museum, like that which he had seen in the city of Innspruck.

The voices he heard were very hushed, and the steps seemed to go away, far away, leaving him alone with Hirschvogel. He dared not look out, but he peeped through the brass work, and all he could see was a big carved lion's head in ivory, with a gold crown atop. It belonged to a velvet fauteuil, but he could not see the chair, only the ivory lion.

There was a delicious fragrance in the air—a fragrance

as of flowers. "Only how can it be flowers?" thought August. "It is November!"

From afar off, as it seemed, there came a dreamy, exquisite music, as sweet as the spinnet's had been, but so much fuller, so much richer, seeming as though a chorus of angels were singing all together. August ceased to think of the museum: he thought of heaven. "Are we gone to the Master?" he thought, remembering the words of Hirschvogel.

All was so still around him; there was no sound anywhere except the sound of the far-off choral music.

He did not know it, but he was in the royal castle of Berg, and the music he heard was the music of Wagner, who was playing in a distant room some of the motifs of "Parsifal."

Presently he heard a fresh step near him, and he heard a low voice say, close behind him, "So!" An exclamation no doubt, he thought, of admiration and wonder at the beauty of Hirschvogel.

Then the same voice said, after a long pause, during which no doubt, as August thought, this newcomer was examining all the details of the wondrous fire-tower, "It was well bought; it is exceedingly beautiful! It is most undoubtedly the work of Augustin Hirschvogel."

Then the hand of the speaker turned the round handle of the brass door, and the fainting soul of the poor little prisoner within grew sick with fear.

The handle turned, the door was slowly drawn open, someone bent down and looked in, and the same voice that he had heard in praise of its beauty called aloud, in surprise, "What is this in it? A live child!"

Then August, terrified beyond all self-control, and dominated by one master passion, sprang out of the body of the stove and fell at the feet of the speaker.

"Oh, let me stay! Pray, meinherr, let me stay!" he sobbed. "I have come all the way with Hirschvogel!"

Some gentlemen's hands seized him, not gently by any means, and their lips angrily muttered in his ear, "Little knave, peace! Be quiet! Hold your tongue! It is the king!"

They were about to drag him out of the august atmosphere as if he had been some venomous, dangerous beast come there to slay, but the voice he had heard speak of the stove said, in kind accents, "Poor little child! He is very young. Let him go. Let him speak to me."

The word of a king is law to his courtiers: so, sorely against their wish, the angry and astonished chamberlains let August slide out of their grasp, and he stood there in his little rough sheepskin coat and his thick, mud-covered boots, with his curling hair all in a tangle, in the midst of the most beautiful chamber he had ever dreamed of, and in the presence of a young man with a beautiful dark face, and eyes full of dreams and fire; and the young man said to him, "My child, how came you here, hidden in this stove? Be not afraid: tell me the truth. I am the king."

August in an instinct of homage cast his great battered black hat with the tarnished gold tassels down on the floor of the room, and folded his little brown hands in supplication. He was too intensely in earnest to be in any way abashed; he was too lifted out of himself by his love for Hirschvogel to be conscious of any awe before any earthly majesty. He was only so glad—so glad it was the king. Kings were always kind; so the Tyrolese think, who love their lords.

"Oh, dear king!" he said, with trembling entreaty in his faint little voice, "Hirschvogel was ours, and we have loved it all our lives; and father sold it. And when I saw that it did really go from us, then I said to myself I would

go with it; and I have come all the way inside it. And last
night it spoke and said beautiful things. And I do pray
you to let me live with it, and I will go out every morning
and cut wood for it and you, if only you will let me stay
beside it. No one ever has fed it with fuel but me since I
grew big enough, and it loves me—it does indeed; it said
so last night; and it said it had been happier with us than if
it were in any palace——"

And then his breath failed him, and, as he lifted his
little eager, pale face to the young king's, great tears were
falling down his cheeks.

Now, the king likes all poetic and uncommon things,
and there was that in the child's face which pleased and
touched him. He motioned to his gentlemen to leave the
little boy alone.

"What is your name?" he asked him.

"I am August Strehla. My father is Karl Strehla. We
live in Hall in the Innthal; and Hirschvogel has been ours
so long—so long!"

His lips quivered with a broken sob.

"And have you truly traveled inside this stove all the
way from Tyrol?"

"Yes," said August. "No one thought to look inside
till you did."

The king laughed; then another view of the matter
occurred to him.

"Who bought the stove of your father?" he inquired.

"Traders of Munich," said August, who did not know
that he ought not to have spoken to the king as to a simple
citizen, and whose little brain was whirling and spinning
dizzily round its one central idea.

"What sum did they pay your father, do you know?"
asked the sovereign.

"Two hundred florins," said August, with a great sigh

of shame. "It was so much money, and he is so poor, and there are so many of us."

The king turned to his gentlemen-in-waiting. "Did these dealers of Munich come with the stove?"

He was answered in the affirmative. He desired them to be sought for and brought before him. As one of his chamberlains hastened on the errand, the monarch looked at August with compassion.

"You are very pale, little fellow: when did you eat last?"

"I had some bread and sausage with me; yesterday afternoon I finished it."

"You would like to eat now?"

"If I might have a little water I would be glad; my throat is very dry."

The king had water and wine brought for him, and cake also; but August, though he drank eagerly, could not swallow anything. His mind was in too great a tumult.

"May I stay with Hirschvogel?—may I stay?" he said, with feverish agitation.

"Wait a little," said the king, and asked abruptly. "What do you wish to be when you are a man?"

"A painter. I wish to be what Hirschvogel was—I mean the master that made *my* Hirschvogel."

"I understand," said the king.

Then the two dealers were brought into their sovereign's presence. They were so terribly alarmed, not being either so innocent or so ignorant as August was, that they were trembling as though they were being led to the slaughter, and they were so utterly astonished too at a child having come all the way from Tyrol in the stove, as a gentleman of the court had just told them this child had done, that they could not tell what to say or where to look, and presented a very foolish aspect indeed.

"Did you buy this Nürnberg stove of this little boy's father for two hundred florins?" the king asked them; and his voice was no longer soft and kind as it had been when addressing the child, but very stern.

"Yes, your majesty," murmured the trembling traders.

"And how much did the gentleman who purchased it for me give to you?"

"Two thousand ducats, your majesty," muttered the dealers, frightened out of their wits, and telling the truth in their fright.

The gentleman was not present: he was a trusted councilor in art matters of the king's, and often made purchases for him.

The king smiled a little and said nothing. The gentleman had made out the price to him as eleven thousand ducats.

"You will give at once to this boy's father the two thousand gold ducats that you received, less the two hundred Austrian florins that you paid him," said the king to his humiliated and abject subjects. "You are great rogues. Be thankful you are not more greatly punished."

He dismissed them by a sign to his courtiers, and to one of these gave the mission of making the dealers of the Marienplatz disgorge their ill-gotten gains.

August heard, and felt dazzled yet miserable. Two thousand gold Bavarian ducats for his father! Why, his father would never need to go any more to the salt baking! And yet, whether for ducats or for florins, Hirschvogel was sold just the same, and would the king let him stay with it—would he?

"Oh, do! Oh, please do!" he murmured, joining his little brown weather-stained hands, and kneeling down

before the young monarch, who himself stood absorbed in painful thought, for the deception so basely practiced for the greedy sake of gain on him by a trusted councilor was bitter to him. He looked down on the child, and as he did so smiled once more.

"Rise up, my little man," he said, in a kind voice. "Kneel only to your God. Will I let you stay with your Hirschvogel? Yes, I will; you shall stay at my court, and you shall be taught to be a painter—in oils or on porcelain as you will—and you must grow up worthily, and win all the laurels at our Schools of Art, and if when you are twenty-one years old you have done well and bravely, then I will give you your Nürnberg stove, or, if I am no more living, then those who reign after me shall do so. And now go away with this gentleman, and be not afraid, and you shall light a fire every morning in Hirschvogel, but you will not need to go out and cut the wood."

Then he smiled and stretched out his hand. The courtiers tried to make August understand that he ought to bow and touch it with his lips, but August could not understand that anyhow; he was too happy. He threw his two arms about the king's knees, and kissed his feet passionately; then he lost all sense of where he was, and fainted away from hunger, and tiredness, and emotion, and wondrous joy.

As the darkness of his swoon closed in on him, he heard in his fancy the voice from Hirschvogel saying—

"Let us be worthy our maker!"

He is only a scholar yet, but he is a happy scholar, and promises to be a great man. Sometimes he goes back for a few days to Hall, where the gold ducats have made his father prosperous. In the old house-room there is a large

white porcelain stove of Munich, the king's gift to Dorothea and 'Gilda.

And August never goes home without going into the great church and saying his thanks to God, who blessed his strange winter's journey in the Nürnberg stove. As for his dream in the dealers' room that night, he will never admit that he did dream it; he still declares that he saw it all, and heard the voice of Hirschvogel. And who shall say that he did not? For what is the gift of the poet and the artist except to see the sights which others cannot see and to hear the sounds that others cannot hear?

MOUFFLOU

Lolo wove the straw covering of wine flasks and plaited the cane matting with busy fingers

MOUFFLOU

Mouﬄou's masters were some boys and girls. They were very poor, but they were very merry. They lived in an old, dark, tumbledown place, and their father had been dead five years; their mother's care was all they knew; and Tasso was the eldest of them all, a lad of nearly twenty, and he was so kind, so good, so laborious, so cheerful, and so gentle, that the children all younger than he adored him. Tasso was a gardener. Tasso, however, though the eldest and mainly the breadwinner, was not so much Mouﬄou's master as was little Romolo, who was only ten, and a cripple. Romolo, called generally Lolo, had taught Mouﬄou all he knew; and that all was a very great deal, for nothing cleverer than was Mouﬄou had ever walked upon four legs.

Why Mouﬄou?

Well, when the poodle had been given to them by a soldier who was going back to his home in Piedmont, he had been a white woolly creature of a year old, and the children's mother, who was a Corsican by birth, had said

that he was just like a *moufflon,* as they call sheep in Corsica. White and woolly this dog remained, and he became the handsomest and biggest poodle in all the city, and the corruption of Moufflou from Moufflon remained the name by which he was known; it was silly, perhaps, but it suited him and the children, and Moufflou he was.

They lived in an old quarter of Florence, in that picturesque zigzag which goes round the grand church of Or San Michele, and which is almost more Venetian than Tuscan in its mingling of color, charm, stateliness, popular confusion, and architectural majesty. The tall old houses are weather-beaten into the most delicious hues; the pavement is enchantingly encumbered with peddlers and stalls and all kinds of trades going on in the open air, in that bright, merry, beautiful Italian custom which, alas, alas! is being driven away by new-fangled laws which deem it better for the people to be stuffed up in close, stewing rooms without air, and would fain do away with all the good-tempered politics and the sensible philosophies and the wholesome chatter which the open-street trades and street gossipry encourage, for it is good for the populace to *sfogare* and in no other way can it do so one half so innocently. Drive it back into musty shops, and it is driven at once to mutter sedition. . . . But you want to hear about Moufflou.

Well, Moufflou lived here in that high house with the sign of the lamb in wrought iron, which shows it was once a warehouse of the old guild of the Arte della Lana. They are all old houses here, drawn round about that grand church which I called once, and will call again, like a mighty casket of oxidized silver. A mighty casket indeed, holding the Holy Spirit within it; and with the

vermilion and the blue and the orange glowing in its niches and its lunettes like enamels, and its statues of the apostles strong and noble, like the times in which they were created—St. Peter with his keys, and St. Mark with his open book, and St. George leaning on his sword, and others also, solemn and austere as they, austere though benign, for do they not guard the White Tabernacle of Orcagna within?

The church stands firm as a rock, square as a fortress of stone, and the winds and the waters of the skies may beat about it as they will, they have no power to disturb its sublime repose. Sometimes I think of all the noble things in all our Italy Or San Michele is the noblest, standing there in its stern magnificence, amidst people's hurrying feet and noisy laughter, a memory of God.

The little masters of Moufflou lived right in its shadow, where the bridge of stone spans the space between the houses and the church high in midair: and little Lolo loved the church with a great love. He loved it in the morning-time, when the sunbeams turned it into dusky gold and jasper; he loved it in the evening-time, when the lights of its altars glimmered in the dark, and the scent of its incense came out into the street; he loved it in the great feasts, when the huge clusters of lilies were borne inside it; he loved it in the solemn nights of winter; the flickering gleam of the dull lamps shone on the robes of an apostle, or the sculpture of a shield, or the glow of a casement-molding in majolica. He loved it always, and, without knowing why, he called it *la mia chiesa*.

Lolo, being lame and of delicate health, was not enabled to go to school or to work, though he wove the straw covering of wine-flasks and plaited the cane matting with busy fingers. But for the most part he did as he

liked, and spent most of his time sitting on the parapet of Or San Michele, watching the venders of earthenware at their trucks, or trotting with his crutch (and he could trot a good many miles when he chose) out with Moufflou down a bit of the Stocking-makers' Street, along under the arcades of the Uffizi, and so over the Jewelers' Bridge, and out by byways that he knew into the fields on the hillside upon the other bank of Arno. Moufflou and he would spend half the day—all the day—out there in daffodil time; and Lolo would come home with great bundles and sheaves of golden flowers, and he and Moufflou were happy.

His mother never liked to say a harsh word to Lolo, for he was lame through her fault: she had let him fall in his babyhood, and the mischief had been done to his hip never again to be undone. So she never raised her voice to him, though she did often to the others—to curly-pated Cecco, and pretty black-eyed Dina, and saucy Bice, and sturdy Beppo, and even to the good, manly, hard-working Tasso. Tasso was the mainstay of the whole, though he was but a gardener's lad, working in the green Cascine at small wages. But all he earned he brought home to his mother; and he alone kept in order the lazy, high-tempered Sandro, and he alone kept in check Bice's love of finery, and he alone could with shrewdness and care make both ends meet and put *minestra* always in the pot and bread always in the cupboard.

When his mother thought, as she thought indeed almost ceaselessly, that with a few months he would be of the age to draw his number, and might draw a high one and be taken from her for three years, the poor soul believed her very heart would burst and break; and many a day at twilight she would start out unperceived and

creep into the great church and pour her soul forth in supplication before the White Tabernacle.

Yet, pray as she would, no miracle could happen to make Tasso free of military service: if he drew a fatal number, go he must, even though he take all the lives of them to their ruin with him.

One morning Lolo sat as usual on the parapet of the church, Moufflou beside him. It was a brilliant morning in September. The men at the handbarrows and at the stalls were selling the crockery, the silk handkerchiefs, and the straw hats which form the staple of the commerce that goes on round about Or San Michele—very blithe, good-natured, gay commerce, for the most part, not got through, however, of course, without bawling and screaming, and shouting and gesticulating, as if the sale of a penny pipkin or a twopenny pie pan were the occasion for the exchange of many thousands of pounds sterling and cause for the whole world's commotion. It was about eleven o'clock. The poor petitioners were going in for alms to the house of the fraternity of San Giovanni Battista. The barber at the corner was shaving a big man with a cloth tucked about his chin, and his chair set well out on the pavement. The sellers of the pipkins and pie pans were screaming till they were hoarse, *"Un soldo l'uno, due soldi tre!"* big bronze bells were booming till they seemed to clang right up to the deep blue sky; some brethren of the Misericordia went by bearing a black bier; a large sheaf of glowing flowers—dahlias, zinnias, asters, and daturas—was borne through the huge arched door of the church near St. Mark and his open book. Lolo looked on at it all, and so did Moufflou, and a stranger looked at them as he left the church.

"You have a handsome poodle there, my little man," he

said to Lolo, in a foreigner's too distinct and careful Italian.

"Moufflou is beautiful," said Lolo with pride. "You should see him when he is just washed; but we can only wash him on Sundays, because then Tasso is at home."

"How old is your dog?"

"Three years old."

"Does he do any tricks?"

"Does he!" said Lolo with a very derisive laugh. "Why, Moufflou can do anything! He can walk on two legs ever so long; make ready, present, and fire; die; waltz; beg, of course; shut a door; make a wheelbarrow of himself: there is nothing he will not do. Would you like to see him do something?"

"Very much," said the foreigner.

To Moufflou and to Lolo the street was the same thing as home; this cheery *piazzetta* by the church, so utterly empty sometimes, and sometimes so noisy and crowded, was but the wider threshold of their home to both the poodle and the child.

So there, under the lofty and stately walls of the old church, Lolo put Moufflou through his exercises. They were second nature to Moufflou, as to most poodles. He had inherited his address at them from clever parents, and, as he had never been frightened or coerced, all his lessons and acquirements were but play to him. He acquitted himself admirably, and the crockery venders came and looked on, and a sacristan came out of the church and smiled, and the barber left his customer's chin all in a lather while he laughed, for the good folk of the quarter were all proud of Moufflou and never tired of him, and the pleasant, easy-going, good-humored disposition of the Tuscan populace is so far removed from the

stupid buckram and whalebone in which the new-fangled democracy wants to imprison it.

The stranger also was much diverted by Moufflou's talents, and said, half aloud, "How this clever dog would amuse poor Victor! Would you bring your poodle to please a sick child I have at home?" he said, quite aloud, to Lolo, who smiled and answered that he would. Where was the sick child?

"At the Gran Bretagna, not far off," said the gentleman. "Come this afternoon, and ask for me by this name."

He dropped his card and a couple of francs into Lolo's hand, and went his way. Lolo, with Moufflou scampering after him, dashed into his own house, and stumped up the stairs, his crutch making a terrible noise on the stone.

"Mother, mother! See what I have got because Moufflou did his tricks," he shouted. "And now you can buy those shoes you want so much, and the coffee that you miss so of a morning, and the new linen for Tasso, and the shirts for Sandro."

For to the mind of Lolo two francs was as two millions—source unfathomable of riches inexhaustible!

With the afternoon he and Moufflou trotted down the arcades of the Uffizi and down the Lung' Arno to the hotel of the stranger, and, showing the stranger's card, which Lolo could not read, they were shown at once into a great chamber, all gilding and fresco and velvet furniture.

But Lolo, being a little Florentine, was never troubled by externals, or daunted by mere sofas and chairs. He stood and looked around him with perfect composure; and Moufflou, whose attitude, when he was not romping,

was always one of magisterial gravity, sat on his haunches and did the same.

Soon the foreigner he had seen in the forenoon entered and spoke to him, and led him into another chamber, where stretched on a couch was a little wan-faced boy about seven years old; a pretty boy, but so pallid, so wasted, so helpless. This poor little boy was heir to a great name and a great fortune, but all the science in the world could not make him strong enough to run about among the daisies, or able to draw a single breath without pain. A feeble smile lit up his face as he saw Moufflou and Lolo. Then a shadow chased it away.

"Little boy is lame like me," he said, in a tongue Lolo did not understand.

"Yes, but he is a strong little boy, and can move about, as perhaps the suns of his country will make you do," said the gentleman, who was the poor little boy's father. "He has brought you his poodle to amuse you. What a handsome dog, is it not?"

"Oh, *bufflins!*" said the poor little fellow, stretching out his wasted hands to Moufflou, who submitted his leonine crest to the caress.

Then Lolo went through the performance, and Moufflou acquitted himself ably as ever; and the little invalid laughed and shouted with his tiny thin voice, and enjoyed it all immensely, and rained cakes and biscuits on both the poodle and its master. Lolo crumped the pastries with willing white teeth, and Moufflou did no less. Then they got up to go, and the sick child on the couch burst into fretful lamentations and outcries.

"I want the dog! I will have the dog!" was all he kept repeating.

But Lolo did not know what he said, and was only sorry to see him so unhappy.

"You shall have the dog tomorrow," said the gentleman, to pacify his little son; and he hurried Lolo and Moufflou out of the room, and consigned them to a servant, having given Lolo five francs this time.

"Why, Moufflou," said Lolo, with a chuckle of delight, "if we could find a foreigner every day, we could eat meat at supper, Moufflou, and go to the theater every evening!"

And he and his crutch clattered home with great eagerness and excitement, and Moufflou trotted on his four frilled feet, the blue bow with which Bice had tied up his curls on the top of his head, fluttering in the wind. But, alas! even his five francs could bring no comfort at home. He found his whole family wailing and mourning in utterly inconsolable distress.

Tasso had drawn his number that morning, and the number was seven, and he must go and be a conscript for three years.

The poor young man stood in the midst of his weeping brothers and sisters, with his mother leaning against his shoulder, and down his own brown cheeks the tears were falling. He must go, and lose his place in the public gardens, and leave his people to starve as they might, and be put in a tomfool's jacket, and drafted off among cursing and swearing and strange faces, friendless, homeless, miserable! And the mother—what would become of the mother?

Tasso was the best of lads and the mildest. He was quite happy sweeping up the leaves in the long alleys of the Cascine, or mowing the green lawns under the ilex avenues, and coming home at suppertime among the merry little people and the good woman that he loved. He was quite contented; he wanted nothing, only to be let alone; and they would not let him alone. They would

haul him away to put a heavy musket in his hand and a heavy knapsack on his back, and drill him, and curse him, and make him into a human target, a live popinjay.

No one had any heed for Lolo and his five francs, and Moufflou, understanding that some great sorrow had fallen on his friends, sat down and lifted up his voice and howled.

Tasso must go away!—that was all they understood. For three long years they must go without the sight of his face, the aid of his strength, the pleasure of his smile. Tasso must go! When Lolo understood the calamity that had befallen them, he gathered Moufflou up against his breast, and sat down too on the floor beside him and cried as if he would never stop crying.

There was no help for it: it was one of those misfortunes which are, as we say In Italian, like a tile tumbled on the head. The tile drops from a height, and the poor head bows under the unseen blow. That is all.

"What is the use of that?" said the mother passionately, when Lolo showed her his five francs. "It will not buy Tasso's discharge."

Lolo felt that his mother was cruel and unjust, and crept to bed with Moufflou. Moufflou always slept on Lolo's feet.

The next morning Lolo got up before sunrise, and he and Moufflou accompanied Tasso to his work in the Cascine.

Lolo loved his brother, and clung to every moment while they could still be together.

"Can nothing keep you, Tasso?" he said, despairingly, as they went down the leafy aisles, whilst the Arno water was growing golden as the sun rose.

Tasso sighed.

"Nothing, dear. Unless Gesu would send me a thousand francs to buy a substitute."

And he knew he might as well have said, "If one could coin gold ducats out of the sunbeams of Arno water."

Lolo was very sorrowful as he lay on the grass in the meadow where Tasso was at work, and the poodle lay stretched beside him.

When Lolo went home to dinner (Tasso took his wrapped in a handkerchief) he found his mother very agitated and excited. She was laughing one moment, crying the next. She was passionate and peevish, tender and jocose by turns; there was something forced and feverish about her which the children felt but did not comprehend. She was a woman of not very much intelligence, and she had a secret, and she carried it ill, and knew not what to do with it; but they could not tell that. They only felt a vague sense of disturbance and timidity at her unwonted manner.

The meal over (it was only bean soup, and that is soon eaten), the mother said sharply to Lolo. "Your aunt Anita wants you this afternoon. She has to go out, and you are needed to stay with the children: be off with you."

Lolo was an obedient child; he took his hat and jumped up as quickly as his halting hip would let him. He called Moufflou, who was asleep.

"Leave the dog," said his mother sharply. " 'Nita will not have him messing and carrying mud about her nice clean rooms. She told me so. Leave him, I say."

"Leave Moufflou!" echoed Lolo, for never in all Moufflou's life had Lolo parted from him. Leave Moufflou! He stared open-eyed and open-mouthed at his mother. What could have come to her?

"Leave him, I say," she repeated, more sharply than ever. "Must I speak twice to my own children? Be off with you, and leave the dog, I say."

And she clutched Moufflou by his long silky mane and dragged him backwards, while with the other hand she thrust out of the door Lolo and Bice.

Lolo began to hammer with his crutch at the door thus closed on him; but Bice coaxed and entreated him.

"Poor mother has been so worried about Tasso," she pleaded. "And what harm can come to Moufflou? And I do think he was tired, Lolo; the Cascine is a long way; and it is quite true that Aunt 'Nita never liked him."

So by one means and another she coaxed her brother away; and they went almost in silence to where their aunt Anita dwelt, which was across the river, near the dark-red bell-shaped dome of Santa Spirito.

It was true that her aunt had wanted them to mind her room and her babies while she was away carrying home some lace to a villa outside the Roman gate, for she was a lace-washer and clear-starcher by trade. There they had to stay in the little dark room with the two babies, with nothing to amuse the time except the clang of the bells of the church of the Holy Spirit, and the voices of the lemonade sellers shouting in the street below. Aunt Anita did not get back till it was more than dusk, and the two children trotted homeward hand in hand, Lolo's leg dragging itself painfully along, for without Moufflou's white figure dancing on before him he felt very tired indeed. It was pitch dark when they got to Or San Michele, and the lamps burned dully.

Lolo stumped up the stairs wearily, with a vague, dull fear at his small heart.

"Moufflou, Moufflou!" he called. Where was

Moufflou? Always at the first sound of his crutch the poodle came flying towards him. "Moufflou, Moufflou!" he called all the way up the long, dark twisting stone stair. He pushed open the door, and he called again, "Moufflou, Moufflou!"

But no dog answered to his call.

"Mother, where is Moufflou?" he asked, staring with blinking, dazzled eyes into the oil-lit room where his mother sat knitting. Tasso was not then home from work. His mother went on with her knitting; there was an uneasy look on her face.

"Mother, what have you done with Moufflou, *my* Moufflou?" said Lolo, with a look that was almost stern on his ten-year-old face.

Then his mother, without looking up and moving her knitting needles very rapidly, said—

"Moufflou is sold!"

And little Dina, who was a quick, pert child, cried with a shrill voice—

"Mother has sold him for a thousand francs to the foreign gentleman."

"Sold him!"

Lolo grew white and grew cold as ice; he stammered, threw up his hands over his head, gasped a little for breath, then fell down in a dead swoon, his poor useless limb doubled under him.

When Tasso came home that sad night and found his little brother shivering, moaning, and half delirious, and when he heard what had been done, he was sorely grieved.

"Oh, mother, how could you do it?" he cried. "Poor Moufflou! and Lolo loves him so!"

"I have got the money," said his mother feverishly,

"and you will not need to go for a soldier: we can buy your substitute. What is a poodle, that you mourn about it? We can get another poodle for Lolo."

"Another will not be Moufflou," said Tasso, and yet was seized with such a frantic happiness himself at the knowledge that he would not need go to the army, that he too felt as if he were drunk on new wine, and had not the heart to rebuke his mother.

"A thousand francs!" he muttered, "a thousand francs! *Dio mio!* Who could ever have fancied anybody would have given such a price for a common white poodle? One would think the gentleman had bought the church and the tabernacle!"

"Fools and their money are soon parted," said his mother, with cross contempt.

It was true: she had sold Moufflou.

The English gentleman had called on her while Lolo and the dog had been in the Cascine, and had said that he was desirous of buying the poodle, which had so diverted his sick child that the little invalid would not be comforted unless he possessed it. Now, at any other time the good woman would have sturdily refused any idea of selling Moufflou; but that morning the thousand francs which would buy Tasso's substitute were forever in her mind and before her eyes. When she heard the foreigner her heart gave a great leap, and her head swam giddily, and she thought, in a spasm of longing—if she could get those thousand francs! But though she was so dizzy and so upset she retained her grip on her native Florentine shrewdness. She said nothing of her need of the money; not a syllable of her sore distress. On the contrary, she was coy and wary, affected great reluctance to part with her pet, invented a great offer made for him by a director

of a circus, and finally let fall a hint that less than a thousand francs she could never take for poor Moufflou.

The gentleman assented with so much willingness to the price that she instantly regretted not having asked double. He told her that if she would take the poodle that afternoon to his hotel the money should be paid to her; so she despatched her children after their noonday meal in various directions, and herself took Moufflou to his doom. She could not believe her senses when ten hundred franc notes were put into her hand. She scrawled her signature, Rosina Calabucci to a formal receipt, and went away, leaving Moufflou in his new owner's rooms, and hearing his howls and moans pursue her all the way down the staircase and out into the air.

She was not easy at what she had done. "It seemed," she said to herself, "like selling a Christian."

But then to keep her eldest son at home—what a joy that was! On the whole, she cried so and laughed so as she went down the Lung' Arno that once or twice people looked at her, thinking her out of her senses, and a guard spoke to her angrily.

Meanwhile, Lolo was sick and delirious with grief. Twenty times he got out of his bed and screamed to be allowed to go with Moufflou, and twenty times his mother and his brothers put him back again and held him down and tried in vain to quiet him.

The child was beside himself with misery. "Moufflou! Moufflou!" he sobbed at every moment; and by night he was in a raging fever, and when his mother, frightened, ran and called in a doctor of the quarter, that worthy shook his head and said something as to a shock of the nervous system, and muttered a long word—"meningitis."

Lolo took a hatred to the sight of Tasso, and thrust him away, and his mother too.

"It is for you Moufflou is sold," he said, with his little teeth and hands tight clinched.

After a day or two Tasso felt as if he could not bear his life, and went down to the hotel to see if the foreign gentleman would allow him to have Moufflou back for half an hour to quiet his little brother by a sight of him. But at the hotel he was told that the *Milord Inglese* who had bought the dog of Rosina Calabucci had gone that same night of the purchase to Rome, to Naples, to Palermo, *chi sa?*

"And Moufflou with him?" asked Tasso.

"The *barbone* he had bought went with him," said the porter of the hotel. "Such a beast! Howling, shrieking, raging all the day, and all the paint scratched off the *salon* door."

Poor Moufflou! Tasso's heart was heavy as he heard of that sad, helpless misery of their bartered favorite and friend.

"What matter?" said his mother fiercely, when he told her. "A dog is a dog. They will feed him better than we could. In a week he will have forgotten—*chè!*"

But Tasso feared that Moufflou would not forget. Lolo certainly would not. The doctor came to the bedside twice a day, and ice and water were kept on the aching hot little head that had got the malady with the long name, and for the chief part of the time Lolo lay quiet, dull, and stupid, breathing heavily, and then at intervals cried and sobbed and shrieked hysterically for Moufflou.

"Can you not get what he calls for to quiet him with a sight of it?" said the doctor. But that was not possible, and poor Rosina covered her head with her apron and felt a guilty creature.

"Still, you will not go to the army," she said to Tasso, clinging to that immense joy for her consolation. "Only think! We can pay Guido Squarcione to go for you. He always said he would go if anybody would pay him. Oh, my Tasso, surely to keep you is worth a dog's life!"

"And Lolo's?" said Tasso gloomily. "Nay, mother, it works ill to meddle too much with fate. I drew my number; I was bound to go. Heaven would have made it up to you somehow."

"Heaven sent me the foreigner; the Madonna's own self sent him to ease a mother's pain," said Rosina rapidly and angrily. "There are the thousand francs safe to hand in the *cassone,* and what, pray, is it we miss? Only a dog like a sheep, that brought gallons of mud in with him every time it rained, and ate as much as any one of you."

"But Lolo?" said Tasso, under his breath.

His mother was so irritated and so tormented by her own conscience that she upset all the cabbage broth into the burning charcoal.

"Lolo was always a little fool, thinking of nothing but the church and the dog and nasty field flowers," she said angrily. "I humored him ever too much because of the hurt to his hip, and so—and so——"

Then the poor soul made matters worse by dropping her tears into the saucepan, and fanning the charcoal so furiously that the flame caught her fan of cane leaves, and would have burned her arm had not Tasso been there.

"You are my prop and safety always. Who would not have done what I did? Not Santa Felicita herself," she said with a great sob.

But all this did not cure poor Lolo.

The days and the weeks of the golden autumn weather passed away, and he was always in danger, and the small,

close room where he slept with Sandro and Beppo and Tasso was not one to cure such an illness as had now beset him. Tasso went to his work with a sick heart in the Cascine, where the colchicum was all lilac among the meadow grass, and the ashes and elms were taking their first flush of the coming autumnal change. He did not think Lolo would ever get well, and the good lad felt as if he had been the murderer of his little brother.

True, he had had no hand or voice in the sale of Moufflou, but Moufflou had been sold for his sake. It made him feel half guilty, very unhappy, quite unworthy all the sacrifice that had been made for him. "Nobody should meddle with fate," thought Tasso, who knew his grandfather had died in San Bonifazio because he had driven himself mad over the dream book trying to get lucky numbers for the lottery and become a rich man at a stroke.

It was rapture, indeed, to know that he was free of the army for a time at least, that he might go on undisturbed at his healthful labor, and get a raise in wages as time went on, and dwell in peace with his family, and per-haps—perhaps in time earn enough to marry pretty flaxen-haired Biondina, the daughter of the barber in the piazzetta. It was rapture indeed; but then poor Moufflou!—and poor, poor Lolo! Tasso felt as if he had bought his own exemption by seeing his little brother and the good dog torn in pieces and buried alive for his service.

And where was poor Moufflou?

Gone far away somewhere south in the hurrying, screeching, vomiting, braying train that it made Tasso giddy only to look at as it rushed by the green meadows beyond the Cascine on its way to the sea.

"If he could see the dog he cries so for, it might save him," said the doctor, who stood with grave face watching Lolo.

But that was beyond anyone's power. No one could tell where Moufflou was. He might be carried to England, to France, to Russia, to America—who could say? They did not know where his purchaser had gone. Moufflou even might be dead.

The poor mother, when the doctor said that, went and looked at the ten hundred franc notes that were once like angels' faces to her, and said to them—

"Oh, you children of Satan, why did you tempt me? I sold the poor, innocent, trustful beast to get you, and now my child is dying!"

Her eldest son would stay at home, indeed; but if this little lame one died! Rosina Calabucci would have given up the notes and consented never to own five francs in her life if only she could have gone back over the time and kept Moufflou and seen his little master running out with him into the sunshine.

More than a month went by, and Lolo lay in the same state, his yellow hair shorn, his eyes dilated and yet stupid, life kept in him by a spoonful of milk, a lump of ice, a drink of lemon water; always muttering, when he spoke at all, "Moufflou, Moufflou, *dov' è* Moufflou?" and lying for days together in somnolence and unconsciousness, with the fire eating at his brain and the weight lying on it like a stone.

The neighbors were kind, and brought fruit and the like, and sat up with him, and chattered so all at once in one continuous brawl that they were enough in themselves to kill him, for such is ever the Italian fashion of sympathy in all illness.

But Lolo did not get well, did not even seem to see the light at all, or to distinguish any sounds around him; and the doctor in plain words told Rosina Calabucci that her little boy must die. Die, and the church so near! She could not believe it. Could St. Mark, and St. George, and the rest that he had loved so do nothing for him? No, said the doctor, they could do nothing; the dog might do something, since the brain had so fastened on that one idea; but then they had sold the dog.

"Yes, I sold him!" said the poor mother, breaking into floods of remorseful tears.

So at last the end drew so nigh that one twilight time the priest came out of the great arched door that is next St. Mark, with the Host uplifted, and a little acolyte ringing the bell before it, and passed across the piazzetta, and went up the dark staircase of Rosina's dwelling, and passed through the weeping, terrified children, and went to the bedside of Lolo.

Lolo was unconscious, but the holy man touched his little body and limbs with the sacred oil, and prayed over him, and then stood sorrowful with bowed head.

Lolo had had his first communion in the summer, and in his preparation for it had shown an intelligence and devoutness that had won the priest's gentle heart.

Standing there, the holy man commended the innocent soul to God. It was the last service to be rendered to him save that very last of all when the funeral office should be read above his little grave among the millions of nameless dead at the sepulchers of the poor at Trebbiano.

All was still as the priest's voice ceased. Only the sobs of the mother and of the children broke the stillness as they kneeled. The hand of Biondina had stolen into Tasso's.

Suddenly, there was a loud scuffling noise; hurrying feet came patter, patter, patter up the stairs, a ball of mud and dust flew over the heads of the kneeling figures. Fleet as the wind Moufflou dashed through the room and leaped upon the bed.

Lolo opened his heavy eyes, and a sudden light of consciousness gleamed in them like a sunbeam. "Moufflou!" he murmured, in his little thin, faint voice. The big dog pressed close to his breast and kissed his wasted face.

Moufflou was come home!

And Lolo came home, too, for death let go its hold upon him. Little by little, very faintly and flickeringly and very uncertainly at the first, life returned to the poor little body, and reason to the tormented, heated little brain. Moufflou was his physician; Moufflou, who, himself a skeleton under his matted curls, would not stir from his side and looked at him all day long with two beaming brown eyes full of unutterable love.

Lolo was happy; he asked no questions—was too weak, indeed, even to wonder. He had Moufflou; that was enough.

Alas! Though they dared not say so in his hearing, it was not enough for his elders. His mother and Tasso knew that the poodle had been sold and paid for; that they could lay no claim to keep him; and that almost certainly his purchaser would seek him out and assert his indisputable right to him. And then how would Lolo ever bear that second parting?—Lolo, so weak that he weighed no more than if he had been a little bird.

Moufflou had, no doubt, traveled a long distance and suffered much. He was but skin and bone; he bore the marks of blows and kicks; his once silken hair was all

discolored and matted; he had, no doubt, traveled far. But then his purchaser would be sure to ask for him, soon or late, at his old home; and then? Well, then if they did not give him up themselves, the law would make them.

Rosina Calabucci and Tasso, though they dared say nothing before any of the children, felt their hearts in their mouth at every step on the stair, and the first interrogation of Tasso every evening when he came from his work was, "Has anyone come for Moufflou?" For ten days no one came, and their first terrors lulled a little.

On the eleventh morning, a feast day, on which Tasso was not going to his labors in the Cascine, there came a person, with a foreign look, who said the words they so much dreaded to hear: "Has the poodle that you sold to an English gentleman come back to you?"

Yes, his English master claimed him!

The servant said that they had missed the dog in Rome a few days after buying him and taking him there; that he had been searched for in vain, and that his master had thought it possible the animal might have found his way back to his old home: there had been stories of such wonderful sagacity in dogs. Anyhow, he had sent for him on the chance; he was himself back on the Lung' Arno. The servant pulled from his pocket a chain, and said his orders were to take the poodle away at once: the little sick gentleman had fretted very much about his loss.

Tasso heard in a very agony of despair. To take Moufflou away now would be to kill Lolo—Lolo so feeble still, so unable to understand, so passionately alive to every sight and sound of Moufflou, lying for hours together motionless with his hand buried in the poodle's curls, saying nothing, only smiling now and then, and murmuring a word or two in Moufflou's ear.

"The dog did come home," said Tasso, at length, in a low voice. "Angels must have shown him the road, poor beast! From Rome! Only to think of it, from Rome! And he a dumb thing! I tell you he is here, honestly: so will you not trust me just so far as this? Will you let me go with you and speak to the English lord before you take the dog away? I have a little brother sorely ill——"

He could not speak more, for tears that choked his voice.

At last the messenger agreed so far as this: Tasso might go first and see the master, but he would stay here and have a care they did not spirit the dog away—"for a thousand francs were paid for him," added the man, "and a dog that can come all the way from Rome by itself must be an uncanny creature."

Tasso thanked him, went upstairs, was thankful that his mother was at mass and could not dispute with him, took the ten hundred franc notes from the old oak *cassone,* and with them in his breast pocket walked out into the air. He was but a poor working lad, but he had made up his mind to do an heroic deed, for self-sacrifice is always heroic. He went straightway to the hotel where the English *milord* was, and when he had got there remembered that still he did not know the name of Moufflou's owner; but the people of the hotel knew him as Rosina Calabucci's son, and guessed what he wanted, and said the gentleman who had lost the poodle was within upstairs and they would tell him.

Tasso waited some half hour with his heart beating sorely against the packet of hundred franc notes. At last he was beckoned upstairs, and there he saw a foreigner with a mild fair face, and a very lovely lady, and a delicate child who was lying on a couch. "Moufflou! Where is

Moufflou?" cried the little child impatiently, as he saw the youth enter.

Tasso took his hat off and stood in the doorway an embrowned, healthy, not ungraceful figure, in his working clothes of rough blue stuff.

"If you please, most illustrious," he stammered, "poor Moufflou has come home."

The child gave a cry of delight; the gentleman and lady one of wonder. Come home! All the way from Rome!

"Yes, he has, most illustrious," said Tasso, gaining courage and eloquence, "and now I want to beg something of you. We are poor, and I drew a bad number, and it was for that my mother sold Moufflou. For myself, I did not know anything of it, but she thought she would buy my substitute, and of course she could. But Moufflou is come home, and my little brother Lolo, the little boy your most illustrious first saw playing with the poodle, fell ill of the grief of losing Moufflou, and for a month has lain saying nothing sensible, but only calling for the dog, and my old grandfather died of worrying himself mad over the lottery numbers, and Lolo was so near dying that the Blessed Host had been brought, and the holy oil had been put on him, when all at once there rushes in Moufflou, skin and bone, and covered with mud, and at the sight of him Lolo comes back to his senses, and that is now ten days ago, and though Lolo is still as weak as a newborn thing, he is always sensible, and takes what we give him to eat, and lies always looking at Moufflou and smiling, and saying, 'Moufflou, Moufflou!' and, most illustrious, I know well you have bought the dog, and the law is with you, and by the law you claim it; but I thought perhaps, as Lolo loves him so, you would let us keep the dog, and would take back the thousand francs, and myself I will go

and be a soldier, and heaven will take care of them all somehow."

Then Tasso, having said all this in one breathless, monotonous recitative, took the thousand francs out of his breast pocket and held them out timidly towards the foreign gentleman, who motioned them aside and stood silent.

"Did you understand, Victor?" he said, at last, to his little son.

The child hid his face in his cushions.

"Yes, I did understand something. Let Lolo keep him; Moufflou was not happy with me."

But he burst out crying as he said it.

Moufflou had run away from him.

Moufflou had never loved him, for all his sweet cakes and fond caresses and platefuls of delicate savory meats. Moufflou had run away and found his own road over two hundred miles and more to go back to some little hungry children, who never had enough to eat themselves, and so, certainly, could never give enough to eat to the dog. Poor little boy! He was so rich and so pampered and so powerful, and yet he could never make Moufflou love him!

Tasso, who understood nothing that was said, laid the ten hundred franc notes down on a table near him.

"If you would take them, most illustrious, and give me back what my mother wrote when she sold Moufflou," he said timidly, "I would pray for you night and day, and Lolo would, too. And as for the dog, we will get a puppy and train him for your little *signorino*. They can all do tricks, more or less, it comes by nature; and as for me, I will go to the army willingly; it is not right to interfere with fate; my old grandfather died mad because he would

try to be a rich man, by dreaming about it and pulling destiny by the ears, as if she were a kicking mule; only, I do pray of you, do not take away Moufflou. And to think he trotted all those miles and miles, and you carried him by train, too, and he never could have seen the road, and he had no power of speech to ask———"

Tasso broke down again in his eloquence, and drew the back of his hand across his wet eyelashes.

The English gentleman was not altogether unmoved.

"Poor faithful dog!" he said, with a sigh. "I am afraid we were very cruel to him, meaning to be kind. No, we will not claim him, and I do not think you should go for a soldier; you seem so good a lad, and your mother must need you. Keep the money, my boy, and in payment you shall train the puppy you talk of, and bring him to my little boy. I will come and see your mother and Lolo tomorrow. All the way from Rome! What wonderful sagacity! What matchless fidelity!"

You can imagine, without any telling of mine, the joy that reigned in Moufflou's home when Tasso returned thither with the money and the good tidings both. His substitute was bought without a day's delay, and Lolo rapidly recovered. As for Moufflou, he could never tell them his troubles, his wanderings, his difficulties, his perils. He could never tell them by what miraculous knowledge he had found his way across Italy, from the gates of Rome to the gates of Florence. But he soon grew plump again, and merry, and his love for Lolo was yet greater than before.

By the winter all the family went to live on an estate near Spezia that the English gentleman had purchased, and there Moufflou was happier than ever. The little English boy is gaining strength in the soft air, and he and

Lolo are great friends and play with Moufflou and the poodle puppy half the day upon the sunny terraces and under the green orange boughs. Tasso is one of the gardeners there; he will have to serve as a soldier probably in some category or another, but he is safe for the time, and is happy. Lolo, whose lameness will always exempt him from military service, when he grows to be a man means to be a florist, and a great one. He has learned to read, as the first step on the road of his ambition.

"But oh, Moufflou, how *did* you find your way home?" he asks the dog a hundred times a week.

How indeed!

No one ever knew how Moufflou had made that long journey on foot, so many weary miles; but beyond a doubt he had done it alone and unaided, for if anyone had helped him they would have come home with him to claim the reward.

And that you may not wonder too greatly at Moufflou's miraculous journey on his four bare feet, I will add here two facts known to friends of mine, of whose truthfulness there can be no doubt.

One concerns a French poodle who was purchased in Paris by the friend of my friend, and brought all the way from Paris to Milan by train. In a few days after his arrival in Milan the poodle was missing; and nothing more was heard or known of him until many weeks later his quondam owner in Paris, on opening his door one morning, found the dog stretched dying on the threshold of his old home.

That is one fact; not a story, mind you, *a fact*.

The other is related to me by an Italian nobleman, who in his youth belonged to the Guardia Nobile of Tuscany. That brilliant corps of elegant gentlemen owned a regi-

mental pet, a poodle also, a fine merry and handsome dog of its kind; and the officers all loved and made much of him, except, alas! the commandant of the regiment, who hated him, because when the officers were on parade or riding in escort the poodle was sure to be jumping and frisking about in front of them. It is difficult to see where the harm of this was, but this odious old martinet vowed vengeance against the dog, and, being of course all powerful in his own corps, ordered the exile from Florence of the poor fellow. He was sent to a farm at Prato, twenty miles off, along the hills; but very soon he found his way back to Florence. He was then sent to Leghorn, forty miles off, but in a week's time had returned to his old comrades. He was then, by order of his unrelenting foe, shipped to the island of Sardinia. How he did it no one ever could tell, for he was carried safely to Sardinia and placed inland there in kind custody, but in some wonderful way the poor dog must have found out the sea and hidden himself on board a returning vessel, for in a month's time from his exile to the island he was back again among his comrades in Florence. Now, what I have to tell you almost breaks my heart to say, and will, I think, quite break yours to hear: alas! the brute of a commandant, untouched by such marvelous cleverness and faithfulness, was his enemy to the bitter end, and, in inexorable hatred, *had him shot!* Oh, when you grow to manhood and have power, use it with tenderness!

THE CHILD OF URBINO

*He took a jewel hung on a gold chain and threw it
over Raffaelle's shoulders*

THE CHILD OF URBINO

I⊤ was in the year of grace 1490, in the reign of
Guidobaldo, Lord of Montefeltro, Duke of Urbino—the
year, by the way, of the birth of that most illustrious and
gracious lady Vittoria Colonna.

It was in the spring of the year, in that mountain eyrie
beloved of the Muses and coveted of the Borgia, that a
little boy stood looking out of a grated casement into the
calm sunshiny day. He was a pretty boy, with hazel eyes,
and fair hair cut straight above his brows; he wore a little
blue tunic with some embroidery about the throat of it,
and had in his hand a little round flat cap of the same
color. He was sad of heart this merry morning, for a dear
friend of his, a friend ten years older than himself, had
gone the night before on a journey over the mountains to
Maestro Francesco at Bologna, there to be bound apprentice to that gentle artist. This friend, Timoteo della Vita,
had been very dear to the child, had played with him and
jested with him, made him toys and told him stories, and
he was very full of pain at Timoteo's loss. Yet he told

himself not to mind, for had not Timoteo said to him, "I go as goldsmith's 'prentice to the best of men; but I mean to become a painter"? And the child understood that to be a painter was to be the greatest and wisest the world held; he quite understood that, for he was Raffaelle, the seven-year-old son of Signor Giovanni Sanzio.

He was a very happy little boy here in this stately yet homely and kindly Urbino, where his people had come for refuge when the lances of Malatesta had ravaged and ruined their homestead. He had the dearest old grandfather in all the world; he had a loving mother, and he had a father who was very tender to him, and painted him among the angels of heaven, and was always full of pleasant conceits and admirable learning, and such true love of art that the child breathed it with every breath, as he could breathe the sweetness of a cowslip bell when he held one in his hands up to his nostrils.

It was good in those days to live in old Urbino. It was not, indeed, so brilliant a place as it became in a later day, when Ariosto came there, and Bembo and Castiglione and many another witty and learned gentleman, and the Courts of Love were held with ingenious rhyme and pretty sentiment, sad only for wantonness. But, if not so brilliant, it was homelier, simpler, full of virtue, with a wise peace and tranquillity that joined hands with a stout courage. The burgher was good friends with his prince, and knew that in any trouble or perplexity he could go up to the palace, or stop the duke in the market place, and be sure of sympathy and good counsel. There were a genuine love of beautiful things, a sense of public duty and of public spirit, a loyal temper and a sage contentment, among the good people of that time, which made them happy and prosperous.

All work was solidly and thoroughly done, living was cheap, and food good and plentiful, much better and more plentiful than it is now; in the fine old houses every stone was sound, every bit of ornament well wrought, men made their nests to live in and to pass to their children and children's children after them, and had their own fancies and their own traditions recorded in the ironwork of their casements and in the woodwork of their doors. They had their happy day of honest toil from matins bell to evensong, and then walked out or sat about in the calm evening air and looked down on the plains below that were rich with grain and fruit and woodland, and talked and laughed among each other, and were content with their own pleasant, useful lives, not burnt up with envy of desire to be someone else, as in our sickly, hurrying time most people are.

Yes, life must have been very good in those old days in old Urbino, better than it is anywhere in ours.

Can you not picture to yourself good, shrewd, wise Giovanni Sanzio, with his old father by his side, and his little son running before him, in the holy evening time of a feast day, with the deep church bells swaying above head, and the last sun rays smiting the frescoed walls, the stone bastions, the blazoned standard on the castle roof, the steep city rocks shelving down into the greenery of cheery orchard and of pear tree? I can, whenever I shut my eyes and recall Urbino as it was; and would it had been mine to live then in that mountain home, and meet that divine child going along his happy smiling way, garnering unconsciously in his infant soul all the beautiful sights and sounds around him, to give them in his manhood to the world.

"Let him alone: he will paint all this some day," said

his wise father, who loved to think that his brushes and his colors would pass in time to Raffaelle, whose hands would be stronger to hold them than his own had been. And, whether he would ever paint it or not, the child never tired of thus looking from his eyrie on the rocks and counting all that passed below through the blowing corn under the leafy orchard boughs.

There were so many things to see in Urbino in that time, looking so over the vast green valley below: a clump of spears, most likely, as men-at-arms rode through the trees; a string of market folk bringing in the produce of the orchards or the fields; perchance a red-robed cardinal on a white mule with glittering housings, behind him a sumpter train rich with baggage, furniture, gold and silver plate; maybe the duke's hunting party going out or coming homeward with caracoling steeds, beautiful hounds straining at their leash, hunting horns sounding merrily over the green country; maybe a band of free lances, with plumes tossing, steel glancing, bannerets fluttering against the sky; or maybe a quiet gray-robed string of monks or pilgrims singing the hymn sung before Jerusalem, treading the long lush grass with sandaled feet, coming towards the city, to crowd slowly and gladly up its rocky height. Do you not wish with me you could stand in the window with Raffaelle to see the earth as it was then?

No doubt the good folks of Urbino laughed at him often for a little moonstruck dreamer, so many hours did he standing looking, looking—only looking—as eyes have a right to do that see well and not altogether as others see.

Happily for him, the days of his childhood were times of peace, and he did not behold, as his father had done,

the torches light up the street and the flames devour the homesteads.

At this time Urbino was growing into fame for its pottery work; those big dishes and bowls, those marriage plates and pharmacy jars, which it made, were beginning to rival the products of its neighbor Gubbio, and when its duke wished to send a bridal gift, or a present on other festal occasions, he oftenest chose some service or some rare platter of his own Urbino ware. Now, pottery had not then taken the high place among the arts of Italy that it was destined very soon to do. As you will learn when you are older, after the Greeks and the Christians had exhausted all that was beautiful in shape and substance of clay vases, the art seemed to die out, and the potters and the pottery painters died with it, or at any rate went to sleep for a great many centuries, while soldiers and prelates, nobles and mercenaries were trampling to and fro all over the land and disputing it, and carrying fire and torch, steel and desolation, with them in their quarrels and covetousness. But now, the reign of the late good duke, great Federigo, having been favorable to the Marches (as we call his province now), the potters and pottery painters, with other gentle craftsmen, had begun to look up again, and the beneficent fires of their humble ovens had begun to burn in Castel Durante, in Pesaro, in Faenza, in Gubbio, and in Urbino itself. The great days had not yet come: Maestro Giorgio was but a youngster, and Orazio Fontane not born, nor the clever baker Prestino either, nor the famous Fra Xanto; but there was a Don Giorgio even then in Gubbio, of whose work, alas! one plate now at the Louvre is all we have; and here in the ducal city on the hill rich and noble things were already being made in the stout and lustrous majolica that was

destined to acquire later on no wide a ceramic fame. Jars and bowls and platters, oval dishes and ewers and basins, and big-bodied, metal-welded pharmacy vases were all made and painted at Urbino while Raffaelle Sanzio was running about on rosy infantine feet. There was a master potter of the Montefeltro at that time, one Maestro Benedetto Ronconi, whose name had not become world-renowned as Orazio Fontane's and Maestro Giorgio's did in the following century, yet in that day enjoyed the honor of all the duchy, and did things very rare and fine in the Urbino ware. He lived within a stone's throw of Giovanni Sanzio, and was a gray-haired, handsome, somewhat stern and pompous man, now more than middle-aged, who had one beauteous daughter, by name Pacifica. He cherished Pacifica well, but not so well as he cherished the things he wrought—the deep round nuptial plates and oval massive dishes that he painted with Scriptural stories and strange devices, and landscapes such as those he saw around, and flowing scrolls with Latin mottoes in black letters, and which, when thus painted, he consigned with an anxiously beating heart to the trial of the ovens, and which sometimes came forth from the trial all cracked and blurred and marred, and sometimes emerged in triumph and came into his trembling hands iridescent and lovely with those lustrous and opaline hues which we admire in them to this day as the especial glory of majolica.

Maestro Benedetto was an ambitious and vain man, and had had a hard, laborious manhood, working at his potter's wheel and painter's brush before Urbino ware was prized in Italy or even in the duchy. Now, indeed, he was esteemed at his due worth, and his work was also, and he was passably rich, and known as a good artist beyond

the Marches; but there was a younger man over at Gubbio, the Don Giorgio who was precursor of unequaled Maestro Giorgio Andreoli, who surpassed him, and made him sleep o' nights on thorns, as envy makes all those to do who take her as their bedfellow.

The house of Maestro Benedetto was a long stone building, with a loggia at the back all overclimbed by hardy rose trees, and looking on a garden that was more than half an orchard, and in which grew abundantly pear trees, plum trees, and wood strawberries. The lancet windows of his workshop looked on all this quiet greenery. There were so many such pleasant workshops then in the land—calm, godly, homelike places, filled from without with song of birds and scent of herbs and blossoms. Nowadays men work in crowded, stinking cities, in close factory chambers; and their work is barren as their lives are.

The little son of neighbor Sanzio ran in and out this bigger, wider house and garden of Maestro Benedetto at his pleasure, for the maiden Pacifica was always glad to see him, and even the somber master potter would unbend to him and show him how to lay the color on to the tremulous fugitive unbaked biscuit.

Pacifica was a lovely young woman of some seventeen or eighteen summers; and perhaps Raffaelle was but remembering her when he painted in his afteryears the face of his Madonna di San Sisto. He loved her as he loved everything that was beautiful and everyone who was kind; and almost better than his own beloved father's studio, almost better than his dear old grandsire's cheerful little shop, did he love this grave, silent, sweet-smelling, sun-pierced, shadowy old house of Maestro Benedetto.

Maestro Benedetto had four apprentices or pupils in

that time learning to become *figuli*, but the one whom Raffaelle liked the most (and Pacifica, too) was one Luca Torelli, of a village above in the mountains—a youth with a noble, dark pensive beauty of his own, and a fearless gait, and a supple, tall, slender figure that would have looked well in the light coat of mail and silken doublet of a man-at-arms. In sooth, the spirit of Messer Luca was more made for war and its risks and glories than for the wheel and the brush of the bottega. But he had loved Pacifica ever since he had come down one careless holy day into Urbino, and had bound himself to her father's service in a heedless moment of eagerness to breathe the same air and dwell under the same roof as she did. He had gained little for his pains: to see her at mass and at mealtimes, now and then to be allowed to bring water from the well for her or feed her pigeons, to see her gray gown go down between the orchard trees and catch the sunlight, to hear the hum of her spinning wheel, the thrum of her viol—this was the uttermost he got of joy in two long years; and how he envied Raffaelle running along the stone floor of the loggia to leap into her arms, to hang upon her skirts, to pick the summer fruit with her, and sort with her the autumn herbs for drying!

"I love Pacifica!" he would say, with a groan, to Raffaelle. And Raffaelle would say, with a smile, "Ah, Luca, so do I!"

"It is not the same thing, my dear," sighed Luca; "I want her for my wife."

"I shall have no wife; I shall marry myself to painting," said Raffaelle, with a little grave wise face looking out from under the golden roof of his fair hair. For he was never tired of watching his father painting the saints with their branch of palm on their ground of blue or of

gold, or Maestro Benedetto making the dull clay glow with angels' wings and prophets' robes and holy legends told in color.

Now, one day as Raffaelle was standing and looking thus at his favorite window in the potter's house, his friend the handsome, black-browed Luca, who was also standing there, did sigh so deeply and so deplorably that the child was startled from his dreams.

"Good Luca, what ails you?" he murmured, winding his arms about the young man's knees.

"Oh, 'Faello!" mourned the apprentice woefully. "Here is such a chance to win the hand of Pacifica if only I had talent—such talent as that Giorgio of Gubbio has! If the good Lord had only gifted me with a master's skill, instead of all this bodily strength and sinew, like a wild hog of the woods, which avails me nothing here!"

"What chance is it?" asked Raffaelle, "and what is there new about Pacifica? She has told me nothing, and I was with her an hour."

"Dear simple one, she knows nothing of it," said Luca, heaving another tremendous sigh from his heart's deepest depths. "You must know that a new order has come in this very forenoon from the duke; he wishes a dish and a jar of the very finest and firmest majolica to be painted with the story of Esther, and made ready in three months from this date, to then go as his gifts to his cousins of Gonzaga. He has ordered that no cost be spared in the work, but that the painting thereof be of the best that can be produced, and the prize he will give is fifty scudi. Now, Maestro Benedetto, having known some time, it seems, of this order, has had made in readiness several large oval dishes and beautiful big-bellied jars: he gives one of each to each of his pupils—to myself, to

Berengario, to Tito, and Zenone. The master is sorely distraught that his eyesight permits him not himself to execute the duke's commands; but it is no secret that should one of us be so fortunate as to win the duke's approbation, the painter who does so shall become his partner here and shall have the hand of Pacifica. Some say that he has only put forth this promise as a stimulus to get the best work done of which his bottega is capable; but I know Maestro Benedetto too well to deem him guilty of any such evasion. What he has said he will carry out; if the vase and the dish win the duke's praise, they will also win Pacifica. Now you see, 'Faello mine, why I am so bitterly sad of heart, for I am a good craftsman enough at the wheel and the furnace, and I like not ill the handling and the molding of the clay, but at the painting of the clay I am but a tyro, and Berengario or even the little Zenone will beat me. Of that I am sure."

Raffaelle heard all this in silence, leaning his elbows on his friend's knee, and his chin on the palms of his own hands. He knew that the other pupils were better painters by far than his Luca, though not one of them was such a good-hearted or noble-looking youth, and for none of them did the maiden Pacifica care.

"How long a time is given for the jar and the dish to be ready?" he asked, at length.

"Three months, my dear," said Luca, with a sigh sadder than ever. "But if it were three years, what difference would it make? You cannot cudgel the divine grace of art into a man with blows as you cudgel speed into a mule, and I shall be a dolt at the end of the time as I am now. What said your good father to me but yesternight?—and he *is* good to me and does not despise me. He said, 'Luca, my son, it is of no more for you to

sigh for Pacifica than for the moon. Were she mine I would give her to you, for you have a heart of gold, but Signor Benedetto will not; for never, I fear me, will you be able to decorate anything more than an apothecary's mortar or a barber's basin. If I hurt you, take it not ill; I mean kindness, and were I a stalwart youth like you I would go try my fortunes in the Free Companies in France or Spain, or down in Rome, for you are made for a soldier.' That was the best even your father could say for me, 'Faello."

"But Pacifica," said the child—"Pacifica would not wish you to join the Free Companies?"

"God knows," said Luca hopelessly. "Perhaps she would not care."

"I am sure she would," said Raffaelle, "for she does love you, Luca, though she cannot say so, being but a girl, and Signor Benedetto against you. But that redcap you tamed for her, how she loves it, how she caresses it, and half is for you, Luca, half for the bird!"

Luca kissed him.

But the tears rolled down the poor youth's face, for he was much in earnest and filled with despair.

"Even if she did, if she do," he murmured hopelessly, "she never will let me know it, since her father forbids a thought of me; and now here is this trial of skill at the duke's order come to make things worse, and if that swaggering Berengario of Fano win her, then truly will I join the free lances and pray heaven send me swift shrive and shroud."

Raffaelle was very pensive for a while; then he raised his head and said—

"I have thought of something, Luca. But I do not know whether you will let me try it."

"You angel child! What would your old Luca deny to you? But as for helping me, my dear, put that thought out of your little mind forever, for no one can help me, 'Faello, not the saints themselves, since I was born a dolt!"

Raffaello kissed him and said, "Now listen!"

A few days later Signor Benedetto informed his pupils in ceremonious audience of the duke's command and of his own intentions; he did not pronounce his daughter's name to the youths, but he spoke in terms that were clear enough to assure them that whoever had the good fortune and high merit to gain the duke's choice of his pottery should have the honor of becoming associate in his own famous bottega. Now, it had been known in Urbino ever since Pacifica had gone to her first communion that whoever pleased her father well enough to become his partner would have also to please her as her husband. Not much attention was given to maidens' wishes in those times, and no one thought the master potter either unjust or cruel in thus suiting himself before he suited his daughter. And what made the hearts of all the young men quake and sink the lowest was the fact that Signor Benedetto offered the competition not only to his own apprentices but to any native of the duchy of Urbino. For who could tell what hero might not step forth from obscurity and gain the great prize of this fair hand of Pacifica's? And with her hand would go many a broad gold ducat, and heritage of the wide old gray stone house, and many an old jewel and old brocade that were kept there in dusky sweet-smelling cabinets, and also more than one good piece of land, smiling with corn and fruit trees, outside the gates in the lower pastures to the westward.

Luca, indeed, never thought of these things, but the other three pupils did, and other youths as well. Had it not been for the limitation as to birth within the duchy, many a gallant young painter from the other side of the Apennines, many a lusty *vasalino* or *baccalino* from the workshops of fair Florence herself, or from the Lombard cities, might have traveled there in hot haste as fast as horses could carry them, and come to paint the clay for the sake of so precious a recompense. But Urbino men they had to be; and poor Luca, who was so full of despair that he could almost have thrown himself headlong from the rocks, was thankful to destiny for even so much slender mercy as this—that the number of his rivals was limited.

"Had I been you," Giovanni Sanzio ventured once to say respectfully to Signor Benedetto, "I think I should have picked out for my son-in-law the best youth that I knew, not the best painter; for be it said in all reverence, my friend, the greatest artist is not always the truest man, and by the hearthstone humble virtues have sometimes high claim."

Then Signor Benedetto had set his stern face like a flint, knowing very well what youth Messer Giovanni would have liked to name to him.

"I have need of a good artist in my bottega to keep up its fame," he had said stiffly. "My vision is not what it was, and I should be loath to see Urbino ware fall back, while Pesaro and Gubbio and Castel-Durante gain ground every day. Pacifica must pay the penalty, if penalty there be, for being the daughter of a great artist."

Mirthful, keen-witted Sanzio smiled to himself and went his way in silence; for he who loved Andrea

Mantegna did not bow down in homage before the old
master potter's estimation of himself, which was in truth
somewhat overweening in its vanity.

"Poor Pacifica!" he thought. "If only my 'Faello were
but some decade older!"

He, who could not foresee the future, the splendid,
wondrous, unequaled future that awaited his young son,
wished nothing better for him than a peaceful painter's
life here in old Urbino, under the friendly shadow of the
Montefeltro's palace walls.

Meanwhile, where think you was Raffaelle? Half the
day, or all the day, and every day whenever he could?
Where think you was he? Well, in the attic of Luca,
before a bowl and a dish almost as big as himself. The
attic was a breezy, naked place, underneath the arches
supporting the roof of Maestro Benedetto's dwelling.
Each pupil had one of these garrets to himself—a rare
boon, for which Luca came to be very thankful, for
without it he could not have sheltered his angel; and the
secret that Raffaelle had whispered to him that day of the
first conference had been, "Let *me* try and paint it!"

For a long time Luca had been afraid to comply, had
only forborne indeed from utter laughter at the idea from
his love and reverence for the little speaker. Baby
Sanzio, who was only just seven years old as the April
tulips reddened the corn, painting a majolica dish and
vase to go to the Gonzaga of Mantua! The good fellow
could scarcely restrain his shouts of mirth at the auda-
cious fancy; and nothing had kept him grave but the sight
of that most serious face of Raffaelle, looking up to his
with serene, sublime self-confidence, nay, perhaps, rather,
confidence in heaven and in heaven's gifts.

"Let me try!" said the child a hundred times. He

would tell no one, only Luca would know.   And if he failed—well, there would only be the spoiled pottery to pay for, and had he not two whole ducats that the duke had given him when the court had come to behold his father's designs for the altar frescoes at San Dominico di Calgi?

So utterly in earnest was he, and so intense and blank was Luca's absolute despair, that the young man had in turn given way to his entreaties.   "Never can I do aught," he thought bitterly, looking at his own clumsy designs. "And sometimes by the help of cherubs the saints work miracles."

"It will be no miracle," said Raffaelle, hearing him murmur this, "it will be myself, and that which the dear God has put into me."

From that hour Luca let him do what he would, and through all these lovely early summer days the child came and shut himself up in the garret, and studied, and thought, and worked, and knitted his pretty fair brows, and smiled in tranquil satisfaction, according to the mood he was in and the progress of his labors.

Giovanni Sanzio went away at that time to paint an altarpiece over at Città di Castello, and his little son for once was glad he was absent.   Messer Giovanni would surely have remarked the long and frequent visits of Raffaelle to the attic, and would, in all likelihood, have obliged him to pore over his Latin or to take exercise in the open fields; but his mother said nothing, content that he should be amused and safe, and knowing well that Pacifica loved him and would let him come to no harm under her roof.   Pacifica herself did wonder that he deserted her so perpetually for the garret.   But one day when she questioned him the sweet-faced rogue clung to

her and murmured, "Oh, Pacifica, I do want Luca to win
you, because he loves you so; and I do love you both!"
And she grew pale, and answered him, "Ah, dear, if he
could!" and then said never a word more, but went to her
distaff; and Raffaelle saw great tears fall off her lashes
down among the flax.

She thought he went to the attic to watch how Luca
painted, and loved him more than ever for that, but knew
in the hopelessness of her heart—as Luca also knew it in
his—that the good and gallant youth would never be able
to create anything that would go as the duke's gifts to the
Gonzaga of Mantua.   And she did care for Luca!   She
had spoken to him but rarely indeed, yet passing in and
out of the same doors, and going to the same church
offices, and dwelling always beneath the same roof, he
had found means of late for a word, a flower, a serenade.
And he was so handsome and so brave, and so gentle, too,
and so full of deference.   Poor Pacifica cared not in the
least whether he could paint or not.   He could have made
her happy.

In the attic Raffaelle passed the most anxious hours of
all his sunny little life.   He would not allow Luca even to
look at what he did.   He barred the door and worked;
when he went away he locked his work up in a wardrobe.
The swallows came in and out of the unglazed window,
and fluttered all around him; the morning sunbeams came
in too, and made a nimbus round his golden head, like
that which his father gilded above the heads of saints.
Raffaelle worked on, not looking off, though clang of
trumpet, or fanfare of cymbal, often told him there was
much going on worth looking at down below.   He was
only seven years old, but he labored as earnestly as if he
were a man grown, his little rosy fingers gripping that

pencil which was to make him in life and death famous as kings are not famous, and let his tender body lie in its last sleep in the Pantheon of Rome.

He had covered hundreds of sheets with designs before he had succeeded in getting embodied the ideas that haunted him. When he had pleased himself at last, he set to work to transfer his imaginations to the clay in color in the subtile luminous metallic enamel that characterizes Urbino majolica.

Ah, how glad he was now that his father had let him draw from the time he was two years old, and that of late Messer Benedetto had shown him something of the mysteries of painting on biscuit and producing the metallic luster which was the especial glory of the pottery of the duchy!

How glad he was, and how his little heart bounded and seemed to sing in this his first enjoyment of the joyous liberties and powers of creative work!

A well-known writer has said that genius is the power of taking pains; he should have said rather that genius *has* this power also, but that first and foremost it possesses the power of spontaneous and exquisite production without effort and with delight.

Luca looked at him (not at his work, for the child had made him promise not to do so) and began to marvel at his absorption, his intentness, the evident facility with which he worked. The little figure, leaning over the great dish on the bare board of the table, with the oval opening of the window and the blue sky beyond it, began to grow sacred to him with more than the sanctity of childhood. Raffaelle's face grew very serious, too, and lost its color, and his large hazel eyes looked very big and grave and dark.

"Perhaps Signor Giovanni will be angry with me if ever he knows," thought poor Luca, but it was too late to alter anything now. The child Sanzio had become his master.

So Raffaelle, unknown to anyone else, worked on and on there in the attic while the tulips bloomed and withered, and the honeysuckle was in flower in the hedges, and the wheat and barley were being cut in the quiet fields lying far down below in the sunshine. For midsummer was come; the three months all but a week had passed by. It was known that everyone was ready to compete for the duke's choice.

One afternoon Raffaelle took Luca by the hand and said to him, "Come."

He led the young man up to the table, beneath the unglazed window, where he had passed so many of these ninety days of the spring and summer.

Luca gave a great cry, and stood gazing, gazing, gazing. Then he fell on his knees and embraced the little feet of the child: it was the first homage that he, whose life became one beautiful song of praise, received from man.

"Dear Luca," he said softly, "do not do that. If it be indeed good, let us thank God."

What his friend saw were the great oval dish and the great jar or vase standing with the sunbeams full upon them, and the brushes and the tools and the colors all strewn around. And they shone with lustrous opaline hues and wondrous flame-like glories and gleaming iridescence, like melted jewels, and there were all manner of graceful symbols and classic designs wrought upon them; and their borders were garlanded with cherubs and flowers, bearing the arms of Montefeltro, and the landscapes were the tender, homely landscapes round about

Urbino; and the mountains had the solemn radiance that the Apennines wore at evening time, and amidst the figures there was one supreme, white-robed, golden-crowned Esther, to whom the child painter had given the face of Pacifica. And this wondrous creation, wrought by a baby's hand, had safely and secretly passed the ordeal of the furnace, and had come forth without spot or flaw.

Luca ceased not from kneeling at the feet of Raffaelle, as ever since has kneeled the world.

"Oh, wondrous boy! Oh, angel sent unto men!" sighed the poor 'prentice, as he gazed and his heart was so full that he burst into tears.

"Let us thank God," said little Raffaelle again; and he joined his small hands that had wrought this miracle, and said his Laus Domini.

When the precious jar and the platter were removed to the wardrobe and shut up in safety behind the steel wards of the locker, Luca said, timidly, feeling twenty years in age behind the wisdom of this divine child, "But, dearest boy, I do not see how your marvelous and most exquisite accomplishment can advantage me. Even if you would allow it to pass as mine, I could not accept such a thing: it would be a fraud, a shame: not even to win Pacifica could I consent."

"Be not so hasty, good friend," said Raffaelle. "Wait just a little longer yet and see. I have my own idea. Do trust in me."

"Heaven speaks in you, that I believe," said Luca humbly.

Raffaelle answered not, but ran downstairs, and passing Pacifica, threw his arms about her in more than his usual affectionate caresses.

"Pacifica, be of good heart," he murmured, and would not be questioned, but ran homeward to his mother.

"Can it be that Luca has done well?" thought Pacifica; but she feared the child's wishes had outrun his wisdom. He could not be any judge, a child of seven years, even though he were the son of that good and honest painter and poet Giovanni Sanzio.

The next morning was midsummer day. Now, the pottery was all to be placed on this forenoon in the bottega of Signor Benedetto; and the Duke Guidobaldo was then to come and make his choice from amidst them; and the master potter, a little because he was a courtier, and more because he liked to affect a mighty indifference and to show he had no favoritism, and declared that he would not himself see the competing works of art until the eyes of the Lord of Montefeltro also fell upon them.

As for Pacifica, she had locked herself in her chamber, alone with her intense agitation. The young men were swaggering about, and taunting each other, and boasting. Luca alone sat apart, thrumming an old lute. Giovanni Sanzio, who had ridden home at evening from Città di Castello, came in from his own house and put his hand on the youth's shoulder.

"I hear the Pesaro men have brought fine things. Take courage, my lad. Maybe we can entreat the duke to dissuade Pacifica's father from this tyrannous disposal of her hand."

Luca shook his head wearily.

There would be one beautiful thing there, indeed, he knew; but what use would that be to him?

"The child—the child——" he stammered, and then remembered that he must not disclose Raffaelle's secret.

"My child?" said Signor Giovanni. "Oh, he will be

here; he will be sure to be here. Wherever there is a painted thing to be seen, there always, be sure, is Raffaelle."

Then the good man sauntered within from the loggia, to exchange salutations with Ser Benedetto, who, in a suit of fine crimson with doublet of sand-colored velvet, was standing ready to advance bareheaded into the street as soon as the hoofs of the duke's charger should strike on the stones.

"You must be anxious in your thoughts," said Signor Giovanni to him. "They say a youth from Pesaro brings something fine: if you should find yourself bound to take a stranger into your workroom and your home——"

"If he be a man of genius he will be welcome," answered Messer Ronconi pompously. "Be he of Pesaro, or of Fano, or of Castel-Durante, I go not back from my word. I keep my word, to my own hindrance even, ever."

"Let us hope it will bring you only joy and triumph here," said his neighbor, who knew him to be an honest man and a true, if overobstinate and too vain of his own place in Urbino.

"Our lord the duke!" shouted the people standing in the street and Ser Benedetto walked out with stately tread to receive the honor of his master's visit to his bottega.

Raffaelle slipped noiselessly up to his father's side, and slid his little hand into Sanzio's.

"You are not surely afraid of our good Guidobaldo!" said his father, with a laugh and some little surprise, for Raffaelle was very pale, and his lower lip trembled a little.

"No," said the child simply.

The young duke and his court came riding down the

street, and paused before the old stone house of the master potter—splendid gentlemen, though only in their morning apparel, with noble Barbary steeds fretting under them, and little pages and liveried varlets about their steps.   Usually, unless he went hunting or on a visit to some noble, Guidobaldo, like his father, walked about Urbino like any one of his citizens; but he knew the pompous and somewhat vainglorious temper of Messer Benedetto, and good-naturedly was willing to humor its harmless vanities.   Bowing to the ground, the master potter led the way, walking backward into his bottega; the courtiers followed their prince; Giovanni Sanzio with his little son and a few other privileged persons went in also at due distance.   At the farther end of the workshop stood the pupils and the artists from Pesaro and other places in the duchy whose works were there in competition.   In all there were some ten competitors: poor Luca, who had set his own work on the table with the rest as he was obliged to do, stood hindmost of all, shrinking back, to hide his misery, into the deepest shadow of the deep-bayed latticed window.

On the narrow deal benches that served as tables on working days to the pottery painters were ranged the dishes and the jars, with a number attached to each—no name to any, because Signor Benedetto was resolute to prove his own absolute disinterestedness in the matter of choice: he wished for the best artist.   Prince Guidobaldo, doffing his plumed cap courteously, walked down the long room and examined each production in its turn.   On the whole, the collection made a brave display of majolica, though he was perhaps a little disappointed at the result in each individual case, for he had wanted something out of the common run and absolutely perfect.   Still, with fair

words he complimented Signor Benedetto on the brave show, and only before the work of poor Luca was he entirely silent, since indeed silence was the greatest kindness he could show to it: the drawing was bold and regular, but the coloring was hopelessly crude, glaring, and ill disposed.

At last, before a vase and a dish that stood modestly at the very farthest end of the deal bench, the duke gave a sudden exclamation of delight, and Signor Benedetto grew crimson with pleasure and surprise, and Giovanni Sanzio pressed a little nearer and tried to see over the shoulders of the gentlemen of the court, feeling sure that something rare and beautiful must have called forth that cry of wonder from the Lord of Montefeltro, and having seen at a glance that for his poor friend Luca there was no sort of hope.

"This is beyond all comparison," said Guidobaldo, taking the great oval dish up reverently in his hands. "Maestro Benedetto, I do felicitate you indeed that you should possess such a pupil. He will be a glory to our beloved Urbino."

"It is indeed most excellent work, my lord duke," said the master potter, who was trembling with surprise and dared not show all the astonishment and emotion that he felt at the discovery of so exquisite a creation in his bottega. "It must be," he added, for he was a very honest man, "the work of one of the lads of Pesaro or Castel-Durante. I have no such craftsman in my workshop. It is beautiful exceedingly!"

"It is worth its weight in gold!" said the prince, sharing his emotion. "Look, gentlemen—look! Will not the fame of Urbino be borne beyond the Apennines and Alps?"

Thus summoned, the court and the citizens came to look, and averred that truly never in Urbino had they seen such painting on majolica.

"But whose is it?" said Guidobaldo, impatiently, casting his eyes over the gathered group in the background of apprentices and artists. "Maestro Benedetto, I pray you, the name of the artist; I pray you, quick!"

"It is marked number eleven, my lord," answered the master potter. "Ho, you who reply to that number, stand out and give your name. My lord duke has chosen your work. Ho, there! do you hear me?"

But not one of the group moved. The young men looked from one to another. Who was this nameless rival? There were but ten of themselves.

"Ho, there!" repeated Signor Benedetto, getting angry. "Cannot you find a tongue, I say? Who has wrought this work? Silence is insolence to his highness and to me!"

Then the child Sanzio loosened his little hand from his father's hold, and went forward, and stood before the master-potter.

"I painted it," he said, with a pleased smile. "I, Raffaelle."

Can you not fancy, without telling, the confusion, the wonder, the rapture, the incredulity, the questions, the wild ecstasy of praise, that followed on the discovery of the child artist? Only the presence of Guidobaldo kept it in anything like decent quietude, and even he, all duke though he was, felt his eyes wet and felt his heart swell; for he himself was childless, and for the joy that Giovanni Sanzio felt that day he would have given his patrimony and duchy.

He took a jewel hung on a gold chain from his own breast and threw it over Raffaelle's shoulders.

"There is your first guerdon," he said. "You will have many, O wondrous child, who shall live when we are dust!"

Raffaelle, who himself was all the while quite tranquil and unmoved, kissed the duke's hand with sweetest grace, then turned to his own father.

"It is true I have won my lord duke's prize?"

"Quite true, my angel!" said Giovanni Sanzio, with tremulous voice.

Raffaelle looked up at Maestro Benedetto.

"Then I claim the hand of Pacifica!"

There was a smile on all the faces round, even on the darker countenances of the vanquished painters.

"Oh, would indeed you were of age to be my son by marriage, as you are the son of my heart!" murmured Signor Benedetto. "Dear and marvelous child, you are but jesting, I know. Tell me what it is indeed that you would have. I could deny you nothing; and truly it is you who are my master."

"I am your pupil," said Raffaelle, with that pretty, serious smile of his, his little fingers playing with the ducal jewel. "I could never have painted that majolica yonder had you not taught me the secrets and management of your colors. Now, dear maestro mine, and you, O my lord duke, do hear me! I by the terms of the contest have won the hand of Pacifica and the right of association with Messer Ronconi. I take these rights and I give them over to my dear friend Luca of Fano, because he is the honestest man in all the world, and does honor Signor Benedetto and love Pacifica as no other can do so well, and Pacifica loves him; and my lord duke will say that thus all will be well."

So with the grave innocent audacity of a child he

spoke—this seven-year-old painter who was greater than any there.

Signor Benedetto stood mute, somber, agitated. Luca had sprung forward and dropped on one knee. He was as pale as ashes. Raffaelle looked at him with a smile.

"My lord duke," he said, with his little gentle smile, "you have chosen my work; defend me in my rights."

"Listen to the voice of an angel, my good Benedetto; heaven speaks by him," said Guildobaldo gravely, laying his hand on the arm of his master potter.

Harsh Signor Benedetto burst into tears.

"I can refuse him nothing," he said, with a sob. "He will give such glory unto Urbino as never the world hath seen!"

"And call down this fair Pacifica whom Raffaelle has won," said the sovereign of the duchy, "and I will give her myself as her dower as many gold pieces as we can cram into this famous vase. An honest youth who loves her and whom she loves—what better can you do, Benedetto? Young man, rise up and be happy. An angel has descended on earth this day for you."

But Luca heard not. He was still kneeling at the feet of Raffaelle, where the world has knelt ever since.

MELEAGRIS GALLOPAVO

He kept up side by side with the pig

MELEAGRIS GALLOPAVO

A TURKEY stood on a wall and saw a drove of black and gray pigs go by on the highroad underneath. The turkey was a very handsome gobbler, and his plumage was of the most brilliant gray and white, and his wattles were of the red of the carnation or the rose. He was very proud, and as he looked down on the pigs he stuck up his tail peacock-wise and fanned the air with it, and strutted up and down on the stone ledge, and said to himself, "What poor, dusty, hard-driven drudges those are in the road there! And not a single feather upon them! Nothing to cover their bodies except a few dingy-looking hairs! And they can only make an odd snuffling noise instead of gobbling! What a contemptible grunting and grumbling! And then what a tail!—a wisp of rope would be better!"

Then he spread his own tail higher and higher and broader and broader, just to show the pigs what a tail could be; and he gobbled loudly, that they might know what intelligible and melodious speech was like.

The poor pigs went snuffling and shuffling along in the mud and stones beneath the wall, and were driven into the straw yard of the turkey's own farmhouse.

Next morning, lo! the turkey was put in a coop and was carried off to market, with a number of ducks and geese and cackling pullets, and who should be next to him but a poor gray pig, with his heels tied together so that he could not stir.

"What a wretched creature!" said the turkey in its pride, for the coop had not taken down its vanity one peg. "What a sorry animal! and such a tail! Of course they are going to cut his throat. As for me, this is a throne: I suppose I am going to the palace. Perhaps the queen has never seen a beautiful turkey before."

Then he began again to spread out his tail-plume and shake his rosy wattles, and began to gobble, gobble, gobble with all his might. But the cart gave a lurch and the coop tilted on one side, and the turkey tilted up with it and lost his balance.

"Dear me! what a price one pays for being of high rank in this world!" he said to himself, as he clung to the side of the wicker-work and tried to preserve his dignity.

The poultry were all in flat baskets, and so were the geese and the ducks.

"He'll be fine for killing three months hence, ma'am!" his driver was saying as he stopped the cart and held up the coop to show our gentleman to a woman who stood on the curbstone.

"For killing!" echoed the turkey, and he swooned away, and fell in a heap of ruffled feathers on the bottom of the wicker-work prison.

For death had never occurred to him as a possible fate for himself, though he saw other creatures go daily to martyrdom.

"You will be sooner or later killed, just as I shall be," said the pig, with a grunt, as the turkey came to itself.

"What do you suppose they fatten you for? For love of you? Ugh! you silly vain thing!"

"I thought it was because—because—because I am a turkey!" sighed the poor prisoner in the coop.

"Because you are a turkey!" echoed the pig. "As if there were not five hundred thousand turkeys in the world! That is all. You will be before Christmas just as I shall be: a knife will slit your throat."

The poor turkey swooned again on hearing this, and did not recover so rapidly as before; therefore the cart had jolted on again and was standing in the market-place, with the horses out of the shafts, before he opened his eyes and regained his consciousness.

The master of the cart was away from it, and it had been unpacked of most of its contents, and the pig and the turkey were left alone.

Suddenly the pig gave a grunt, and the turkey started, for his nerves were on edge and the least thing frightened him.

"What a hideous voice you have!" he said pettishly. "You should hear *me!*"

And he began to gobble with all his might.

"I don't see that your noise is a bit prettier than mine," said the pig. "But it is very silly to lose your time squabbling about voices. We could get out if you would help me a little."

The turkey was silent.

To get out would be delightful; but to go into partnership with piggy hurt his pride so much that he would not even ask in what way escape could be accomplished. But the pig was in too much haste and too much in earnest to stand upon etiquette.

"I can get my snout to your coop," he said eagerly,

"and I will gnaw it asunder—it's nothing but wicker—if you will promise to peck my cords to pieces when you are out. Now, don't you see what I mean?"

The turkey was so enraptured that his pride all tumbled down like a broken egg, and his wings began to flap in a tremendous flurry.

"Make haste! make haste!" he cried, and gobbled till he was red in the face.

"Don't make such a noise, or they'll hear you," said the pig, getting his teeth well onto the wicker, "and then you and I shall go up as the alderman and his chains on to some horrid man's table."

"Alderman?" said the turkey.

"They call a roast turkey and its sausages so," explained the pig.

The turkey thought it very ghastly pleasantry.

The pig meanwhile was hard at work, and in a very little time he had gnawed, and pulled, and bitten, and twisted the coop on the side near to him in such an effectual manner that the turkey soon got his head through, and then his throat, and then his body. He gave a gobble of glory and joy.

"But undo me!" squeaked the pig.

Now, the turkey was in a fearful hurry to be gone; his heart beat and his wings flapped so that he almost fell into convulsions; but he was a bird of honor and good faith. He bent down and pecked with such frantic force at the knots tying the pig's legs that he filled his beak with frayed cord, and in less time than I take to write it piggy tumbled in his heavy fashion off the cart on to the ground—free.

"Now run," said the pig; and nobody knows how fast a pig can run who has not seen him put his mind and his will into it. The turkey could not fly, because his wings were

cut, and tame turkeys seldom know much about flying; but, what with a stride and a flutter mixed in one, he managed to cover the ground rapidly, and kept up side by side with the pig, who, for his part, knowing the country, kept steadily on down the road, which fortunately for them was a solitary one, and made straight for a wood which he saw in the distance. The wood was about a mile and a half off, and the two comrades were in sore distress when they came up to it; but they did reach it unstopped, and sank down on the grass under some larches with a sigh of content.

"Such a useless tree the larch!" murmured the pig; "not an acorn on it once in all its days!" For, of course, the pig viewed all trees only in relation to acorns.

"I can't eat acorns," sighed the turkey, as soon as he got his breath.

"You ungrateful creature," said the pig in reproof. "Be content that you have escaped with your life."

"Are you *sure* we have escaped?"

"We have escaped for the time," said the philosophic pig, "and to be loose in a wood is heaven upon earth. There must be grain, or berries, or something you can pick up, if only you will look about for it."

Now it was easy for the good pig to be philosophic, because near at hand he had smelled out a savory spot in the mossy ground, and he was right in the very middle of a hearty meal of truffles.

"I never thought to have to beg my bread," sighed the turkey.

"Who do you suppose would take the trouble to feed you if it was not to kill you?" grunted the pig, with his mouth quite full. "You need not *beg* your bread, as you call it; *look* for it—as I do."

The turkey, pressed by hunger, did begin to look. A tame turkey, you know, knows nothing about feeding itself; food is thrown out to it; and our turkey, at any rate, had always supposed that was an ordination of Providence.

But little by little, watching the pig devouring the truffles, natural appetites and instincts awoke in him. No doubt his grandparents a hundred times removed had been wild turkeys by the borders of the Missouri or in the woods of Arkansas, and hereditary instincts revived in him under the all-potent prick of hunger. He did begin to look about, and spied a wild strawberry or two and ate them, and saw a blackberry bush and stripped it, and, finding a big grasshopper and a small frog, found an appetite also for them.

"I never knew so much natural nourishment grew about one," he remarked to the pig, who snorted—

"There is food enough; only men take it all. Your people are all in America, but men can't let them alone even there, so I have heard. Oh, there is a pretty hen pheasant! Good morning, Madame Phasiani."

"Is that her name?" asked the turkey.

"It is her family name; and your own is Meleagris Gallopavo, and I don't suppose you knew that," said the pig very snappishly.

The turkey was silent. Meleagris Gallopavo! That really was a very fine name!

"Is one well off in this wood, Madame Phasiani?" asked the pig of the pheasant, who sighed, and replied that the wood was very nice, and Indian corn was thrown out twice a day; but then when there was the trail of the beater over it all, who could be happy?

"There is the trail of the butcher over me," said the pig,

"but I enjoy myself while I can. You mentioned Indian corn, madame. Is the keeper's cottage unfortunately near us, then?"

She said it was perhaps half a mile off.

"This is a preserve, then?" said the pig.

She sighed again, and said it was, and sauntered pensively away with her head on one side, as pheasants always do.

"I hoped it was a bit of wild coppice," said the pig. "Ah, here is a kingfisher. How do, Mr. Alced?"

But the kingfisher, who is the shyest creature upon earth, skimmed away in silence.

"Why do you call them all those fine names?" said the turkey.

"It costs nothing, and it pleases them," said the pig curtly. "It is part of men's tomfoolery," he added, after a pause; and then, seeing a turtledove, he grunted in his most amiable fashion, "Sir Turtur Auritus, good day. We are resting in your wood a little while; it is very cool, and green, and pleasant. May I ask if it be also *safe?*"

"Safe!" said the turtledove, sitting down on a cranberry bough. "There are guns, guns, guns, from morning to night."

"Surely not this time of the year? No!"

"There are for us," said the turtledove sorrowfully, "and when there are not guns there are traps. They have no mercy on us. We only eat the pine kernels, the wood spurge, grain, the little snails. We do no harm. Yet they hunt us down; they put poisoned colza for us; they kill us by thousands; and I have heard—though it seems too terrible to be true—that they pack us alive in hampers, keep us shut up one atop of another for days, then pull

our tail feathers out, and shut us up again in another box; when that box flies open they shoot at us, so I have heard."

"Oh, yes; my gentlemen call that their *'poules,'* and give each other prizes for doing it," said the pig, with a grim sympathy. "They think it vulgar when the lads at village fairs grease our tails and hunt us. Dear Sir Turtur Auritus, is there such a gigantic sham, such an unutterable beast anywhere as Man?"

"I should think there is not," said the turtledove. "Myself I live out of the world, on the top of that lime tree you see there, and if I can only alight safely to feed and drink twice a day, I ask no more."

A pretty partridge went tripping by at that moment, with some finely grown sons and daughters after her. She was a charming and lovely creature, only she had a sadly nervous manner.

"When it grows near the first of September," she said in a tone of apology to the pig, who saluted her as Lady Starnacineria, "every sound, the very slightest, sends my heart up into my mouth, and I take every stone for a dog. What is the use or the joy of bringing these dear children into a world of shot? Their doom is to be huddled alive into a game bag, with broken limbs and torn bodies, and my lord will think himself a saint fit for heaven if he send a hamper of them up to a hospital."

"All men's hypocrisy, madame," said the pig. "I prefer the frank, blunt snap of the fox, who makes no pretense of Christian charity, but only wants his dinner."

"If it were only the fox," sighed the partridge, "that would be very bearable; and he likes a common hen quite as well as ourselves—and better, because the poor vulgar creature is bigger."

With a sigh she devoted herself to laying open an ants' nest, and called to her young to devour the eggs in it.

"This seems a very nice home of yours," said the pig, to provoke conversation.

The partridge sighed as the pheasant had done.

"It is too charming among these turnips," she said, "and there is most excellent fare all over these fields; but, alas! for what a fate do I live and hatch these dear children—the gun, the dog, the bag! Ah, dear sir, life to a partridge, where man is, is only a vale of tears, though led in the best of cornfields!"

And she said, "Cheep, cheep," and made a restless little flutter of all her feathers, and crept under the rail again back among the turnips.

At that moment a fine black rabbit, with a white tuft for a tail, darted by too quick for the pig to stop him.

"Ah, he has a sad life—almost as sad as mine!" said the turtledove. "He dwells in quite a humble way underground, but they never let him alone. When they can shoot nothing else, they are forever banging and blazing at him. And they put a ferret through his hall door without even knocking to say they are there. Have you ever seen the poor bunnies sitting outside their warrens cleaning their faces like pussycats in the cool of the early morning! Ah, such a pretty sight! But men only want them for their pelts or to put them in a pie."

"What is your opinion of men, dear lady?" said the pig, as a cow came and looked over the fence.

"Oh, don't mention them!" said the cow, with unfeigned horror. "Don't they massacre all my pretty children, and drive me to market with my udders burst-

ing, and break my heart and brand my skin? And when I am grown old will they not knock me on the head, or run a knife through my spine, and turn me into a hundred uses, hide, and hoofs, and everything? It is all written in their children's lesson books. 'The most useful animal in the kingdom of nature is a cow.' That is what they say. Ugh!"

"My dear friend," said the pig, turning to the turkey, "you see that every living thing is devoured by man. Why should you suppose you were to be the exception?"

"No one has such a tail as I have," said the turkey.

His fright over, he had come to the conclusion that nobody would ever do anything except adore a being with such a tail as his.

"What is your tail compared with the peacock's?" said the pig, with scorn. "You are only so vain because you are so ignorant."

"Do they kill peacocks?" asked the turkey.

"No; I don't think they do," replied the pig, truthful, though truth demolished his theories, which is more than can be said for human philosophers.

"Then why do they keep them?" said the turkey.

"Because they have such wonderful tails," said the pig incautiously.

"There!" said the turkey triumphantly; and out he spread his own tail, making it into a very grand wheel, and crying with all his might in that peculiar voice which nature has given to turkeys, "I am Meleagris Gallopavo! I am Meleagris Gallopavo!"

He had never known his new name till five minutes previously; but that made no difference: he was just as vain of it as if he had borne it all his life. Ask the Herald's College if this be uncommon.

He had stretched his throat out, and his rosy wattles glowed like geraniums, and he turned slowly round and round so that everyone might admire him, and he stuck his tail up on high as stiff and as straight as if it had been made of pasteboard.

"I am Meleagris Gallopavo!" he cried, with a very shrill shriek, and scattered the sandy soil of the wood all about him with his hind claws.

Crack! A bludgeon rolled him over, a mere ball of ruffled, crumpled feathers, on the ground, and a lurcher dog ran into him and gripped him tight and hard.

"We're in luck, mate!" said an ill-looking fellow who was prowling along the edge of the field with another as ill favored. "Mum's the word, and he'll go in the pot worth twenty rabbits. Who'd ha' thought of finding a darned turkey out on the spree?"

Then the cruel man rammed poor Meleagris Gallopavo into a bag that he carried with him. He was a village ne'er-do-weel, seeing if he could trespass with impunity and knock over a bunny or two on the sly, knowing that the keepers were away from that part of the wood that day. The pig lay hidden among the wood spurge and the creeping moss, and looked so exactly like a log of grayish brown timber that the ruffians never noticed him.

"I knew his tail would be the undoing of him!" he said sorrowfully, as his poor friend was borne off dead in the poachers' sack.

He himself had never looked so complacently on his own gray hairless wisp as he did now. How convenient it was! Anybody would take it for a bit of dry grass or a twig.

I may as well add that the mistress of the wood came through it next day, and the pig followed her home, and

ate an apple which she gave him so cannily that she sent him into her yard, and has kept him like a very prince of pigs ever since. But he is always sorry for his poor friend's fate; and he has never since told any turkey that its family name is Meleagris Gallopavo.